COMFORT FOOD

A Novel

Noah Ashenhurst

Copyright © Noah Ashenhurst, 2005

All rights reserved.

ISBN 0-9769735-0-2

LCCN 2005905332

Printed in the United States of America

For Natasha

1

COMFORT FOOD

Stan Gillman-Reinhart watched the water bead and form into tiny streams on the glass. The steamy Wash-o-mat windows and the warm, moist air increased his sensation of being in a pungent sauna. His skin itched through his thick wool sweater as he began to sweat. He ran his finger along his collar. He scratched his scalp through his black wavy hair and rubbed bits of sleep from the corners of his brown eyes.

The sweet, hot, and dark liquid, which had become tepid in the paper cup he held, seemed to surge through his veins. His senses were assaulted by the smell of dryer sheets, bleach, powdered laundry soap, the cacophony of the washing machines, and clattering of drying clothes.

Moments ago he was enveloped in the bleak, psychological violence of Dostoevsky's *Crime and Punishment*. He had already read the novel three times and yet each time he sat down with it, and let the words draw him in, he gleaned something different.

He had taken his first Russian Literature class on a whim, attracted to the romantic allure of pre-Revolutionary Russia. He imagined it as a country rife with decadence and feudalism and ripe for disaster. It was like reading about the apocalypse after it had happened. With his brown eyes and naturally jet-black hair he secretly believed he was somehow connected to the paupers, princesses, or bourgeoisie. There was also a questionable Finnish bloodline on his mother's side of the family that his great grandmother always said was close to the Czars.

The novel had changed his life, or at least the direction that it took. After being transported and transcended by the novel he had decided to pursue literature, wherever it took him. His parents were not surprised when he told them but merely nodded—a silent indication that they had always known his romantic depth.

Still, he had little patience for literary criticism. He found it to be a poor, secondhand substitute for the visceral experience of the actual reading and discussion. Literary discussion was like communal passion. He had never been more attracted to or repulsed by his classmates' intellect than when they discussed a work Stan held sacred. Some used it as an opportunity to show off their amazing analytical skills, speaking ability, or pseudo-intellect. On those days ignorance was a welcome relief. He found it difficult to believe that a group of his peers (twenty-something-year-olds) could be so convinced that they were so right. He sometimes felt that way, too. Even without a lifetime of experience he saw things and thought things which he knew would amaze his parents. Stan felt like he lived on the edge of a wealth of ideas and change.

He remembered the spring of his third year at the University of Colorado. Frustrated and desperate to fill his literature requirements, he blindly registered for a Russian Literature class. Until the day he walked into the small classroom, he knew very little about Russian history and culture. Professor Ivanof, who had defected to the United States in the late 1970s, was a soft-spoken and yet undeniably forceful lecturer. By the end of the first week Stan was hooked. By the time he had finished Dostoevsky's *Crime and Punishment,* for the first time, he was convinced that he could be wholly satisfied immersing himself in the writings of a people who had changed, suffered, and at times triumphed even when there was no hope.

Professor Ivanof took great pains explaining and discussing the nuances of the works of Tolstoy, Dostoevsky, Chekhov, Turgenev, and others with him. While Stan grew to love and respect Vladimir Ivanof like an older uncle. He pushed Stan to study and excel. When Stan expressed doubts about graduate school Professor Ivanof became a fury of persuasive energy. He convinced Stan to apply to a number of graduate schools and played up the romantic aspects of each.

The day Stan got his first acceptance letter he practically ran to Professor Ivanof's office, where they rejoiced and celebrated by finishing off a bottle of vodka. Stan packed his bags that night. He was determined to get to Bellingham, Washington, as quickly as possible. The next week of packing, preparing, and saying goodbye was a blur. As he left Boulder he thought to himself, *I'm 22 and I'm finally free.*

Immersed in his thoughts, Stan didn't even notice the man standing against the pale yellow washing machine.

"Hey, Stan the man," said the man.

Stan recognized the voice immediately, and he looked up reluctantly from his book. It was the pervasively annoying John Snyder.

John was wearing his usual uniform: black leather jacket, faded black jeans, and a worn concert T-shirt. His greasy wet brown hair was held back in a long ponytail. In his hand he held a white grocery bag, full of clothes that dripped slightly.

"Hey John," Stan said as he looked back at his book hoping that John would get the hint.

"You reading?" John asked as he sat down three seats away from Stan.

Too late, Stan thought as he inhaled a whiff of stale cigarettes and wet leather.

"Did you go out last night?" John asked.

Stan knew that John wouldn't go away unless he at least tried to fake conversation. He folded down the corner of the page he was reading, set the book down, and half turned his body toward John.

Stan thought about John's question. Stan knew that it was a classic "John Snyder lead-in" which translates to "let me tell you about how fucked up I was, how cool I was, etc."

"No," Stan answered, "I was working on my thesis."

"Oh," John responded and looked out toward the street.

Stan's answer was only partially true. He'd worked on his thesis for about an hour and then got distracted by *Doom* on his computer. One beer became three. Pretty soon he was trying to play drunk while chomping on cheddar popcorn. Sometime after that he had passed out until about three A.M.

"Me and the guys were playin' at this party down on Iron Street and they had about three or four kegs, John said. "I was so fucked up. Then, uh, it was weird, I saw Delany and Dave together."

"You mean *together*, together?" Stan asked, his interest suddenly piqued.

"Yeah, they were all over each other."

"But I thought," Stan paused. He finished the sentence in his head, *that they were history.* "Last time I heard they were through," he said, trying not to sound surprised.

"Yeah," John said. "After he was messing around with Bridgette."

Stan remembered the fallout from Delany and Dave's last break-up distinctly. Delany Richardson and Stan were old friends from high school. She had even let Stan sleep on her couch for a week until he found his own place. He felt indebted, even though she had repeatedly said that it was no big deal.

Eventually Del had confronted Dave about his promiscuous behavior. Vicious words were exchanged and doors were slammed. In the middle of the night she had shown up at Stan's house upset and distraught. They shared a bottle of Kahlua with coffee and talked until the warm light of the sun draped itself across the bay.

At Stan's insistence she had also introduced him to Bridgette.

"But I mean Bridge, hey," John said. "She is unbelievable, who can blame him?"

"Yeah," Stan quietly mumbled.

"Oh, I'm sorry I forgot about you two," John said.

"There was never an *us two*," Stan explained.

"That's *not* what Dave said."

"Dave exaggerates and is basically an asshole," Stan said, exasperated.

"True, true," John conceded, "But still."

"It was really nothing," Stan said dismissing the whole idea more dramatically than he intended with a broad sweep of his hand.

John pulled up his damp sleeve and glanced at his battered Timex.

"Hey I gotta go," he said making his way to the door. "Me and the guys are practicin' at Ric's."

Stan nodded, grateful for any reason John wanted to duck out.

Stan picked up his book and began to find the place where he left off.

John with his hand on the door said, "You goin' to the party up at

Dave's tonight?"

"Doubt it," Stan said reflexively, "I gotta lot of work to do."

"Sure," John said flatly, as he stepped out into the wet February day, the small bag of damp clothes in his hand.

Stan picked up his book again, but agitation gnawed at him and he was unable to slip back between the words. He shook the last drops of his now cold coffee into his mouth and grabbed his black courier bag, slipping his book inside. He made his way past the wall of uncomfortable orange plastic seats and down a long narrow corridor that led to the bathrooms, storage, and payphone. As neared the women's bathroom a young woman dressed in black velvet stepped into the hall. The narrow hallway forced them to squeeze past each other. Stan inhaled her patchouli oil and nearly vomited in her reddish-black, greasy hair. He stumbled past her and was relieved when he finally made it to the phone.

In the hallway he noticed the sounds of agitated water, metallic thumps, and hum of heated air reverberated off the narrow walls.

He lifted the receiver and panicked, afraid that it might be a mistake. Frustrated, he hung up and turned to make his way back down the corridor.

"Oh, fuck," he mumbled, cursing himself for his cowardice.

He walked back and stood in front of the black pay-phone staring at the greasy, fingerprint-covered surface.

"What the hell," he thought, as he dug into the pocket of his faded, torn jeans for a quarter.

He picked up the receiver and began to put the quarter in, letting it rest on the threshold. He let the quarter slip and it clinked through the phone's innards. He dialed her number from memory. It rang. It rang again. It rang again. It rang twice more. He heard a click.

"Hello," Stan said.

Silence.

He was about to say hello again until he heard the tinny, distant sound of her voice on the answering machine.

"We're not home right now," Del's voice said, "But if you talk after the beep we'll get back to ya."

Stan recognized the familiar, corny message.

"Beep!"

"Hey, Del, call me when you get back, I'll be up late." He paused for a few seconds, wondering if he should add something else, but he felt annoyed by the impersonal machine, so he quietly hung up and walked back down the hallway.

Stan packed up his dry clothes into a black plastic garbage sack and walked out into the wet cold. He walked home, about four blocks, because he rarely drove anywhere. It was a miracle that the faded, rusting, red '79 Corolla, that he loathed driving, had made it to Bellingham. Stan had gunned it over the passes, and it had crept along, threatening to overheat and leave him stranded. Once he had parked it he was reluctant to take it out again since he figured he was already pushing his luck.

Everywhere he wanted to go was usually within walking distance, or he took the bus, or he bummed a ride from Del. Walking gave him an opportunity to contemplate. He solved problems and had revelations in the short jaunts he made to get some coffee or groceries. Often he was so preoccupied that he would suddenly realize he had walked a block past where he wanted to be.

His thoughts now drifted to Delany and Dave.

What a waste, he thought. *I mean what is Dave, like a third—or forth—year senior and a total loser.* He shook his head unconsciously.

But Stan remembered that Dave Greibing was actually in his sixth year in his on-again, off-again undergraduate career. When it came to school Dave always seemed to be going nowhere in a hurry. On the surface he appeared totally together. He was outgoing and capable of engaging conversation. He had backpacked and climbed all over the world from China to Patagonia to the Rockies. He had made his first ascent of Mt. Kilimanjaro when he was nineteen, and he went on to climb it twice more. He had scaled mountains in Nepal that Stan had only seen in National Geographic. And he had the good fortune of being born beautiful.

Dave Greibing was what most women would consider drop-dead gorgeous. His long blond hair draped to his strong shoulders, and his eyes were the color of pale-blue arctic glaciers. His teeth were straight and, naturally, gleaming white. He seemed to relish the opportunity to show off his smooth, tanned physique in spandex and no shirt.

Dave seemed to be perpetually preparing for the next adventure, the next expedition. Del said that Dave's lavish lifestyle was supplied by a lavish trust fund. She said that Dave's dad had made his money as an ambulance chaser in California, but was killed in a car accident at forty-five. While Dave had inherited a huge chunk of the settlement and had come to Bellingham to climb, sea kayak, and mountain bike. He had bought a huge, beautiful Victorian house with a sweeping view of the bay. When he got bored with traveling and partying he took a couple of classes and began to think about getting a degree. Del said that it seemed his heart was never in it, and besides, there was no rush—he was young and solvent.

When Stan had harped to Del about Dave's cavalier attitude, she had defended him. She angrily dismissed Stan's complaints as pure jealousy, and their afternoon had dissolved into a heated argument.

Stan emerged from his thoughts as he rounded the corner to his place on Garden Street, a rented room in a dilapidated house on the edge of the student slums. The two-story Victorian hadn't felt a paint brush in at least fifteen years. The faded white paint was chipped and graying. In spots the exposed wood had turned green, molding and rotting from the moisture. The house sagged to one side, away from the small addition which included Stan's room. It was built on a hill and, at times, it looked liked the dark green ivy and thick blackberry bushes were its sole anchors.

He walked up the short wooden stairway, careful not to slip on the rain slime-coated steps. Weeds reached into the light through the cracks. The porch was covered with an assortment of green and brown beer bottles and old cigarette butts. An old orange-brown couch, propped up with cement bricks, sagged in the corner. On its cushions someone had knocked over an almost empty box of Lucky Charms. Once bright marshmallows were now darkened with age.

Stan shook off his coat and wiped his feet on the worn-out mat that read "W—c—me." He felt worn and tired; his day was slowly slipping into an unmistakable craving for mind-altering substances.

He set his bag down and fumbled for his keys, then dropped them, and swore. As he slipped his key into the dead bolt the door swung open. It wasn't locked.

Nice, he thought.

As he walked down the hall he could smell baked cheese and salsa and heard someone in the kitchen loudly chomping their food. The TV was on, echoing. Stan guessed it was Brian.

Brian Fetzler was the only one of Stan's five housemates that he was on a first name basis with. Brian spent most of his waking hours taking bong hits, watching TV, eating nachos, and drinking Bud Light. He was an okay guy, but somehow insincere. It seemed like his whole slacker persona was an affectation. Stan had noticed it in his eyes, the way he watched for reactions. He was somehow too self conscious.

As Stan walked past Brian's room and into the kitchen, he could smell just-smoked reefer that mingled with the scents of Velveeta, Pace Picante Sauce, and corn chips. It had become a familiar homey smell.

Brian was sitting at the kitchen table, a white plastic patio set complete with open umbrella. He was wearing a worn dark gray sweatshirt and dark blue shorts stained with salsa and pizza sauce. His pudgy frame was hunched over an enormous plate of nachos as he stuffed the chips into his mouth with one hand and flipped through the most recent issue of *Omni* magazine with the other. His greasy, long dirty-blond hair hung over his face in places, almost touching his food. Brian didn't look up as he took a swig of Bud Light and said between bites, "Hey Stan."

Stan was slightly disgusted by Brian's eating habits, particularly that he almost always spoke with his mouth full.

"Hey, Brian," Stan said as he opened the refrigerator door. He peered into the packed fridge, unable to tell what was his or even edible. He decided he wasn't really hungry, anyway.

"Wan' som' nachos?" Brian asked, as he chomped away.

"Ah, sure," Stan said. He wasn't really in the mood to watch Brian eat, but he knew that if he didn't eat something his stomach would churn with coffee-laced indigestion.

Stan put his bags down and squeezed in opposite Brian.

The area where the table sat was barely big enough to contain it and people seated. It was a glassed-in extension of the kitchen, part of the many half-assed renovations. Although the area was small, the sloping hillside and the absence of trees behind the house offered an incredible view of the bay through the enormous floor to ceiling windows. Sometimes, in the middle of the night, Stan would sit and watch the freighters lumber through the bay, lit by bright lights. Today the clouds obscured the green tip of Orcas Island and the San Juan Islands.

Stan grabbed a few nachos carefully, to avoid watching Brian eat. He ate the chips one at a time, bite by bite. He found the neon colored cheese unusually tasty.

"W'a' s'up?" Brian asked as he reached for another clump of cheese-laden chips.

"Nothing really," Stan said as he watched the white gulls hovering over the pilings in the wind.

Brian glanced out the window and seemed confused. He shrugged and used a smaller chip to spoon the cheese onto a larger one.

Stan looked over at Brian just as he stuffed a large wad of cheese and chips into his mouth.

Yuck, Stan thought.

"You awight?" Brian asked.

Stan didn't hear him. He was distracted by the white gulls. They floated on the wind, seemingly undaunted by the cold wet drizzle. Their white bodies and outstretched wings were framed by the dark clouds and the murky water of the bay. Some flew to the dock while others settled on the floating logs. The logs were pushed together and secured like small islands near the water's edge. Once a week the longshoremen would pull up their small boats, walk gracefully across the slick wet logs, and secure a large portion to the boat. The logs were then taken to the paper mill where they were made into toilet paper. The gulls had made the log platforms their floating sanctuaries. Their solitude was interrupted only by the longshoremen and an occasional large sea lion.

"Huh?" Stan said snapping out of his thought-induced stare. Before

Brian could ask again, Stan's brain quickly processed his question and he answered, "Yeah, sure, I'm fine."

"Hey, I ah," Brian said, his tone becoming serious, "got some good shit."

"You mean dope?"

"Shh, shh," Brian said putting his finger to his lips, unable to conceal his huge grin.

"I mean, if you want we could get so very lusciously baked."

Stan thought about Brian's offer. It had been ages since he had taken a hit and even longer since he was stoned out of his mind. The way his day had been going he figured it couldn't hurt. His funds were extremely low and he knew he could ill-afford to splurge on green euphoria.

Brian watched Stan was mulling it over.

"I owe you money from the last time we went out," Brian said. "It's on me."

"Really, you sure?"

"What am I going to do? Smoke it all myself?" Brian said, with a smile devoid of sarcasm.

Possibly, Stan thought to himself.

"You wanna go to a party tonight?" Stan asked. He was surprised that he invited Brian since he hadn't even known, until that moment, that he wanted to go.

"Well," Brian said pausing while he chewed. "That would be really cool. We could get really, really baked and head on over."

Yeah, Stan thought. *What a fucking excellent idea.*

"Look," Stan said, "I've got to work on some stuff for a few hours and then we can smoke-up."

"Sure, sure," Brian said. "*Lost in Space* re-runs are on in a half an hour."

Stan smiled to himself as he got up from the table. Brian seemed to plan most of his life around the TV and his taste was far from discriminating. He watched almost anything.

Brian took a large swig of beer and belched, "Later!"

Stan cringed. *Man, he is disgusting,* he thought.

Stan walked down the short hallway, which connected his room to the kitchen. He fumbled with his keys again. When he first moved in, he didn't bother to lock the deadbolt on his door every time he left. Eventually it became a habit after one of his roommates had borrowed one of his CDs without asking.

He opened his door and set his courier bag down on his bed, a mattress on the floor, and tossed his bag of clean clothes near his closet.

His room was fairly large compared to other rooms in the house, and he was thankful that he had two large windows that drenched him in sunlight, when there was sun. He had books everywhere. They were stacked on a huge cinderblock and particle board bookshelf, on the floor, and on his small desk. He had kept almost every book that he had ever read. He couldn't bear to part with them, even though he realized that he would never read many of them again.

His job at Lolita's Used Books had further swelled his collection. It was the first job that he actually felt passionate about. He loved to walk through the small, cavernous, interconnected rooms, organizing and straightening the walls of books. He loved the musty smell of old books, their pages creased and faded. There was also the sensual feel of a worn paperback held open in his hand, the spine worn and loose. The store had a reverent quietude. Late at night, just before closing, he would pull out an old record from the extensive store collection and put it on the turntable, with the volume turned down low. He would hum along to Billie Holiday, Chet Baker, Miles Davis, or an old forgotten artist.

Stan sighed as he noticed his clean clothes were spilling out of the bag. He sometimes regretted that he had purged his closet at home, full of barely worn clothes, just before he moved because he had begun to hate doing laundry.

Each time he walked into the stuffy, muggy, fragrance-laden air of the Wash-o-mat in Fairhaven he felt overcome with a despairing sadness. At all hours of the day the lighting was harsh and cold and people stood around anxious and bored. He found it depressing and numbing. There was no solace in the hard plastic chairs amid the dull hum of pale yellow metal. When he was still an undergrad, he loved to drive home to do his laundry. He would dump his pile of clothes on the floor and sort it into piles of darks and lights, cold and hot. He would make himself a sandwich, usually cheese and mayo on rye, and he would visit with his folks, watch TV, or read through the stack of their magazines.

He stared at the pile of clothes illuminated by the pale, rain-filtered light and felt completely drained. He grabbed a pillow off his bed and lay down on the carpet.

I'll just rest my eyes, he thought to himself.

Stan woke to the sound of someone knocking loudly on his door.

"Hey, you alive?" Brian asked, as he opened the door wide enough to poke his head in.

Stan rubbed his eyes.

Brian pushed opened the door and walked in, leaving the door wide open.

Brian chuckled. "What'd you fall asleep or somethin'?"

"Appears so," Stan said as he sat up. He felt groggy and out-of-sorts.

"What time is it?"

"Just after six," Brian said. "You've been out for almost an hour and a half."

"Shit!" Stan said a bit alarmed. He felt like he had just lain down except that the room was dark. "Can you get the light?"

Brian walked over to the lamp on the desk and twisted the switch.

Stan squinted as his eyes slowly adjusted to the warm yellow light.

"Yeah, you were really dead to the world. I was knockin' for about five minutes before you woke up."

"Shit," Stan said quietly to himself. "Oh well," he thought, "Another unproductive afternoon."

"You still feel like goin' out and stuff?" Brian asked.

"Oh, yeah, sure," Stan said as he stood up and stretched.

"I figure we could smoke up in my room, watch TV, and then eat somethin'."

"I'm game," Stan said smiling, amused at Brian's predictable plan.

He followed Brian to his room.

The door to Brian's room was wide open. As soon as Stan came within five feet of the door he was hit with the overpowering aroma of pot smoke. Stan figured that Brian had been smoking, continuously, since he finished eating.

Brian's TV was on with the sound turned down. He was playing Soundgarden's latest album. Strangely, Stan had never been in Brian's room before, and it took him a couple of minutes for everything to sink in.

Brian had covered every inch of wall space with pictures, posters, advertisements, and old snapshots. It was a collage of *High Times* pot posters, Pink Floyd, Led Zeppelin, scantily clad women, beer commercials, snowboarders, skateboarders, blurred pictures of parties and old friends, strange advertisements, and other odd, indecipherable things.

Stan closed the door behind him and Brian made his way to a large collection of pipes and bongs, which he kept neatly arranged on a table by his bed.

Stan noticed a plethora of lava lamps arranged haphazardly throughout the room. Brian had a small fridge with a case of Pepsi and a case of Bud Light on top. His stereo and TV sat on a shelf near the door. The rest of the shelf was covered with stacks of CDs. Stan had never seen so many outside of a music store. Clothing was strewn across the floor.

Yuck! Stan thought as he stepped off a pair of Brian's boxers.

He realized that there was no closet in the room and no dresser, and Brian was now fumbling though a shoebox filled with different types of lighters.

On the floor there was an old, green vinyl beanbag chair covered with patches of duct tape, its white contents seeping out. Stan sat down on the beanbag, carefully avoiding stepping all over Brian's clothes.

Brian packed a multicolored bong and a large ceramic pipe and grabbed a cold Bud Light out of the fridge. "You wanna beer?"

"Sure, why not."

Brian tossed him the beer and then carefully handed him the pipe and a lighter.

Stan opened his beer and took a couple of sips, letting the cold fluid slide down his throat. He grimaced at the cheap aftertaste.

Brian began taking huge bong hits, holding each one until his face turned a slight crimson.

Stan put down his beer, put the pipe to his lips, and inhaled deeply. The smoke burned slightly as he sucked it down into his lungs. He held it until he thought he would suffocate and then let it out with an enormous sigh and a slight cough. He took another sip of his beer. The coldness helped ease the slight burning of his throat. After the third or fourth hit he felt a creeping euphoria. At first he simply thought he was a bit light-headed from all of the deep inhaling, but as he examined his reflexes and the strangeness of the usually banal TV he knew he was genuinely stoned.

Ah, the old familiar, he thought to himself.

Stan looked at Brian on his second beer, the strange colorful walls, the piles of clothes on the floor, and the lava lamps. Everything seemed different.

He found himself examining his own thoughts and reactions. His gaze drifted to the TV, and he began to stare at the familiar images and wonder what each one meant and symbolized. Brian flipped the channel every couple of minutes. Stan knew that he would usually be annoyed, but he was captivated by the seemingly unrelated images, which had a choppy flow.

He looked over at Brian who was grinning madly at the latest video from R.E.M., his mental presence somewhere else. Stan began to chuckle. Brian looked over, his facial expression unchanging, and then he began to laugh. Soon they were rolling on the floor, in near convulsions of laughter, unable to stop. To Stan it was like a delicious reflex gone out of control. They continued to writhe and shriek with laughter until their stomachs hurt. Then, exhausted and out of breath they stopped.

Brian looked over just as Stan picked up his beer and accidentally grabbed one of Brian's socks in the process. Brian burst into hysterical laughter and Stan was caught up in the contagious euphoria. Once again they laughed until their sides hurt and they could hardly breathe.

"Oh shit!" Stan thought as he lay with his head back, trying to catch his breath, "I gotta call Del."

"I gotta take a piss," Stan lied.

Brian nodded, his gaze once again glued to the TV.

Stan got up and walked out into the dark hallway. Standing up, he felt much more stoned and even a little disoriented. He walked slowly toward the front entryway, as his eyes adjusted to the darkness. The old white phone sat on a small table near the door. For reasons unknown to Stan, the answering machine was under the table on a pile of phone books. The red light on the machine was not flashing.

No messages, Stan thought.

But Stan worried that maybe the phone had become unreliable, after all it was old and maybe broken. He picked it up and listened for the dial tone.

Well, just because the phone works and it looks like no one called doesn't mean it works, he reasoned.

Stan remembered that there were more than a few times when someone had forgotten to write down his messages or save them. The house seemed to be filled with generally unreliable strangers. He wasn't even sure he remembered what all of his housemates looked like.

Stan knew that he told Del he would call her and she probably hadn't called. He figured what the hell. Stan dialed her number from memory.

The phone rang. It rang again. It rang again. It rang twice more. The line clicked but he knew it was the answering machine. He heard the familiar beginning of their message, "We're not…" Disappointed, he quietly hung up.

As he walked back to Brian's room he grew increasingly irritated. He couldn't figure out where she would be, because she *couldn't* be with Dave. He wished she would call.

He pushed open Brian's door and stepped into a thick wall of smoke.

"Whoa!" Stan said amazed.

"Sorry," Brian said trying not to exhale. "Paahh!"

"I packed another bowl. It's *juicy* stuff!"

"I imagine," Stan thought.

"You wannanother beer?" Stan asked, as he opened the small fridge.

"Sure. Hit me!" Brian said in a throaty imitation of Jim Carrey.

Stan sat down on the beanbag and exchanged the beer for a large, red plastic bong.

He noticed that the bong was dark blood-red in the dim light. He took a large hit and inhaled it deeply. He held his breath, counting. At forty-six his lungs felt like they would burst, and he exhaled a small wisp of smoke and hot breath.

He felt different immediately. He was relaxed. He sank down into the deep crevice of the beanbag. He didn't feel the underwater, hazy, and stupid sensation that he felt every time he got drunk. He simply felt undeniably mellow.

But his thoughts flowed. The flashing images of the TV moved too fast for him to concentrate upon. Each time he felt he truly saw the image and its cultural, sexual, or social connotation it was gone. He felt the television itself was creating an attention deficit disorder on the sensory perceptive surface of his pot-altered mind.

Brian got up. Stan didn't even realize he had left until he sat back down. Then it seemed as if he had been gone for hours.

"Where ya been?" Stan's words seemed to slide, smooth and slippery from his mouth.

"Snackin'," Brian said as he cracked a slight grin and chewed on something.

Stan was almost finished with his beer, and he was beginning to get cottonmouth. Food, snack food, sounded distractedly appealing. He looked over at Brian as he sat down carefully, so he wouldn't spill the beer he had just opened. Even in the dim light Stan could see that Brian's blond hair looked especially thin on top. Stan thought about Brian, drinking Bud Light, getting stoned, trying to comb long wisps of hair over his bald spot. He could imagine him watching late night infomercials alone. He imagined him ordering every balding remedy and joining the Hair Club for Men. As sad as it seemed, he couldn't help but chuckle.

Brian looked sheepishly at him and Stan burst into a full-blown laugh. The contagious laughter infected Brian, as well, and they both laughed until they almost pissed in their pants.

"We're getting loopy," Stan said, catching his breath.

Brian grinned, oblivious to the fact that he spilled beer all over his shirt.

Stan looked around the room, his gaze settling upon a large pink lava lamp to his right. He was fascinated with the movement, the coagulation and floating of the shifting shapes. He thought of blood or bombarding amoebas. He was reminded of the movie *The Blob*.

When he was a kid, Stan and his brother, Patrick, had gone to a summertime, classic horror movie festival at the local library. Their mom had chauffeured them for four consecutive weekends. They had seen *The Birds*, *Swarm*, *The Creature from the Black Lagoon*, *The Blob,* and many others. Stan and his brother convinced themselves that nothing scared them, and they would relentlessly tease each other for gasping or covering his face with his hands. Stan was also a very rational child, even at the tender age of ten.

The Blob had seemed so ludicrously fake. They laughed through the whole movie. "Besides," Patrick had said, "It wasn't even in color. Who would be sacred of a big, gray mass of hard pudding?"

When their mom had told them she was terrified by it as a little girl they laughed again.

Stan reached over and touched the lava lamp. "Ouch!" He yelled and he quickly withdrew his hand.

"Hey, careful," Brian said, his eyes never leaving the TV. "That's hot."

"Thanks for the warning."

Stan turned his attention to the TV, and for the next hour and a half he watched the contents of Brian's imaginary world. Although his senses were captivated by the images, he was having long continuous thoughts which seemed to move in concentric circles and fold in upon each other. He wondered if Brian, sitting motionless, the only movement in his eyes, was thinking the same things.

Inevitably, his thoughts turned to Del.

What if she called and I didn't hear it? he thought, suddenly tense and panicked.

He jumped up from the beanbag and ran out of the room. In the hallway he could see that the small red light on the answering machine was not flashing. He picked up the phone to check for a dial tone. It worked. He figured he would call Del anyway, just in case she had called.

He waited for the answering machine to pick up, and for the beep.

"Hey Del, this is Stan, I, uh... Brian and I are over here watching TV and I called to see what you were up to. I wasn't sure if you called. I mean maybe you called and I didn't hear it or maybe you got sick of listening to the machine."

Shit, he thought, *I'm rambling like a lunatic.*

"Uh, yeah. Call me when you get back...later and all."

Stan was about to hang up when he realized that he had forgotten to say goodbye. "Bye!" he said loudly at the receiver he held at arm's length, and he hung up.

She's gonna think I'm a total and complete moron, Stan thought morosely. He mulled over what he said. He was so absorbed in his thoughts that he didn't realize that he had walked down the hallway into the kitchen and was standing in front of the fridge.

"Hey, I'm hungry," Stan said aloud.

He opened the fridge and light flooded into the dark kitchen.

He stared at the unorganized mess of leftovers, condiments (he counted four different kinds of salsa), vegetables, lunch meats, cheeses, milk, beer (an abundance in all shapes and sizes), Coke, Pepsi, root beer, and containers of unmarked, mystery objects.

Stan picked up an old cottage cheese container that was expired by two months. Reflexively, he opened the side of the lid and took a whiff. He was hit by the stench of moldy dairy products.

"Whoa!" Stan exclaimed as he tossed the whole container in the garbage.

The whole fridge is probably full of spoiled, rotten, half-eaten garbage, he thought. He started pulling the containers out one by one, dumping out the contents if the container could be recycled.

Brian walked out of his room and noticed Stan in the dark kitchen, illuminated by the door light, sitting on the floor with the entire contents of the fridge spread out on the floor around him. Stan was absorbed in his task and continued to sniff the contents of a mystery container.

"What're you doin'?" Brian asked.

"Oh, heh," Stan said a bit embarrassed, as he realized that his small project had gotten a bit out of hand. "I'm, ah, cleaning."

"Yeah, I noticed."

Stan attempted to ignore Brian so he wouldn't be distracted from his mission.

"Are you gonna do that all night?" Brian asked.

"No, no. I'll be done real quick here."

Brian shrugged and went back into his room to watch the end of *He-Haw*.

It took Stan almost half an hour to sort, dispose, and clean the fridge and its contents. When he was done the fridge looked empty and the garbage was almost overflowing. He sealed up the garbage and hauled it outside to the dumpster. He was happily surprised that the misty rain had abated and the air had warmed a bit.

He felt glowing satisfaction in the task he had accomplished, although he knew the effect would be temporary. His housemates were lazy slobs.

Brian didn't even look up from the TV when Stan walked back into his room and sat down. Brian had a glazed look in his eyes and seemed to be thoroughly engrossed in *Leave It to Beaver*.

"Hey, Brian," Stan said trying to get his attention.

Brian sat motionless and unresponsive.

"Hey Brian!" Stan yelled.

Brian jumped. "What, what?"

"Let's go," Stan said.

"Go where?"

"To the party."

"Oh, oh yeah, right," Brian said, as his eyes wandered back to the TV. "I'll just throw somethin' on."

Brian made no movement to get up. Stan stood in front of the TV, blocking Brian's view.

"Hey!" Brian yelled, "I can't see."

"Ten minutes," Stan said holding up his fingers. "We're leaving in ten minutes."

"OK, all right already!"

"With or without you," Stan said, as he walked to his room.

Stan lowered his blinds and changed his clothes, attempting to pick ones that weren't visibly dirty or stinky. He wanted to take a shower, but it was getting far too late and he didn't feel like getting wet. He loaded on deodorant and some cologne. He knew he would reek of cigarettes, pot smoke, and beer five minutes after he got to the party anyway. He brushed his teeth, drank some water, and checked his appearance in the mirror.

As Stan stepped out onto the porch, he could smell wet cedar and grass. Brian looked anxious and distracted.

"You got your own key?" Stan asked Brian.

"Uh, yeah."

Brian was wearing his party garb: wrap around shades, a plaid polar fleece sweatshirt, shorts, and Tevas.

They made their way down Garden Street and up Ivy Street to Dave's party. Stan was phazing from all the dope he smoked. He was experiencing strange loops in conscious thought, each thought linked to the other in unbroken, looping circles. Occasionally, he would be jarred from his altered state and momentarily disoriented until his mind caught up with his senses.

Walking and phasing set his body on auto-pilot. Neither Stan nor Brian talked both were deeply immersed in their own separate realities, which seemed substantially more concrete than the world around them.

"Like a treadmill," Brian said suddenly.

It took Stan a few seconds to mentally shift gears and bring himself out of his reflection on the relationship between the contemporary United States and the fall of the Roman Empire.

"What?" Stan asked.

"Ya know," Brian said softly, "Like we're walking on this huge moving sidewalk, like at the airport."

"You mean, like, we're walking even faster or slower?"

"Faster. I guess. Or maybe slower."

"Yeah, faster I could see," Stan said, as he began to feel like he was moving more quickly than his legs could carry him.

They were, once again, lost in contemplative thought, considering and noticing the moving-sidewalk feeling.

Stan felt like they were walking at a car's pace, making their way rapidly through the side streets and alleys.

When they were almost a block away they began to hear the familiar sounds of a party: loud music, yelling, occasional screaming, and drunken laughter.

As they got closer they could hear the thumping bass and feedback of John Snyder's band *Burn*.

They walked up the alley behind Dave's house where couples shared a smoke or an intimate moment. They walked under an ivy-covered archway and onto the narrow path that snaked through the backyard.

Stan smelled the faint aroma of spilled beer and cigarettes. Stan didn't recognize anyone. He wasn't surprised because Dave's parties often consisted of underage underclassmen trying to look cool as they fumbled their way to inebriation, basically "amateur night."

"Hey! Brian!" A long-haired male yelled from a circle of people hacky sacking.

"Hey! Billy!" Brian yelled back and made his way toward the group.

Stan hung back. He didn't know any of Brian's friends and he was feeling particularly antisocial. "I'll catch up with you later!" Stan yelled at Brian's back.

Brian acknowledged with a wave as he kicked the hackysack.

Stan walked up the steps to the back porch and passed by a couple making out. They didn't even notice that he was there. He opened the back door and his senses were assaulted by the jarring, thump, and whine of the music, the smell of beer, cigarettes, perfume, and sweat.

He walked though the laundry room and into the hall where people were either yelling at each other over the music or content not to speak. He walked by the kitchen, which was crowded with people in groups and pairs leaning against the counters or sitting at the large Formica kitchen table.

He had noticed the last time that he came to one of Dave's "shindigs" that there was almost no furniture. He knew it wasn't a money thing, Dave was loaded. When he asked Del she said that Dave loved to party and so he bought or found cheap old junk, tore up the carpet, and refinished and super-sealed the wood floors. She added that he should see the nice stuff in Dave's generally locked bedroom. Stan was sorry he asked.

He made his way down the hall and into the enormous living room, where the music was unbearably loud. *Burn* was set up on a small makeshift stage in one corner of the room, gyrating and jumping wildly as they played their own version of *AC/DC's* "Back in Black." Stan recognized John Snyder immediately. He wore an *Alice in Chains* concert T-shirt that was soaked with sweat. His hair was braided into two greasy ponytails, which swung around like whips when he moved his head. The whole band seemed to be having an incredibly good time considering that only a few people in the large crowd were dancing.

As loud and rambunctious as the music was Stan could still tell that John was talented. He had heard him play an acoustic set once, a beautiful classical piece for guitar. He couldn't figure out how such a talented musician had gotten stuck playing for beer and tips. When Stan asked around he found out that John's past was a mystery. The most Stan had discovered was that he had gotten kicked out (or quit) an elite music school and had traveled extensively around Europe. Somehow, he always easily irritated Stan. He seemed to know just how to get under Stan's skin.

Stan thought that he vaguely recognized a few faces as he glanced around the crowd. Almost everyone was standing, usually in groups. A few lucky people had staked out the long tattered couch, which sat against the wall. To his right Stan noticed a tall woman with silky smooth long auburn hair whose back was turned towards him. She wore tight-fitting jeans and a short black suede jacket. A group of young men stood in front her, an enraptured audience. Stan couldn't hear what she was saying, and they probably couldn't, either, but he nearly laughed out loud when he saw the expressions on their faces. They smiled, almost constantly, each one seeming to hang on her every word and gesture. She looked around, bored, and Stan recognized her full, dark lips, high cheekbones, and small nose. It was Bridgette.

He knew that he should have immediately guessed that it was her. She was beautiful and charismatic enough to attract men like a magnet. Every time she moved she was noticed by men, and possibly some women, and they were captivated.

She was sublime, but Stan wanted to run and hide. Bridgette's very presence made him feel panicked, uncomfortable, and unattractive. The first time he saw her on campus he was instantly in lust. She moved with confidence and grace. She was impeccably dressed in a white silk blouse and black, flowing silk pants.

When he told Del about her she smiled a wry smile and casually said, "Oh, yeah, that's Bridgette Jonsen."

Stan, in a fit of desperation, asked her if she could set them up, introduce them or something. Del felt sorry for him so she introduced him, and much to his surprise Bridgette agreed to go out with him.

Their date was a complete disaster.

They went to a very fancy French restaurant, which he really couldn't afford. Throughout the meal she seemed bored and aloof. He had ordered expensive wine, but she didn't seem impressed. Afterwards she wanted to go to a club in Vancouver, B.C. but they got lost on the way. After they finally got there she saw Dave Greibing and ended up leaving with him. Depressed and distraught, Stan left. About five miles from town Del's SAAB broke down, and he ended up walking home.

Stan decided it was time to leave before she noticed him. He was tired of the party, and seeing Bridgette was too much. He turned around and began to make his way though the crowd. He didn't even notice Dave until he ran into him, spilling Dave's drink.

"Shit, I'm really sorry," Stan said.

"Hey, hey, no…" Dave took a long look at Stan. "Wait, you're Stan, right? Del's friend from New Mexico."

"Colorado actually."

"Yeah, yeah sure, whatever."

"Why don't you come have a drink," Dave said as he flopped his arm around Stan's shoulder and half-dragged him to the kitchen.

"But, I ah," Stan began, but realized that it was useless. Dave was extremely drunk and notorious for not liking to drink alone.

Dave behaved as though Stan was his best friend, rambling about his last trip to Nepal.

Stan didn't hear a word Dave said but he kept thinking, *Where the hell did Bridgette go?*

"Pretty amazing, huh?" Dave said as they rounded the corner into the kitchen.

"Yeah, yeah," Stan said, unsure what he had just agreed to.

Bridgette was standing in the kitchen. She saw Dave and Stan before they saw her.

"Dave, honey," she said. "Where have you been, I was looking all over for you." She put her hand on his cheek, oblivious to Stan's presence.

Up close Stan could tell that she was hammered as well.

"I was with my buddy here, Steve," Dave answered.

"It's Stan," Stan said, slightly irritated.

"Yeah, yeah, sure."

"Wait," Bridgette said, "You're Del's friend, right? I'm Bridgette." She held out her hand.

Stan was dumfounded. She was introducing herself as though they had just met. She seemed to have no recollection of their date. The worst night of Stan's life, and she didn't even remember it.

She stood for a few seconds looking awkward until Stan reached out and shook her hand.

"Delighted to finally *meet* you," Stan said.

She merely smiled, the irony lost on her.

"I think I'm going to be sick," Stan said, meaning it, metaphorically.

"Not on my new outfit!" Bridgette said, quickly backing up.

Dave took his arm off Stan's shoulders and he stepped over next to Bridgette.

"Hey, would you mind puking outside, away from the house," Dave said as he put his arm around Bridgette's waist.

"No, I'm fine really," Stan said feeling an incredible urge to get as far away from these two as possible. "I think I'll take a walk, fresh air and all."

"Sure, sure," Dave said, as Bridgette kissed the back of his neck.

Stan wandered out of the kitchen, and as he stepped into the laundry room he looked back to see Dave and Bridgette, their arms around each other, making their way toward the stairs to Dave's room.

Stan suddenly felt genuinely nauseous. He was relieved when he stepped out onto the porch and felt the cool night air. He figured he should sit down. The couch in the dark corner looked like a comfortable and out of the way spot.

A woman was sitting on the other end of the couch, her dark hair pulled back in a ponytail. She was looking away and smoking a cigarette. Stan rarely smoked, but the smell and his nerves made him crave one.

"Hi," Stan said, "Can I bum a smoke?"

"Stan?" the woman asked, as she turned.

It was Del. Stan couldn't believe he hadn't recognized her.

"Del!" he said and they hugged. He was incredibly thankful to see a familiar face, especially hers.

"Wait," Stan said, "You don't smoke."

"Only after long drawn-out fights with philandering assholes."

"Yeah, I'm sorry."

"C'est la vie."

"He *is* such an asshole Del, you deserve so much more."

"Do I?" she asked, as she flicked the ash from her cigarette. Her brown eyes looked large and glassy in the shadows. "I keep asking myself, why am I attracted to these self-centered shit-bags who are sweet only when it suits them?"

Stan was silent.

"I mean what is it in me that needs his attention? He is such a fucking worm!"

Del sniffled. Stan knew she hated to cry, but he had also seen her worse than this. She quietly began to sob.

Stan felt awkward and uneasy. He knew she didn't want to be held or patronized, but she also didn't want to be left alone. So he put his hand on her cheek, lifted her head, and kissed her fully on the mouth. She kissed back. For a moment there was no one else, no Dave, no Bridgette, no party, no world other than the pure heat of their kiss. They each broke away, tenderly, slowly.

Stan felt enveloped in warm silence.

And Del reached across and clasped Stan's hand in the darkness.

2

THRESHOLD

The loud scraping of steel against steel jarred him from the deep fluid of unconsciousness. His eyes began to open almost against his will. John noticed the young French couple sleeping tightly together on the soft, orange bench seat across from him; they were covered by a large gray wool coat. Sweeping his eyes across the floor he saw the empty bottle of vodka, a crumpled pack of Camels, and his old black leather shoes. As he sat up and placed his feet upon the floor his temples began to throb. He painfully remembered the previous evening's revelries.

He had met the young French couple in the station in Prague as they waited for the train to Budapest. They shared their travel secrets in broken English and he told them about America. They pooled their cash for a bottle of cheap Russian vodka and a pack of Camels. During the night they talked about European politics, American movies, beer, and terrorism. The bottle was slowly emptied and their conversation lubricated by its loosening qualities. They never exchanged their names; they never really introduced themselves. It would seem like they had never really met or parted.

John rubbed his head. His tongue felt like a dirty tube-sock. Even after he had passed out he never really slept. Every few hours various customs officials scrutinized their passports. At one point the officials in their muted green, gray, and brown uniforms, guns strapped to their hips, moved about in an almost comical line. Each one seemed fascinated by his small blue book inscribed on the outside with the eagle seal and the words "PASSPORT" and "United States of America." Inside, laminated against the flap, was his picture looking far too serious in a slicked-back ponytail and a black shirt beside which read: "SNYDER, JOHN JASON, 1 FEB/FEB 70, M, NEW YORK, U.S.A." Just thinking about the superficial importance of the small book almost made him smile.

He parted the heavy, dirty, faded orange curtains and peered out into early morning. The sky was a cold, pale gun-metal gray. They had entered the rail yard, which meant that they would be at the station any minute. He gently shook the couple awake, and stepped outside the compartment. The narrow passageway ran between the front of the compartments and the outside windows of the train. He looked down the passageway at the few other passengers who stood at the windows. A young man to his right, two compartments down, had opened the window and he leaned out, his elbows resting on the sill and the cold air blowing his thin, dark hair in every direction. He had propped his small hard-sided suitcase between his toes and the wall. He wore an old green and brown acrylic sweater. In his left hand he held a cigarette, which he smoked carefully, leaning back away from the rush of passing air. To John's left, three compartments down, stood an older man in a tweed suit, smoking a large, dark pipe and blowing the smoke through a small opening in the window in front of him. Smoke swirled about him, hanging suspended until it was sucked into the morning air.

John opened a window and put his face out into the cold air. He inhaled deeply. The air was crisp and smelled faintly of oil and diesel exhaust. He stuck his head out farther and let the coldness slap him in the face. He went back into the compartment feeling refreshed, his face tingling. His head throbbed, his knees hurt, and his mouth tasted like wet newspapers. The young French couple nodded silently to him as he entered. They had opened up all of the curtains and were putting their things together.

He checked his pockets for his passport, cash, and credit cards. He pulled his large blue pack from the shiny steel rod shelf above his seat and groaned under the weight as he laid it on the floor. Then he carefully lowered his guitar case. He set the case on his lap and inspected his guitar, turned it over in his hands, ran his hand over the smooth, pale face, and gingerly plucked the strings. He was too tired to play and so he gently put the guitar back in its worn case and closed the latches. He cradled it in his lap and watched out the large window as the train began to slow into the station.

Holding the guitar case triggered faint memories and faded moments from many years ago. He remembered his first guitar, dinged-up and worn.

When John was six his dad had picked it up in a pawnshop after he haggled the giant of a man down to a reasonable price. It was child-sized, looking like a damaged toy in the man's hands but when John held it and plucked the strings it seemed to come alive like a long caged bird. He carried that guitar everywhere he went, like some children would carry around an old blanket or teddy bear with the stuffing seeping out. At school when the teacher would take it away from him he would scream until it was returned. He spent many nights crouched under his covers in the darkness, quietly strumming and plucking the strings to strengthen his fingers.

By the time he had begun music lessons he had already taught himself a couple of songs. He got his second guitar when he was ten and a third at fourteen. At sixteen, he got his first electric guitar and worked diligently at trying to imitate Hendrix and Page. He received accolades and was placed in special classes for gifted musicians. He performed at recitals and concerts. Before he graduated from high school he was accepted into a prestigious, private music school in Seattle.

During his first semester he realized just how much he had to learn. His classmates were child prodigies and his professors were experts and performers. He felt enormous pressure from everyone to reach a certain standard. Eventually he stopped caring, because he knew that he would never measure up. They had shown him how to kill his love of music through intense repetition, a condemnation of mistakes, and an affinity for conscripted compliance.

His unease was compounded—he was uncomfortable in his own skin. He found himself questioning his sexuality and his growing attraction to men. It was something he had secretly feared for years and he had pushed it back, focusing on his music. He stopped going to class and began to spend his days bored, drinking, getting high on whatever his friends passed along to him, sleeping, and watching TV. For almost two months he didn't even touch his guitar.

One wet October night he stayed up all night drinking and doing speed. He had passed out in the bathroom and pissed in his pants. He woke up later, in the shower, fully dressed, shivering under the scalding hot water. After he sobered up he realized that he was wasting his life on nothing and for nothing. He scraped together what cash he had and bought a one-way coach ticket to London. He packed his backpack, grabbed the passport he had never used but always intended to and a couple of credit cards his parents had given him, and left without telling anyone. He called his parents, in New York from the airport, and left a message on their voice-mail attempting to sound subdued, since they were not even aware that he had dropped out of school.

When he had stepped off the plane at Heathrow he felt alive for the first time. And yet he was frightened. He had almost no money and his parents could cancel the credit cards he was using at any time. He carried his guitar, some clothes, and a faint notion that he was venturing into the unknown.

London ended up being far different than he had envisioned. It was dirty and crowded and a lot like New York. But the people were friendly and he managed to scrape by. He made his way onto the Continent and busked at train stations and other public places for loose change thrown into his guitar case. He kept moving, sleeping in parks. It was as though he was being pulled further eastward into cities and locales that had only vaguely existed in his consciousness until now.

The train lurched forward unevenly, the brakes screaming and squealing. The train slowed to a stop, jerking slightly. He could hear people rustling about in the other cabins as they moved out into the narrow passageway. They spoke in hushed and reverent tones, unwilling to disrupt the morning's relative silence. John watched the tired travelers as they moved slowly past the cabin. The French couple and John said their adieus hugging and smiling. He felt a strange connection to these two strangers whom he was sure he would never see again. They were only staying in Budapest for a few hours and then they were off to visit the Black Sea.

The couple stepped into the passageway, squeezing between the exiting passengers as they looked back at him one last time and smiled. John stayed in his seat, with his guitar in his lap and his worldly possessions in the bag next to him. He looked out the large window into the yellow sodium lights of the station and the posters, signs, and advertisements in a language he didn't understand. He saw families embracing, a trio of men in uniform smoking cigarettes with their hands resting on their machine guns, and a young mother who dragged her child by the hand and held an old suitcase in the other. He sighed as the tired departing passengers slowed to a trickle.

He stood up and hoisted his heavy pack over his shoulders and picked up his guitar case, adjusting his hand on the handle. He moved out and walked down the narrow passage to the exit. He pulled on his shoulder straps, unsuccessfully trying to spare his back the strain.

At the end of the passage he turned and stepped through the threshold. His senses were assailed with the acrid smells of burning brakes, diesel oil, and the faint smell of urine. The station above him was expansive and cold. Announcements echoed in Hungarian. He walked down the platform, slowly, as his pack seemed to push him downward into the floor. His temples throbbed more acutely now as though someone was tapping his head with a pair of ball peen hammers. In front of him a crowd blocked his way, like a human net draped across the platform. A few young foreign tourists had been ensnared by the locals hawking lodging, cheap accommodations, and the like. Even though the young tourists were Japanese, Americans, Canadians, and assorted Northern Europeans, the sales pitches were all in English. As he grew closer he could hear the pitches being made.

"This place cheap, nice, you like," said a small, frail elderly man to the group of wide-eyed Japanese.

"Just four metro stops away, hot showers, breakfast," said a young college-age man in a bulky red sweater with a scarf wrapped around his neck.

"Cheap, good place," said a balding man with a pockmarked face to a pair of Northern Europeans.

As John neared the group of locals, who had been turned away by the others and had been watching him lumber down the platform, they began vying for position. They casually pushed passed each other, some with color brochures held tightly in their fists. The first person who spoke to him was the young, college-age man who spoke perfect English with no trace of an accent.

"Are you an American?" he asked.

John didn't feel like answering, so he merely nodded his head and tried to move forward, but the young man stepped back with him blocking his way.

John looked at the young man as he held out a brochure and began to extol the virtues of the National Student Hostel. John tried to ignore him but felt dizzy, his senses bombarded with the activity.

"No thanks," John said. "I have a place to say."

A lie, but it was enough. The young man shrugged, thrust the brochure into John's hand, and began to scan the platform for another prospect.

John moved through the crowd, avoiding direct eye contact with the other hawkers. He didn't have a place to stay and although he knew he should care he had a feeling that he should wait. He ignored the stragglers who stood behind the crowd, attempting to pick up any of the leftovers. As he started to walk down the stairs to the metro station a small, squat woman blocked his way.

"You need place to stay, no?" the woman asked, with a thick accent.

John looked down at her. She was short, around five-feet. Her hair was dark brown, wavy, and short. She wore a dark leather jacket, new-looking jeans, and had a pale-yellow silk scarf around her neck. She wore no gloves, despite the slight chill, and he noticed the pronounced bluish veins on her hands as she brought out a map of Budapest.

"We here," she said pointing to the train station on the map, which was outlined in red. "Here, my place," she said, pointing at another area circled in red a couple of inches away. "Two metro stops," she said, as she pointed at the two stops with her finger.

John looked at the map and over her shoulder, contemplating how he would get past the small woman without being overly rude.

"Parliament across street," she said, with increasing enthusiasm. "Close to everything."

"How much?" John asked, almost involuntarily, surprising himself.

"For you," she said with a small smile, "Twenty U.S."

"Twenty bucks?" John asked surprised. Suddenly, he remembered the most basic law of negotiation: never settle for the first offer.

He said, "How 'bout ten?"

The small woman scrunched up her face as though she had just bit into a lemon. "Eighteen," she said.

John was drawn in by the prospect of haggling, even though he wasn't sure he even wanted to stay at her place. "Twelve," he said folding his arms across his chest.

"Seventeen."

"Thirteen."

"Sixteen."

"Fourteen."

"Fifteen," she said. "U.S. dollars."

John thought about it, pausing mainly so that the woman wouldn't think he was a complete sucker.

"OK," he said, and held out his hand.

She looked at him awkwardly, and with a small grin on her face she shook his outstretched hand firmly.

"Follow," she said turning and moving spryly down the steps.

He lumbered after her, barely able to keep up, the pack cutting into his shoulders.

In the corner a group of men squatted around a game that looked like craps as they drank out of a bottle in a paper bag and smoked cheap-smelling cigarettes.

The stench of urine and alcohol grew stronger as they walked across a small open-air area where groups of men dressed in dirty clothes stood about or despondently watched passengers. An old man with a long, gray matted beard and dressed in dirty blue overalls and a dingy white shirt, torn and stained, was lying on the concrete floor by a bench, babbling. There was a strange absence of police or uniformed guards, and John felt uneasy.

With his pack and guitar he knew that he stood out. He could feel the men staring at him, their eyes dark with alcoholic rage and desperation. But he found himself wanting to watch, question, and examine. Their evident misery seemed profound, and yet it was as though he was looking at them from behind a wall of glass, detached, and saddened. He realized that he had been holding his breath when they descended down the next flight of steps and into the ticket area.

They neared the small ticket booth, and she spoke rapidly to the ticket seller through the small holes in the scratched glass.

"Sixty five forint," she said to John.

He realized that he had no Hungarian money because he had expected to change over his traveler's checks before he found a place to stay. He only had traveler's checks, credit cards, and a roll of American bills stuffed into his sock.

"I, ah, only have checks," he said, and shrugged.

"No worry, I take care," she said. "You pay back later."

"Thank you," John said, grinning gratefully.

They made their way through the turnstiles and down to a slow-moving escalator. The escalator descended almost vertically, seeming to defy the laws of perception and gravity. It was so steep that John felt as though he would tumble downward into the abyss if he lost his balance. He gripped the rail tightly and peered downward, unable to definitively see the platform below.

Until that moment he thought that he had become immune to the steep descents from the various subway systems in New York, Paris, London, and Prague.

As they descended the acrid, stale air, which smelled of burning rubber and oil, grew more distinct.

He followed the woman onto the platform and they walked behind the row of people facing the track. Old women stood with suitcases or old paper bags in their hands, their heads covered with kerchiefs and their stockings sewn together with thread. A few young people loitered about, glancing at John with looks of disdain, envy, or curiosity. Unlike Seattle, John noticed that everyone was dressed in clothing that looked worn-out and drab. No one wore the latest basketball shoes, fancy suits, or urban-casual GAP outfits. Looking down at his black leather jacket, Levis, and Doc Martins he began to understand exactly how much he stood out. Coupled with the pack he felt very much out of place. Just as he was growing more anxious the subway rushed into the station, grinding and squealing to a halt. The doors opened with a whoosh of air and they stepped into the old, rickety car.

The blue short, squat cars resembled the Russian-made cars in Prague. The seats filled up quickly, but John decided to stand, unwilling to remove his pack despite the pain it was causing him. He held onto the vertical bar as the doors closed and something was said in slow Hungarian over the loud speaker. He tightened his grip as the subway jerked forward and accelerated. As the subway sped along he stared at the floor, avoiding the gazes of the other passengers. Occasionally, he stole a quick glance around him. When he looked up no one seemed to notice him. No one smiled. All the faces were dour, eyes vacant and distant. The inside of the car glowed with florescent lights that gave the passengers' skin a sickly greenish-yellow hue. Outside the tunnel sped by unlit.

Ahead he could see the light of the approaching station. As the train ground to a halt it threw him forward, and he lost his footing. He stepped forward to regain his balance and nearly knocked over the small woman traveling with him.

"Sorry," John said quietly.

She shrugged as if it was no big deal.

The doors opened with a whoosh and a few of the passengers made their way through the crowd and onto the platform. More passengers came into the car, pushing John and the others against the wall. John leaned against his pack, trying to take some of the weight off his shoulders.

The doors slammed shut and the subway lurched forward, forcing John to adjust his footing while he gripped the bar tightly.

The air inside the car was stuffy and thick with the smells of sweat and stale breath.

The train plummeted forward, swaying through the cavernous darkness for ten long, loud minutes. As it approached the distant light it shuddered, jerking to a stop.

More people waited to get on the train, and as the doors whooshed open they began to push and shove their way inside. The small woman grabbed John by one of his pack straps and dragged him though the crowd. She pushed other people aside as she yelled at them in a rapid staccato of Hungarian.

They emerged from the crowd wriggling and shoving their way onto the platform. John barely extracted his guitar as the doors slammed shut.

"This way," the small woman said, motioning to the escalator.

Again they rode an escalator that seemed to stretch straight up into empty space. John imagined that if hell had escalators this would be what they would look like. He struggled to see the end, but quit when he began feeling queasy with vertigo. Tired, he turned toward the wall and the peeling and indecipherable advertisements posted there.

At the top of the escalator they came into a large room that led to three sets of escalators. John followed the woman up the short escalator in front of them, and they made their way though the turnstile by a small ticket booth. The green-tiled walls reflected the dim sunlight and as they rounded the corner he realized they were finally above ground.

They walked out of the subway entrance and into a large street. Trucks and small cars waited for the light, many belching dark diesel exhaust. He didn't recognize the makes of any of the cars. They were boxy and dull colored or white, some heavily rusted. He figured they must be Eastern European or Russian.

"Parliament," the woman said, her voice devoid of emotion. She gestured toward the park across the street and the ornate, enormous building which stood behind a black wrought iron fence.

John squinted, staring across the street, and nodded unconsciously.

The woman quickly rounded the corner and took a left along the building they just emerged from. As John rounded the corner he nearly ran into a Gypsy woman and her small child. The near collision startled him, and he found himself staring directly into her pale-green eyes.

Her skin was dark and wrinkled. Her greasy dark hair was pulled back by a worn red kerchief. Her dress looked as though it was once elaborate, but now it was faded, patched, and dirty along the hem. She was barefoot and had a green blanket wrapped around her body; she carried a small child whose only visible feature was its fine black hair.

For a few seconds the woman looked at John impassively. He no longer noticed the traffic or other people passing on the street.

Then the woman smiled, her teeth yellowed, many of them missing, and said, "Dollar?"

John was jerked back to reality when his small Hungarian tour guide pulled him roughly away by his sleeve.

She pulled him along the sidewalk as she said, "Never talk to them, never give money, steer clear, heh?"

John looked back at the woman. Her hand was outstretched and she said something in a language that he could not understand.

"You hear?" the small woman shouted, jerking his sleeve.

"Sure, yeah," he said, nodding unconsciously. He shook his head trying to clear his thoughts.

The small woman released him and they made their way down a narrow side street of old buildings in a state of decay. John could tell by the elaborate decoration and large windows that these buildings were once impressive and probably elegant. Now the decorations were covered with years of grime and soot, and some of the lower windows were enclosed by bars, while others were broken.

On the sidewalks there was broken glass and trash.

They crossed the street and walked into a shallow courtyard. It smelled overwhelmingly of ripe garbage. The woman jiggled her key in the lock and they stepped inside. The entryway reeked even more strongly of garbage, and John held his nose just as he started to quietly gag.

Maybe this was a major mistake, he thought to himself.

They walked to the elevator. A black, wrought iron cage surrounded the open shaft, and John could see the cables and wiring stretching into the floor below. She pushed the button and the elevator creaked and moaned to life. The cables pulled up slack as it slid into view and stopped with a jerking thud.

John thought, *I am not getting on that thing*. He glanced longingly at the narrow staircase which wound upward out of sight.

"Come on, you fit," the woman said, as though that was his primary concern.

John sighed and stepped into the elevator, feeling it shift slightly beneath his weight. He squeezed into it surprised by how small it was. The woman squeezed around him and swung the door closed. She pushed a button and the elevator jumped to a start.

The whole way up John felt like he should close his eyes. Every floor they passed caused the elevator to make a grinding noise. He felt like he was traveling in a cable-suspended coffin, each foot they traveled upward assuring him a longer drop into the basement below.

They jerked to a stop and the woman opened the door, holding it open for John. He stepped onto the hard marble surface and was grateful for its solidity.

They walked down the hallway and she produced a large ring of keys. As she unlocked the door, she showed him the keys and how he had to jiggle this one and that just so. He tried to pay attention but he couldn't. He was beyond exhausted. His feet were killing him, his back ached, and his head throbbed with a new intensity. His eyes burned and his throat was sore. All he wanted was the reassuring feel of deep sleep.

They entered the apartment and she called out something in Hungarian. A dark haired man dressed in a navy-blue cardigan, slacks, and a dirty T-shirt and a young college-aged man, dressed in jeans and a sweatshirt stepped into the kitchen.

"This is my husband and son," the woman said.

"Nice to meet you," John said, and shook their hands. The husband muttered something, smiled at John, and went back through the door.

"Are you from America?" the son asked, with a distinctly British accent.

"Yes. Seattle, actually."

"Really," the son said. "I have never been to the States, some day perhaps."

"Sure," John said.

There was an awkward silence.

"I'm sure you are very tired."

"Quite."

"Well, enjoy your stay then."

"Thank you."

"I show you the room," the woman said.

They walked through the kitchen and turned left down a narrow hallway.

"Here is bathroom." She flipped on the light and illuminated the large claw tub, surrounded by a yellowed, faded curtain, a small sink, and an archaic toilet with its small tank mounted far above it on the wall.

John nodded, unconcerned.

She stepped into the bathroom. "Here, the shower," she moved the curtain aside and exposed a large black cylinder that had a red lever on the side, and open area at the base from which the shower head emerged.

"For water to be hot you move the lever here, you take match." She held up wooden matches and lit it against the box. "Then match here."

Just as she placed the match into the small open area at the base of the cylinder there was a small explosion of blue and yellow flames.

At the sound of the gas igniting, John jumped backward. He was tired and his reflexes were dulled, but for a split second he was convinced that his life was going to end in a Budapest flat because a strange woman had forgotten to turn down the gas as she lit the shower. But the flames had quickly subsided into a small cool, blue flame in the base of the cylinder.

It was too much for him. His knees felt weak, and he had no inclination to even attempt to take a shower there.

From the bathroom they made their way down the hall.

"Watch your step," she said, as she stepped up into a shorter, narrower hallway.

John followed her up the step.

"Here is the other water closet," she said, motioning to a small closet that had been had hastily converted to hold a small sink and old-fashioned toilet.

John nodded. He didn't care.

"And here is your room," she said, and turned around and stepped into the small alcove. She jiggled the key in the lock, cursing slightly under her breath. Then she turned the handle and pushed the door open.

Stepping into the room he noticed that it was bright and small. The room was built just under the eaves and the two small windows were actually skylights. There were no curtains or window coverings and the room was bathed in anemic sunlight. The wall opposite the door was actually the roof and it sloped downward at a steep angle, where it met a small wall that ran vertically to the floor. A single bed was pushed up against the small wall like a berth on a ship. Its position would require the sleeper to roll out of bed and stoop or crawl until he reached a place where he could stand. John also noticed that the bed could be moved on its small wheels. The floor was made of wide wooden planks and looked worn with age. John noticed a colorful woven rug, a closet without a door, and a small unstained pine dresser, on top of which was a small brown reading lamp with a metal shade.

He walked to the closet and propped up his pack and guitar. He sighed with relief and stretched his back and shoulders as he stood up.

He noticed that the woman was looking at him pensively, waiting for a signal of approval.

"This is just fine," he said with a slight smile.

"Good, good," she said, and handed him the room keys. "If you need me, down the hall."

"Thank you," he said, practically closing the door in her face.

Sleep called him. It whispered in his ear and gnawed upon his consciousness. He felt fatigue in almost every muscle and joint in his body.

He opened up his pack and pulled out a small plastic water bottle he had been carrying since Prague. He emptied the entire contents of the bottle in three short gulps and shook the last drops into his mouth.

He carefully put the bottle back into his pack. He rolled the bed away from the wall and into the center of the room. In the lowest dresser drawer he found a couple of blankets and an old pillow. He took off his shoes and his coat and threw them on the floor. He lay down and pulled the blankets over his head.

When he opened his eyes the sunlight was blinding. He squinted against the glare and realized he was looking into the deep blue of open sky dotted with small puffy clouds. Startled, he quickly sat up and then nearly fell over as his bed moved beneath him. He looked around him and realized that he wasn't in a bed at all but was in the bottom of a small, white wooden rowboat. The paint on the boat was chipped and the wood smoothed with age. There was nothing but deep green water as far as he could see. A faint breeze blew through his hair and he could smell the briny odor of a salt-water sea. He looked over the side of the boat, gripping the gunwales so he wouldn't fall into the water, and he could see the sandy bottom deep below. A small school of dark fish moved silently through the clear water, their shadows visible below. He shook his head, confused and disoriented.

He sat back up in the boat and jerked backward, shaking the small boat, when he realized that someone was sitting across from him. It was the Gypsy woman he had seen on the street. She sat almost motionless, her back erect as she bobbed with the motion of the boat. She looked like a statue, her green eyes fixed on John. He shivered despite the warm sun. There was nowhere to go, no land or ship in sight, only the wide expanse of endless water. He looked down and then up from his hands, expecting her to be gone, but she hadn't moved. He soon found himself staring into her eyes. They were the same color as the sea they floated on, translucent, green and endless. The breeze stopped, there were no sounds, and the boat was perfectly still. Then she opened her mouth to speak.

A door slammed and John's eyes snapped opened. He was disoriented. The room was dark and stiflingly hot. For a few seconds he began to panic, his heart raced, and he felt as though he was going to suffocate. Abruptly, he realized that he was sleeping with the blankets over his face and he threw his covers off the bed, wildly gulping and gasping. As he lay there, his heart rate began to slow and he took deep breaths, remembering where he was. He knew that he must be overtired from traveling. He smiled an easy smile. His eyes became heavy and as his body relaxed he had passing flashes of the Gypsy and her sea-green eyes. He turned on his side and pulled one of the blankets over his shoulder. As he slipped into unconsciousness he thought he could feel the slight rocking of the sea.

When he woke again the room was dimmer. The shadows were long and stretched out across the floor of his small, dingy room. He rubbed his eyes. For a long time he lay on the bed, covers strewn onto the floor, and contemplated getting up. He felt as though a weight held him upon those uncomfortable polyester sheets and the flat pillow, on an old, hard mattress. He was uncomfortable in a way that moving would not help. Craning his neck he could see out the skylight, a dark blue sky speckled with gray clouds. John lay there and realized that when he tried to decide what he would do next, what his agenda would be, he could not. He felt paralyzed by a strange nothingness as if all of the color of the world had been rubbed over with dull charcoal.

He wondered why the hell he had left Prague. There was something for him there, an intangible thing, but something none the less.

John had spent almost four and a half weeks in Prague. He had spent his days sipping coffee at the Globe Café, under the bright-green awning, the sounds of the street mixing harmoniously with Ella Fitzgerald and the whoosh of the espresso steam. Much of the rest of the day he spent at the park, just across the slow-moving Valta from tourist-infected Old Town. He swapped stories with the long-haired, time-tripped hippie kids from Germany, France, England, and the States. The days were deliciously warm, and he had spent many hours snoozing in the sunshine, resting his head on his folded arms, the wind rustling his hair as he inhaled the sweet smell of growing grass. At night he left the park for a place that served Mexican food. The food was a fairly poor Czech imitation of Mexican fare, but the Budvar was exquisite and cheap. There was always some ex-patriot or pretty-boy American tourist to talk to.

In fact, there were Americans everywhere. Mostly they were kids who came with money and were bored with bland American pop culture. They craved the image of the exotic, their preconceived notions clouding their perception of reality. Most of them, even those that had lived in Prague for months, knew neither the language nor the history of the place they visited. They lived largely unconcerned because they were living the image, one which they would parade in front of their friends when they moved back to the States. Years later, when they had settled into their staid day jobs, they would lament leaving Prague not knowing that they had never really been there. Like so many tourists they lived on the outside: they glimpsed only the physical beauty and trappings.

It irritated John that these kids seemed wholly unaware of the world outside of their immediate sphere. When John asked them what they thought about Sarajevo or Bosnia they merely shrugged. They seemed unperturbed by the terrible devastation, massacres, genocide, and bloodshed not so far away. These ex-patriots made John sick, so he mostly stuck to himself. When he became lonely he would use a trick he had learned in school: banter with them about things that didn't make them uneasy, and they would have surface conversations which were as meaningless as they were forgettable.

A couple of times he tried to get jobs, with a halfhearted effort. Besides, he knew that they would never pay well enough for him to give up his leisure: his time to play, watch beautiful people, sleep in the park, and feel the sun on his arms.

He never really decided that he would leave. He had simply packed his things and left. He had spent a long time packing and unpacking, trying to get things just right. He settled his bill at the youth hostel and took a bus to the train station. As he waited for his train, everything around him felt strangely surreal.

Looking back at his time in Prague seemed like a story he was told by someone else. Reality, in all of its stark coldness, was beginning to settle in. He realized that he was waking from the kind of reverie which makes waking life unusually boring and cruel. When it was time to leave he saw that although he had really believed he loved Prague, he, too, had been on the outside. He had been enamored by Prague's old, twisting cobblestone streets and mix of internationals, its beautifully maintained buildings, its warm sunshine, and its quiet spaces. But he had never really known, or understood, Prague's soul. Somehow, sitting near the train platform, he knew that he would never be back. He was pushing eastward into places which sounded like exotic foods as their names passed between his lips.

He lay there for what seemed like hours. Someone next door was cooking. He could hear the clamor of pans and the sizzle of oil. The smells of fish, vegetables, peanut oil, and spices wafted into his room. He caught small snippets of conversation in a language he didn't understand but sounded like Thai.

The odor soon became overpowering, and he could almost taste what they were cooking. The smell reminded him of a time he had eaten in the International District in Seattle, sort of a small Chinatown. Many East Asian immigrants shared the area, operating everything from quaint cafes to small markets. He had gone there with his mom and step dad when they came to get him settled into college.

They had eaten at a hole in the wall Thai place. John had the best pad

Thai jay he had ever tasted. The peanut taste wasn't overpowering and the sauce just sweet, tart, and spicy enough. The crystal spring rolls, of rice noodles, fried tofu, and vegetables, were fantastic and dipping them in the sweet, tart sauce delectable. His mom and step dad's dinners were also unbelievable. His parents also had some Thai beer, which John had sipped.

They had eaten and talked. For the first time John actually had an adult conversation with his parents. He felt as though he was being treated as an equal. It was a wonderful high, to be so connected to the people who had given him everything and so at ease. He still held onto the lucid memory of that night. To look back now, John could hardly believe that things would go so unbelievably wrong in school. That night there was no hint of things to come.

As he sat in his small room in Budapest he felt overwhelmed. He was beginning to unravel. It was a sickening sensation and, coupled with the smell of oil and seafood, made the bile rise up in his throat. He knew if he stayed in that room he would either puke or throw himself from the tiled roof.

John put on his shoes, threw on his jacket, grabbed his guitar, and backpack, and headed out. He made his way down the narrow hallway, walked through the kitchen, placed the keys on the counter, and walked out the door. As he made his way down the stairs, he held his nose against the stench of garbage. Eventually he was out on the street.

He set down his guitar and lit a cigarette.

He stood there for a moment listening to the sounds of the cars and voices as they echoed down the canyon of concrete. He picked up his guitar.

It was time to go home.

3

THE LONG DAYS BETWEEN

Delany Richardson looked up from the large salmon carcass to the clock high up on the gray wall. It read six after seven. She had been on her feet for almost twelve hours now. At noon she had slept through her short thirty-minute lunch break. She stood in a film of red fish blood and bluish guts, which lapped over the toes of her black rubber boots. Through her glove liners and yellow rubber gloves she could barely feel the smooth insides of the headless six-pound Coho salmon.

She hooked one hand just under the place where its jaw used to end, where the slit in its belly began between the pectoral fins, and she held its tail in the other. Carefully she turned around, lifted the slime-covered fish onto the six-foot metal cart, and slid it onto the second of seven metal trays. She pivoted and bent down again into the large, five by five foot square, white plastic tub and reached into the pile of fish.

She kept one eye on the graders that pulled the fish off the conveyer belt and tossed them over their shoulders into the plastic tubs. She had been hit more than once with a large, wet, cold salmon; its lifeless decapitated body, covered with a sticky film, slapped her in the head and arms.

She picked a greenish-silver-skinned salmon from the pile hooking two fingers, and her thumb under the jaw, and grabbed its tail with the other hand. She turned around and slid the fish next to the other on the stainless steel rack so they lay side by side, their tails barely.

The cutters and conveyer belts roared, nearly drowning out the music blasting from the old boom box, which hung on a hook on the side of a square white pillar near the slime line. She could just barely hear "No Quarter" by *Led Zeppelin*.

Greer, standing next to her, stacked the top rack. His long gangly arms were covered with yellow gloves and elastic gaiters. Greer's yellow PVC overalls were draped on his thin frame, hanging by thick suspenders, touching him only where they met his boots and inviting in the occasional spilled blood, water, or fish to soak his faded jeans. He looked down at Delany and smiled a distant smile that conveyed the fatigue they both felt. She nodded almost imperceptibly, turning up the corners of her mouth as if to answer his silent complaint.

She adjusted her yellow PVC jacket and pants, which seemed to slide around on their own. Through the cuffs and collar, fish blood and water soaked through, slowly saturating her clothing so that she would stay wet until long after she had left work. Despite the knit cap, jeans, T-shirt, and two sweatshirts she wore under her yellow plastic slickers, she was still cold. Normally the temperature inside the plant hovered around fifty, but today it was cold and rainy outside, with a high of fifty-one. Cold air and gusts of water blew in through the large metal doors, kept open for the forklifts.

As she exhaled she could see faint wisps of steam from her breath.

So this is Alaska in July, she thought as she shivered slightly.

She had been working at the Anchorage Salmon Packing Plant for almost four weeks. But it seemed like years. Each day she dragged herself out of bed at six, showered, ate some breakfast, and John and Cynthia picked her up around six forty-five. They got to work just after seven. She squeezed out from the back seat of Cowboy John's rusty blue Datsun 210 and followed John and his girlfriend Cynthia across the hard dirt lot to the back stairs. As soon as they stepped out of the car they could smell the distinct stench of dead salmon that coated everything. It was a pervasive perfume that reminded Del of fatigue and boredom.

The metal stairs, slightly wet with fish blood and grime tracked in from the factory floor, were always a challenge. The pitch and length alone were enough to make Del clutch the railing three-quarters of the way up, nearly out of breath as her thighs, never seeming to recover from hours of standing, pleaded for mercy.

One morning she had ascended the stairs only half-awake. Her eyes closed by themselves and a dreamy haze clouded her other senses. Halfway up she took her hand off the railing and, in her almost treadles Nikes, she tried to hop up the last few steps. When she slipped the sharp green metal seemed to reach out and smack her. For a couple of seconds she lay on the stairs slightly stunned. It was Greer's deep Caribbean-tinged voice that had snapped her back.

"Cha! Catsplattle! You OK?" he said, as he stood near the huge factory door, smoking. He started to make his way to help her.

"Oh yeah fine, fine," she said picking herself up and brushing herself off.

Greer stopped at the bottom of the stairs, his long dark fingers resting loosely around the smooth steel railing.

She rubbed her arm, which she knew would develop a nasty bruise, and she felt her face growing red. She knew the "cancer crew," the smokers who loitered outside the plant and puffed away before their shift started, had seen the whole thing. They watched her with sick, detached fascination or concern.

Del grabbed the railing tightly and walked up the rest of the stairs as fast as she could. She didn't turn around as she opened the door and stepped into the break room.

On the many other days that she made it up the back stairs safely, she would squeeze into the narrow, dilapidated women's locker room, where she changed into her overalls, boots, liners, gloves, gaiters, and jacket. With her fingers uncoordinated and reflexes slow and tired, she spent far more time than usual getting dressed.

She punched in on the time clock and work started at seven thirty. When she was lucky she was done with work at seven or seven thirty at night, which meant she got home around eight. But it had been an unusually busy season and she was working until almost nine every night. And every day it started all over again, one day blending into the next, a seemingly endless stream of dead fish to rack.

The first week she had dreamt of millions of headless bloody fish almost every night. She would wake, slightly queasy, and take deep breaths until she fell back asleep. Later she was too tired to dream. Every night she stripped off her clothes, took a quick shower, and fell into bed, oblivious of the pale light of the midnight sun, which dimly lit her room even with the blinds closed. When the alarm went off she was almost always disoriented, convinced that she had just shut her eyes, that only a few seconds had elapsed since she last lay down.

Her first day she had been put on the slime line. The salmon, which had suffocated after they had been pulled from the water, were packed with ice in large plastic tubs on the fishing boats. Then they were brought into the plant on flatbed trucks and unloaded by forklifts, which dumped them into large metal containers high above the factory floor. When the cutter was turned on, the fish were fed, with the help of a hapless worker, into the cutters and decapitated in one powerful chop. They were gutted by the same machine, their insides spilling out. Next they slid down a short conveyer belt to the slime line.

The slime line consisted of approximately ten to twelve people, who stood on either side of a steel table through which the conveyer belt passed. As the fish came sliding onto the table the slimers, each armed with a small, extremely sharp, plastic-handled steel knife, scraped the insides of the fish to remove any of the excess guts or blood. If all of the blood wasn't removed the meat would dry out. The Japanese who owned the plant were paranoid about the slightest compromise in quality because the salmon would be frozen into filet size salmon steaks and sent to Japan, where the prices were ludicrously inflated.

At the slime line they had handed Del a knife, and one of her fellow workers showed her how to scrape out the fish in two quick motions. She stood at the table and diligently tried to clean fish as fast as she could, but they soon piled up in front of her. The slimer standing next to her tried to help her, giving her instructions in Filipino-speckled English, and cleaning some of Del's fish himself. She couldn't keep up with the other workers at the table, who cleaned about three fish a minute. After her lunch break she was moved to the tank.

The just cleaned fish were pushed, and slid, into the huge tank, which resembled a tall horse trough, where they were dipped and washed of excess blood. The two or three workers on the tank had to reach into the frigid, dirty water, pull the fish out, and put them on another conveyer belt, where they would be graded according to quality.

For almost five hours Del had to lean down into the tank, pull the fish out of the cold water, and put them on the conveyer belt. After the first hour her hands started to feel numb and the water had begun the seep through her gaiters and onto her sleeves. Occasionally, a fish slid too fast into the water off the slime line and splashed her. The dirty cold water and briny saltiness stung her lips. By the second hour her back had begun to ache. Before the end of her shift she began to dread the thought of reaching into the tank.

Once again the forewoman, June Schmitty, had noticed her less than stellar performance, but because of her willingness to work hard and she was placed at the racks. It was better work than the slime line or the tank, and the only hazard was the occasional misdirected, flying fish carcass and utter and complete boredom.

At first she thought that having so much time to think would be almost luxurious, since she seemed to never have a solid minute at school to reflect on anything. Eventually, when the fatigue and the repetitive motions had worn her down physically, her mind seemed to shut down as well. She became a zombie. Her only thoughts were directed at counting the time until the next break, or the hot shower when she got back to her rented room, or the last time she had a cold beer with friends. She felt as though she had become a cog in the fish factory—a human answer to a production need, which was cheaper than a machine.

Even the pay was ridiculously bad. She made five fifty an hour and time and a half after she worked forty hours a week. At first she was delighted at the thought of making about sixty bucks a day, but after the first pay day she realized that she hadn't accounted for the big chunk taken out for taxes, Social Security, and union dues. Plus she had to pay for the dinky room she rented and overpriced food. She had settled into a regimen of peanut butter and jelly sandwiches, chips, raisins, canned green beans, and an occasional chocolate bar. There was never enough time to go out to eat, unless she chose to stop sleeping.

In Washington her friends and acquaintances went on and on about all of the money you could make working in Alaska. They made it sound like another gold rush, as though just being there was enough to make you rich. She knew now that the only people who made money in southwestern Alaska were the Japanese who owned the plants, the tour companies, and the fishing boat owners who flew up from the Lower Forty Eight once a year and made a small killing. The only other place that paid was the North Slope. But Del had heard stories of the desolate and miserably cold place and decided it wasn't where she wanted to spend her summer break. She was resigned to making as much money as she could while the short season lasted so she could buy a used car.

She looked up again at the clock. It read seven forty seven.

Christ, only forty one minutes since I last looked, Del thought. She sighed.

Del noticed Greer watching her.

"Wha' don you take break?" he said. "Is cool."

Del' looked up into Greer's large, dark-brown eyes, framed by almost iridescent whiteness. He frowned, his dark wrinkled skin creasing around the corners of his mouth. He rested his hands on his hips and tilted his head to one side, and seemed to Del as through he was trying to read her thoughts.

Even though he was serious, Del couldn't help but chuckle at Greer's demeanor.

"Kaffofle! Wha' chu laughin' at, girl?" he asked.

"Just tired that's all," she said. "I'll be up in the break room."

Greer nodded knowingly and returned to stacking the fish in one fluid motion.

Del took off her yellow coat, overalls, and gloves and hung them on a long row of pegs just inside the large open doorway. She made a conscious effort to remember exactly where she put them; although her name was written on it, it was easy to lose track amid the wall of yellow PVC outfits.

She stepped out into a light drizzle. It was surreal to step outside in the middle of her shift. Management frowned upon people taking unscheduled breaks, but they also seemed to be afraid of the union. Besides, she knew some people who left in the middle of their shift to go sleep on top of the folded boxes in the upstairs warehouse. Somehow they never seemed to get caught. Standing in the cold, her breath coming out in faint wisps of steam, it was tempting to go upstairs, climb up onto the highest stack of dry, clean boxes, and fall asleep surrounded by the smell of cardboard.

The stairs were slippery and she made her way up them carefully. She was tired and her reflexes slow, and she had no desire to fall and hurt herself. At the top of the stairs she turned left and went into the women's locker room. She peed and washed her hands with hot water and liquid soap. Still her hands smelled like fish. Around the cuffs of her sweatshirt was a two-inch wide stain of pinkish fish blood and water. It was still wet to the touch and it smelled distinctly of dead fish.

She sighed again. She hadn't brought another clean shirt, not that it really mattered since it would get as dirty as the first. She sat down on the narrow wood bench which ran between the lockers. Sitting there she felt more than tired. She felt hollow. It was as though there was an emptiness consuming her from inside. She lay back on the bench, covered her head with her arms, and began to quietly cry. She wasn't sure how long she lay there. Thankfully no one walked in.

When she started to feel better she got up and went to the sink to splash cold water on her face. She dried her face with paper towels and looked into the mirror. For the first time in a long time she really looked at her reflection. It was alarming because she didn't recognize herself. She was normally very thin, but her face was drawn and sallow with dark circles and slight bags under her dark brown eyes. She looked like death warmed over, as her mom used to say.

Del rubbed her eyes and turned away from the mirror.

The door squeaked open and an older woman she didn't know stepped into the locker room.

"Hello," the woman said, and made her way to the toilets and sink.

"Hi," Del said, feeling awkward and uncomfortable. She stepped out into the hall, took a deep breath, and walked into the break room.

The break room was fairly small considering that there were about a hundred and fifty employees at the plant. At most, about forty to fifty employees could sit comfortably and eat or chat. At the entrance to the break room was the new digital time clock and pale yellow time cards, each in their respective slots, sorted by number. To the right of the time clock was a small dirty co-ed restroom.

There were three rows of folding tables scrunched together so tightly that one had to walk sideways between them. Opposite the entrance was a counter, sink, a full-sized fridge, which was always overflowing with workers' lunches, two soda machines, and an overpriced vending machine with stale snacks.

A small group of workers she didn't recognize was sitting at one of the far tables smoking. The break room had begun to fill up with smoke. There were no windows in the break room and so the stench of smoke, food, or the bathroom always lingered. Out of courtesy and an unofficial management policy, no one smoked during lunch breaks, but it was well after lunch and the afternoon break. The thick smell of secondhand smoke was disgusting.

Her head began to throb just behind her eyes. The strange sensation of the heat and pressure was spreading to her sinuses, and she thought that she might be getting a caffeine withdrawal headache.

She walked back to the locker room, dug around in her dark-blue nylon coat for some quarters, and went back and bought herself a soda. Even before her first sip she was craving the euphoria of a caffeinated rush. She stood by the time clock and guzzled half of the can of too sweet, cold yellow liquid. She carried her soda into the warehouse, which was permeated by the smell of dust and cardboard. Her head continued to throb.

To her right, twenty feet away, was the small supply/first aid station, the logistical supply point for almost all of the workers at the plant. It was run by Florence Schmitty who was known to everyone as Flo. June, the forewoman, was Flo's daughter. But Flo seemed to lack the good-natured, positive joviality that June was so famous for. Flo was in charge of checking out uniforms—coats, pants, gloves, glove liners, and boots; she was also in charge of first aid, which consisted mainly of doling out powerful pain medication and band aids. Flo did her job with a serious, stern, slow consternation.

Del quietly walked up to the open half-door of the supply/first aid station. She was careful to avoid leaning on the top of the half-door, a move that had earned other workers a stern tongue-lashing. Flo was seated on a tall wooden stool, her rail-thin frame hunched over a newspaper, folded on the counter in front of her. She wore a worn pink sweatshirt and faded jeans. Her white and pewter-colored hair was thin and cropped short. A pair of black-framed half glasses sat on the end of her slightly crooked nose. A lit cigarette hung from her lips as though it was glued there. In her right hand she held a blue ballpoint pen; her left hand lay on the counter, the fingers curled together in a loose fist.

All around Flo, in every conceivable space, on every shelf, were boxes of gauze pads, rolled-up glove liners, and other random items.

Somehow, Del felt this narrow closet of a room, steel shelves packed to its high ceiling, symbolized Flo's very nature.

Del made a soft squeak with the toe of her boot against the worn wooden floor.

Flo looked up from her paper, slowly. Although she was only about fifteen feet away she squinted, trying to make out the face of her visitor. She put her paper and glasses down, stiffly got off her stool, and walked to the half-door.

Del waited, her head throbbing, the soda in her hand chilling the tips of her fingers. She almost held her breath in anticipation of the response of the small, frail-looking woman who shuffled toward her.

Flo gazed at Del with a look of irritation and curiosity.

"What'd you want?" she asked, putting her right hand upon her hip as her other hand dangled by her side, still clenched in a fist.

"Uh, I, ah," stammered Del. "Could I get something for my headache?"

Flo let out an exasperated sigh and narrowed her eyes in a manner that made it clear she was in no mood to be bothered for something so trivial.

"Yeah, one minute," Flo said, shuffling back to pick up her glasses.

She pulled a small white cardboard box off the shelf, using only her right hand, and placed it carefully on the counter. Again with her right hand, her left dangling at her side, she pulled two plastic-wrapped samples out of the box and laid them on the counter. She picked up her blue pen, scribbled something on a yellow legal pad, and carried the pills back to Del.

"Read the directions," Flo said as she placed the packets in Del's outstretched hand.

"Thank you very much," Del said, as Flo turned around without acknowledgment.

Del shrugged unconsciously and walked back to the break room.

The small party of smokers was gone, and only the smell of cigarettes and cheap coffee lingered. She read the back of one of the packets of pills. It read: "two tablets every four to six hours." Del ripped open the packet and swallowed two with a gulp from her soda. She rubbed her temples with her hands, took off her old baseball cap, and scratched her scalp. She took her hair out of the "scrunchy," running her fingers through her hair. It was the most relaxing thing that she had done all day. She decided not to go back down to the floor, but sat sipping her drink until the shift whistle sounded and the workers began milling into the break room.

Del grabbed her time card and punched out just as a line was beginning to form. She waded through the cluster of other workers who were immersed in nervous conversations that seemed to suggest something about a strike.

She walked into the locker room, grabbed her coat and bag, and was about to walk out the door when Cynthia grabbed her arm. Cynthia was a short, stout bleach-blond girl who always seemed overly dramatic to Del.

"Did you hear?" Cynthia asked, as though she were imparting items concerning life or death. "The fishermen are going to strike and our union is going to recognize it and soon some of us will be out of work."

Del found it interesting, but coming from Cynthia it sounded like pure speculation. But her curiosity was definitely piqued, and she would have to ask a few other people what they thought.

"It's those damn Japs," Cynthia said, "I mean this is the U.S., they can't just do whatever they want here just 'cause they own the place."

That's my cue, Del thought.

"I gotta take care of some stuff before we leave," she said to Cynthia.

"Oh, okay," Cynthia said, with obvious disappointment, as she released Del's arm. "See you back at the car then."

Outside on the landing, Del could feel the wet mist of the cold night air upon her face. Below, a few workers were hosing off floors while others scrubbed with citrus-smelling disinfectant. The smells of dead fish, citrus, and impending rain mixed strangely. Leaning against the railing, she looked out over the railroad tracks behind the plant, and into the low clouds which obscured her view of Anchorage. She considered the possibility of a strike. It would mean she would have to go back to Washington early, with little of the money she had planned on earning. So far she had saved about a thousand dollars, which now seemed like almost nothing. Though her headache had abated it seemed to begin anew as she clenched her jaw with anxiety. She knew it was premature to get over excited about something that hadn't even happened yet.

Del walked down the stairs and into the maze of steel racks covered with frozen remnants of fish blood, water, and slime waiting for Greer to hose them off.

Greer watched her walk through the racks and turned off the hose.

"Hey!" she said, smiling, and stepped into a small open area that was surrounded by racks.

Del knew she would find Greer washing the racks, as he did every night after work. He worked longer and harder than anyone else at the plant. He had told her he was trying to make enough money to help support his wife and kids back in L.A., as well as to send some money to the rest of his family in Barbados. He originally wanted to be on a fishing or crab boat, despite his wife's fears. Later, he found out the owners were reluctant to take him aboard anyway, making lame excuses.

Greer smiled back at Del his large brilliantly white teeth luminescent in the dim light. Del noticed that the yellow PVC jacket he wore over his wool sweater was too short to fully cover his long arms. He saw her looking at the jacket.

"Not mine," he said, "don' know where mine at."

There was a moment of silence as Del tried to figure out how to broach the subject.

"You heard?" she asked.

"Yeah."

"Worried?"

"'Bit," he said, shifting his weight and looking slightly uncomfortable.

"Are you going to stay?"

"Don' know."

They were both silent again. Greer reached into his shirt pocket and fished out a cigarette and lighter. "Dis cool? Tis okay if I smoke, right?"

"No, no," Del said, shaking her head even if she did a bit. "I don't mind."

He cupped his hands and lit his cigarette, taking long puffs, turning his head, and carefully exhaling away from Del.

It was the longest conversation they had had. Despite the long silences, Del didn't feel especially uncomfortable, because the silence somehow seemed as important as the words themselves.

"Feelin' betta?" Greer asked.

Del was puzzled for a moment, and then remembered how Greer had been the one who suggested she take a break.

"Oh yeah," she said, "much better." Her headache was now nonexistent, and she felt more awake. She realized that she could hear Cynthia and John yelling for her from the parking lot.

"I ah, should go," Del said.

"Sure t'ing," Greer said. "See ya."

Del ran over to the parking lot and apologized profusely to Cynthia and John, who looked visibly irritated.

They dropped Del off at her place, which was on the edge of town. The white one-story apartment building looked somewhat out of place against the backdrop of the dark green marshes and woods. She checked her mail. There was a single letter from her parents, in Denver. She put the letter inside her coat pocket, opened the dead bolt, and pushed open the white metal door, which squeaked slightly on its hinges. Her apartment was dark, the shades drawn, and the only light filtered in through spaces and cracks in the blinds. She flipped on the light.

The apartment was one large room and a separate bathroom. There was a movable fabric partition that separated the bedroom from the rest of the apartment. Del figured that someone, most likely the owner, had cheaped-out and decided not to put an actual wall between the bedroom and the rest of the apartment. However, privacy wasn't really an issue, since only two other people had been in her apartment: her landlord, Clay, and her elderly next door neighbor, Hazel Dorn.

There was no closet. A rod and some shelves were built into one wall of her bedroom. She found that it worked well. She had only brought what she could carry on the plane. Sometimes she found herself wanting something that she had put in storage in Bellingham, but on the whole she was fairly content making do with less.

The apartment seemed particularly cavernous because there was almost no furniture. She had one chair that Hazel had lent her and an air mattress. The kitchen had a counter and cabinets that gave the illusion that it was separate from the rest of the apartment. The counter had been extended into the living room, as Del sarcastically called it, where she sat propped up on a couple of pillows to eat.

She had also brought her small CD/tape/radio boom box and a smattering of her favorite CDs and tapes. She kept it in the kitchen where she could listen to the news or her music.

She took off her coat and hung it on a hook by the door. She slipped off her shoes without bothering to untie them.

Del walked across the brown shag carpeting to the bathroom. She peeled off her multiple layers of clothes and stepped into a scalding hot shower. One of the reasons she had picked her apartment was because the rent included utilities and she loved to take long showers. She scrubbed herself with soap and a loofah. She shampooed her hair twice and then conditioned it. After she had rinsed out the conditioner she stood under the spray of hot water which eased the aches in her neck and back. She stayed under the water until the bathroom was so full of steam she could barely see. Then she got out, dried off, wrapped a towel around her hair, and slipped into her soft fleece robe. She picked up her pile of clothes and threw them into a wrinkled brown plastic bag.

She walked into the kitchen and turned on the light. Her journal sat on the counter, unopened, since she had arrived. She felt a pang of guilt for avoiding something that had been such a cherished routine. But she felt like she had nothing left today and nothing she wanted to remember. She slid it into an empty drawer.

Then she checked the contents of her fridge. There were five bottles of beer, a couple of eggs, a stick of butter, a small wedge of cheddar cheese, a half gallon of milk, a jar of peanut butter, jelly, and a large container of salsa. Standing in front of the open fridge she debated if she felt like having a beer.

What the hell, Del thought, and pulled a Sam Adams from its cardboard holder.

She took her Swiss army knife out of the drawer that also contained a couple hard plastic camping forks, spoons and knives. She popped the beer open and took a sip. It was deliciously cold. As she leaned against the counter, she realized she was hungry. She put the beer down and pulled out the eggs, milk, cheese, butter, and salsa. On the counter top was a bag of stale corn chips. The old skillet, borrowed from Hazel, sat on the stove. It looked clean enough to Del, so she turned the burner to medium high.

With a knife she spread a small amount of butter on the pan, lifted the pan off the burner, and moved it from side to side so that a thin coating of butter covered the whole inside of the pan. She cracked the eggs into the pan; they turned white almost instantly as they sizzled and crackled from the heat. She took the fork and scrambled the eggs in the pan, adding a little milk.

She took another sip of her beer, stepped over to her stereo, and pushed play on the CD player. She knew what disk it was: Bob Marley and the Wailers, *Legend*. The slow rhythm, and then Bob Marley's voice asking, "Is This Love?" filled the room. She turned it up, feeling the sound of the music as it washed pleasantly through her apartment. The beer was beginning to give her a buzz, and as she stood at the stove poking the eggs to see how done they were, she could only smile. "No Woman No Cry" came on, and she felt almost lost within the message: "Here little darlin', don' shed no tears. No woman, no cry." For the first time in awhile, she felt really good, for no other reason than she was living deep within this moment, and it filled her up.

With the eggs still slightly runny she took a handful of corn chips, crushed them in her hand, and scattered them over the eggs. Then she took her Swiss army knife and cut the cheese into small, thin slices. She placed the slices of cheese on top of the chips and they melted down into the eggs. Opening up the salsa jar, she poured a little over the top of the cheese. With her fork she mixed the eggs, chips, cheese, and salsa around in the pan, making sure everything cooked evenly. She turned the broiler on, took out two slices of wheat bread, and placed them on the oven rack to toast.

With the beer in her hand she began to sway and spin to the music.

When the eggs were cooked, a little browned on the outside, she took her single plate from the cupboard. It was a blue, steel enameled plate, covered with white flecks. She had found eight settings in her parents' garage before she had left for school. Her family had had them ever since she was little, and they were a regular part of camping mealtimes. One plate, one bowl, and one cup was all that she felt she would need, and she knew her folks wouldn't miss them.

She slid the eggs, chips, cheese, and salsa onto her plate, grabbed her toast out of the oven, and a clean fork. She pulled her chair up to the counter and sat on the two pillows she had left on the seat. She set down her beer down took a bite, using her toast as a wedge to keep it on her fork. It was heavenly—spicy and hot. She nursed her beer to quell the heat.

Halfway through the eggs, and after eating a piece of toast, memories of this same dish came back to her. Her mom, Julia, called them Chili Killies, an Americanized version of the Mexican name: "chilaquiles."

Del's grandfather, Raul Ortiz, was born into a middle-class Mexican family who lived in south central Mexico. Raul met Del's grandmother, Samantha Furbidge, when he was visiting relatives in Mexico City. Samantha had gone to Mexico to study art and culture. Raul and Samantha had fallen in love in a small museum looking at samples of traditional weaving. They eloped to El Paso a month later, and neither of them looked back.

Julia Ortiz had grown up in California speaking some Spanish. After Raul had reconciled with his family, ten years after he left, she began to learn about her roots. But Julia grew up surrounded by the white upper-middle class affluence of Samantha's family. Her complexion was much fairer than her father's, with light brown eyes and slightly olive skin. The only other Mexican kids she knew were recent immigrants who were unofficially segregated from their white peers. When she was thirteen, unsure of who she was and wanting nothing more than to fit in, Julia decided she wanted to be white. She made up her mind that she would forget her heritage and be exactly like all her other friends at school.

Much to her father's surprise, disappointment, and quiet sadness, she stopped speaking Spanish with him around the house. She stopped celebrating Catholic holidays and even went so far as to take on bad habits during Lent. Her father felt he was being pushed away, but her mother said it was only a phase. But the phase never really ended. By the time she was in college she was going by "Julie" and she no longer mentioned her last name, Ortiz, if she could avoid it.

In college, Julie met and fell in love with a boy from upstate New York named James Richardson. They were married during the summer after her junior year and Julia was pleased to have become Julie Richardson. It wasn't until almost twenty years later, when Raul Ortiz lay dying from pancreatic cancer, at his family's house in Mexico, that Julie realized that she would always be Julia. She traveled to Mexico and stayed with her parents for fourteen long, torturous months while the cancer ate her father alive. She spent long hours speaking with him in Spanish and reading to him when he could no longer bear to sit up. When she came back she was transformed and saddened because she had spent so many years running from a father she deeply loved.

Del had never really gotten to know her grandfather, since he died when she was young. But her mom made it a point to make sure that Del saw her grandmother on holidays and during summer break. They would spend long hours sitting in the kitchen or out on the deck talking about old times and long-lost relatives.

Del sighed as she realized that she would miss visiting with her this summer. She remembered she had slipped her parents' letter in her pocket and almost forgotten about it. She pulled out the slightly creased envelope and opened it.

Dearest Delany,

We are so sorry that we missed your birthday. Big 19! We called Hazel's and she said that you had gone out with some friends. I can't believe that you are nineteen! I remember the day you were born. It was a beautiful day! Just after you were born, as I held you in my arms and looked at your tiny face, I was moved to tears. Your father and I are so proud of you! Hazel said that you are working long hours. Don't wear yourself out. If you need us to send you anything don't hesitate to call.

We got your last letter, thanks so much for writing. Last Saturday your grandma flew up from Taos to visit. We had a wonderful time. But your brother is so testy. He is every bit as difficult as any sixteen-year-old kid. We are having a terrible time trying to get him to come in by his curfew time. You were so much more responsible, or maybe we're getting too old. Take care of yourself and tell us if you need anything.

Love,

Mom, Dad, Billy and your favorite dog, Peaches

Del smiled. It was good to hear from her folks. She probably would have had a better time on her birthday if she were back in Denver. John, Cynthia, Ryan, Doreen, and a few other people had taken her out to a bar in Anchorage that never checked IDs. She tried to have a good time, but she ended up getting drunk and sick. The next day, fighting a hangover at work she realized she had almost nothing in common with the people she had gone out with. They were shallow and only concerned about appearances and wanted so badly to be cool in just the right way. They were so full of insecurities that it only made Del feel sorry for them. She had tried to find out their interests or what they cared about. It was like talking to adolescents. They were not passionate about anything and complacent about everything. Their conversation had turned to talk about work and work gossip. Drinking was all Del could do to tolerate them.

So far Del wasn't even sure what she thought about Alaska. She had started her job four days after she had landed in Anchorage, and she had spent those days finding a place to live and a ride to work, filling out paperwork, setting up a local bank account, and chatting with Hazel.

When Del had first moved in Hazel had come over to see how she was getting along. She hobbled into Del's apartment with the hand-carved birch cane her grandson had given her. She stood in Del's doorway, back hunched and squinting with her one good eye. Del looked up from the bag on the floor that she was unpacking to see Hazel's silhouette framed by the bright afternoon sunshine.

Del jumped slightly. She was caught off guard, deep within her own thoughts and hadn't realized that she left the door wide open.

"Heh," Hazel chuckled. "Didn' mean to surprise ya."

"No, it's OK, really," Del said, standing up from her scattered clothes.

"Got a man friend comin' over or somethin'?" Hazel asked, her false teeth parted in a wry smile.

Del looked down at her bag. There was a long strip of condoms poking out from the center of her T-shirts like a flat orange snake.

Del blushed, quickly knelt down, and pushed the condoms back into her bag. "My kid brother insisted on me bringin' them," Del said quickly.

"Pshaw," Hazel said, brushing her hand through the air as though she was swatting away a small fly. "A lady's gotta be careful these days."

Del nodded unconsciously. She realized that she hadn't invited the woman in.

"I'd invite you in but there is no place to sit," Del said.

"You mean you ain't got no furniture?" Hazel asked, concerned.

"Well, not really," Del' answered, a bit embarrassed.

"Guess we'll just have to remedy that, won't we." It wasn't a question. "I ain't got much but the good Lord's been kind to me and I'll see if I don' have something' you can use."

"I don't want to be a bother," Del said.

"Pshaw!" Hazel exclaimed, "Ain't no bother." She motioned Del to her with her arm.

Del got up and took her arm.

"I'm Hazel," Hazel said, "Hazel Dorn."

"Good to meet you. I'm Delany," Del said. "Delany Richardson, but my friends call me Del."

Hazel smiled, and they went over to Hazel's for some coffee and three and a half-hours of conversation.

Hazel told Del about growing up poor in rural Arkansas, moving to Alaska with her husband just after they were married, and the long months they spent apart.

Hazel's husband, Theo, was drafted in WWII and sent to Anchorage and then to a remote listening post on a tiny Aleutian island. Hazel had followed him as far as Anchorage and would have followed him farther, the ends of the earth she told him, but there were no wives allowed at the remote radio outpost.

For the first two months she had a lot of trouble adjusting to her new life. She spent long sleepless nights sitting on her couch staring into the starless summer nights. Eventually she developed a routine: meeting with other military wives, organizing bridge clubs, and working part-time. After her first child was born she settled into a comfortable life. The house was hers, not in name, but in truth. She fixed the water pipes, which had burst in the middle of winter, she replaced the worn railing, and she tended the garden. Sometimes it was almost like Theo was a phantom, an apparition, who came and went with warm embraces and sleepless hot nights. His letters made him more tangible, and she read them over and over, letting the words wander through the recesses of her brain.

With all of the long hours of solitude Theo had become a modestly accomplished writer and reader. He educated himself and spent hours composing poetry that Hazel treasured. Sometimes it was so blatantly erotic that she locked it away in a chest where her children wouldn't find it. When the war was over and Theo came home, he had some trouble fitting in. Hazel was adept and used to doing everything herself. For a few months Theo spent his days tottering around the fifteen acres that surrounded their house, working on their car, and writing. Eventually he took a job selling appliances, but his heart was never in it. But when he came home, to his warm house full of childhood laughter, his mind cleared.

After dinner he would sit down at the typewriter and write. He wrote whatever came to mind. Hazel figured that he had written about five novels, two dozen or more short stories, and countless poems over forty years. He sent his work to every publishing house and magazine he could think of, but no one was interested. He wrote stories about quiet lives and ordinary people, not the kind of stories that magazines wanted from unpublished authors. They always asked him to change a few things; twist around some other things. He wasn't interested. And just before he died he told Hazel that in the long run it didn't matter that his work had never been published. What mattered was that he had the chance to write it. Five months after his death, a poem that Theo had written about rebirth, deliverance, and the power of nature was published by an obscure literary publication in Berkeley. For Hazel it was an indication that the world had finally wised up, that someone had figured out what she knew all along: what Theo wrote was worth reading.

That afternoon Hazel and Del became great friends. Despite their differences in age and experience there was an almost instantaneous bond between them. When Del talked to Hazel it was nothing like talking to her mother, her grandmother, or even her friends. Hazel listened without judgment and with interest. To Hazel, Del was brand new. She hadn't formed long, callused judgments or preconceived notions about her. Hazel said she was glad to have the company since her children moved away and rarely visited. She said that she was glad to have someone to relive old memories, almost forgotten. Each was a prism through which the light of each other's stories passed, white to brilliant rainbow-colored hues.

Hazel had insisted that Del use her phone, since Del didn't have one of her own. When Del's parents called they were surprised when an older woman, slightly hard of hearing, answered the phone and seemed to know all about them. Ultimately, Del's mom and dad were thankful that someone was looking out for her and she had access to a telephone.

Del folded the letter and put it back into the envelope. The small clock on the stove read 9:06. Del realized it was getting late but she wasn't the least bit tired. She felt like talking to someone, but Hazel was asleep by eight. She walked to her bedroom, flopped down on her air mattress, and picked up the book she was reading, *Atlas Shrugged,* by Ayn Rand. The book was interesting, when she felt like reading, but now was not one of those times. She was beginning to feel bored. It was a sensation she hadn't had outside of work for quite some time. Usually she was too tired to feel bored. Del walked back to her seat at the kitchen counter and she turned on the radio to an NPR affiliate she had discovered the previous night.

She tuned in at the tail end of the local news. Although she had missed most of the story she quickly assessed that it was a short piece about the imminent fishing strike. One of the first things she had realized about living in Anchorage was that the fishing industry was in bad shape. The entire industry was sick with greed and lack of foresight.

The 1992 salmon season had gotten off to a bad start due to excessive flooding in local rivers where the salmon spawned. Factory trawlers were sucking the seas dry and, along with the foreign factory farms, they were driving down the price of fish. The huge trawlers, with their death traps of drift nets, were harvesting many more fish than could be sustained. To the fishing industry, fish were a natural resource, like ore in the ground. No one owned them and so they were fair game, and it seemed that everyone was getting involved in fishing.

There were small towns, whose names Del couldn't remember or pronounce, who were entirely dependent on the fishing industry. If the strike lasted very long she knew that those were the people who would be hit the hardest. In a way she felt guilty for thinking about her own situation and her involvement in an industry that was so blatantly exploiting its workers and the ocean.

Del believed strongly that unions were essential to protecting the rights of workers. One of the things she had learned in her college courses was that no one gave a damn about the working person except unions. But things now seemed all twisted around. The biggest reason that the fishermen wanted to strike was because the price the processors paid them had steadily decreased over the years and was cutting into their profits. Del worked for one of these processors. She knew the plant workers were making a little more money than previous years, but not much more than they had when they first started. If they went on strike, the fish would still run but no one would make any money this season. Fishing, except with a trawler, which most people didn't consider fishing, was already a job that depended on luck and making the best use of the fishing seasons. If they missed the salmon runs there wouldn't be a chance until the next year.

Del didn't think she would work in a cannery again next year. She had enough fish guts to last her the rest of her life. In fact, she knew would never even eat fish again. But she had signed up for the entire season and she wanted her end-of-the season bonus. If there was a strike, and it lasted for the rest of the season, she knew there was no way she would be able to afford to stay. She owed almost a thousand dollars on her credit card from school expenses, her plane ticket, and other now long-forgotten items.

When she had planned to come to Alaska and work a crappy job with long hours she justified it by telling herself she was working for a car. Somehow it hardly seemed worth it. Here she was getting stressed out about a strike, which might or might not happen, and which would prevent her from standing in cold fish guts and slinging dead salmon for twelve hours a day. The thought made her chuckle.

Her headache was back and she was tired, although her mind was abuzz with thoughts. After the news the radio station played blues and jazz. She listened for a while to Coltrane, Dizzy Gillespie, and others she recognized only by the sensation that the music seemed to have on her. Del turned up the music, rested her chin in her hands, and listened, trying not to let her thoughts and fears of uncertainty overwhelm her. After about an hour she decided she should lie down and try to sleep.

She turned the music down to an almost inaudible hum and went into the bathroom. Del brushed her teeth, washed her face, and put on an old nightshirt and boxers. She turned off the lights and got under her covers. She felt uncomfortably awake lying there in the half darkness; the light of the midnight sun seeped in through the crevices of her blinds. She took deep breaths and yawned. She tried to clear her head.

The first night she had spent in Alaska, before her life revolved around so much fish blood, she had marveled at the lack of darkness. In Washington, she had been amazed at the long days in summer and long nights in winter, but this was something else. It fooled her eyes and her mind. That night she had to take a couple of ibuprofen and slept with the covers pulled over her head. She hadn't slept well until the second or third day of work, when sleep overtook her like a wall of water dropped upon her all at once.

For a long time Del tossed and turned. She got up to go to the bathroom four times, got some water, and generally cursed her luck. At some point she had nodded off only to wake to the sound of someone pounding on her door.

"Hey Del, you in there?" Cynthia yelled, her voiced muffled and distorted by the closed door.

For a few seconds Del was disoriented and then, when she looked at her watch, she began to panic: it read 7:42. "Shit!"

"That you, Del?" Cynthia asked. "You still asleep?"

"No, no I'll be right there!" Del yelled, as she jumped out of bed and scrambled for some clothes.

Del got dressed in five minutes flat and was out the door when she realized she had almost forgotten the four bucks for lunch. She ran back into her apartment and tore open the plastic bag she had stuffed her dirty jeans into. She grabbed the money and ran out the door, slamming it behind her. As they sped away, Cowboy John was cursing about being late; Del noticed Hazel's door open and Hazel wander out, squinting in the sunlight. When she recognized Del she waved and said something that Del couldn't hear. Del waved back and then slumped down into her seat, hoping to catch a few winks.

Soon after she got to work Del realized that her throat was scratchy and sore. She drank some water and ate an orange that Jesse gave her. Until the first break she was tired but her throat felt better. During break she drank a soda and had some more water. By the time lunch rolled around her head and sinuses began to ache and she found herself clearing her throat every few minutes. After lunch she got a couple of more packets of headache pills and cough drops from Flo. The afternoon flew by, and when break rolled around she was convinced she would be fine. Her headache was gone and her throat was only slightly scratchy. She had another soda and popped a couple more headache pills, for preventive care more than anything else. She was surprised when June Schmitty stomped into the break room and announced that she had some important news.

"I know you have all heard about the possibility of a strike," June said calmly, her face bearing no trace of emotion.

The room fell completely silent. The workers, including Del, stared intently at June.

June didn't seem the least bit unnerved the eyes upon her. She paused, hooked her thumbs into the belt loops on her old Levis, and said, "The fishermen met with the producers and nothing came out of the discussions. Because we are allied with the fishermen's union, and they have officially called a strike, as of midnight tonight we are officially on strike."

The crowd reacted with exasperation and some cursing. Side conversations started up decrying the fishermen, the processors, or both. It was obvious to Del that everyone was extremely disappointed by the news.

"People! People! Hello!" June yelled, waving her hands. Eventually the crowd quieted down to a few whispers and an occasional cursing.

"I understand that you're pissed."

A few workers yelled out affirmatively or nodded their heads.

"But the good news is that we still have some more work."

The break room grew quiet again.

"There is still some fish to be processed and we will be sending some people to the roe plant downtown."

There were more disappointed remarks, cursing, and sniping.

"Hey! Hey! Folks! Let's listen up here!" Flo yelled loudly from the back of the crowd. Her coarse, deep voice cut through the noise.

The room was mostly quiet again.

"Thank you, Flo," June said. "Here's the situation. We will not be able to work everyone so the work will be split up by seniority."

The newer workers yelled their disdain. It took June a couple of minutes to quiet them down.

"We're only going to need about half the staff, and so we'll rotate those with less than two years of seniority and other people will be sent to the roe house."

"Call tomorrow! Listen for your last name!" June yelled over the increasingly boisterous crowd. "Those whose names are on the voice mail come into work as usual, the rest of you try to get some rest!"

The workers were up, making their way to the exits. June seemed to realize that the short meeting had ended, and she walked down to her office to do some paperwork.

In the break room conversations escalated, accusations were leveled, and general discontent verbalized. Del was glad when she finally left.

On the drive home she tried unsuccessfully to ignore the complaining and whining of Cynthia and Cowboy John. Cynthia had worked at the plant for the last three summers, so she knew she would still have work. This was Cowboy John's first season and he was visibly upset that he wouldn't be working. Initially, Cynthia tried to console him, but eventually she grew angry as well. When they got to Del's place she practically ran from the car to her front door, yelling goodbye, and waving without looking back. Inside she leaned against the door, exhausted physically and emotionally. Her neck and shoulders began to feel tight with tension.

She took a shower, washing off the smell of fish blood and slime, and then settled into a long bath. She didn't have any bubble bath and so she made do with some tropical fruit shampoo. With a towel rolled behind her head, the hot water around her shoulders, she felt blissfully relaxed. She closed her eyes.

She woke sometime later, a bit surprised. The water had cooled and she began to shiver. Groggy from a dreamless nap she drained the water and turned the shower on as hot as she could tolerate. She stood under the hot water that cascaded over her back and neck and through her hair until the shivering subsided. Warm from the water and steam of the bathroom, she wrapped her head in a towel and put on her robe.

She was somewhat hungry, but too tired to eat. She drank a couple of glasses of water, brushed her hair, and got ready for bed.

She dropped off into sleep just after her head hit the pillow.

A morning mist enshrouded the deep green forest where Del now stood. She was surprised to be there, surrounded by cedars, moss-covered stumps, large rocks, ferns, and small flowering bushes. In front of her she could see a narrow path, almost covered in places by overhanging plants. Something urged her forward and she walked along the path. She walked for what seemed like hours, over small rises, through trickling creeks filled with green moss-covered stones underneath the canopy of cedars. Everything was verdant, full of life and lushness. Eventually she came to a large clearing. The clearing was carpeted by green grass and a few shrubs but not much else. The misty fog had begun to burn off, and the clearing was bathed in sunlight.

The path ended in the grass, which seemed to stretch out forever. In the distance she could see two large four-legged animals. Against her will she was suddenly ten feet away from the creatures. Del slowly realized that the animals were large brown moose: a mother and a child, heads bent, grazing. She stood admiring them: their thick, chocolate-colored fur, tall spindly legs, large noses, and large dark eyes. Del wanted to reach out and touch them, to feel the smoothness of their snouts. Slowly the mother moose looked up, noticing Del for the first time. Looking into the animal's eyes, its head lowered, Del was gripped by fear and a metallic taste in her mouth. Like a splash of cold water on her face she knew she stood on perilous ground. She remembered hearing of the hazard of being too close to a moose and her offspring. The moose began to snort loudly and pawed the ground. Del turned to run but her feet wouldn't move. She felt as though her feet were stuck to the earth. For a very long time she stared into the animal's eyes, unable to decipher the emotions hidden behind them. Del knew that she would be trampled in a moment. The moose lowered her head, sprung forward, and charged. Del screamed out in terror.

She awoke in her bed, her mouth formed in a scream, but the noise trapped within her throat. She quickly sat up, disoriented. Her breathing was labored and her heart thumped rapidly against her rib cage. As her head cleared she began to recognize her surroundings. It had only been a dream. Cold sweat had drenched her nightshirt and her sheets felt damp to the touch. In the warm room she felt chilled. She was now completely awake, and she didn't feel comfortable enough to go back to sleep. She got out of bed, changed her clothes, and pulled back the sheets with the hoping they would dry out. Her head ached behind her eyes, her mouth was dry, and she had a strange taste in her mouth. She went into the bathroom, wrapped her robe around herself, and drank more water.

She sat on the closed toilet seat, sipped the water, and marveled at the strangeness of her dream. The meaning of it was unclear, but the anxiety obvious. As she sat there she felt strange, not quite right. She was beginning to come down with something. Although she had chosen to ignore the way she had been feeling lately, the sick dream and now the strange taste in her mouth told her that she was becoming ill.

Del loathed being sick, and weak. As a child she sometimes faked being well, despite feeling horrible, so that she wouldn't have to stay home. Illness gave Del a feeling of being helpless; she grew bored being physically limited.

After a half an hour of sitting in the bathroom she took a couple of ibuprofen and decided it was time to sleep. She fell asleep quickly, despite the damp and clammy sheets.

The rest of the night she had no dreams she could remember. She woke around seven and stayed in bed for another hour dozing fitfully. When she finally got up her muscles ached and her head pounded. She took three more ibuprofen and drank some water. She had no appetite and her stomach churned. Getting up had left her completely exhausted and so she went back to sleep. When she woke up again it was around noon and she felt worse. Although she was thankful to have the day off it was depressing to spend it in bed. She got up and tried to eat, but the most she could choke down was a piece of dry toast.

Del turned on the radio and tried to read for a while, but soon she was tired again and went back to bed. Sometime around two Del heard a quiet knock at the door. From her bed Del yelled out, "Who is it?"

"It's Hazel."

"One sec," Del said. She threw on her robe and let Hazel in.

"Oh, Del, my goodness, you look dreadful," Hazel said, reaching out and feeling Del's forehead.

Del nodded in agreement. "I feel worse."

"I didn't hear you leave this morning, so I was worried," Hazel said. "Didn't you have to work today?"

"Strike was called; we won't be working for a while."

"Ain't that just the way it goes? My goodness."

I'm gonna fix you some tea," Hazel said matter-of-factly. "Think you can eat anything?"

"I'm not sure."

"Well I'll bring over some soda crackers and ginger ale just in case."

"Thanks, Hazel," Del said, relieved to have someone to take care of her.

For the rest of the day and the next Hazel took care of Del. She brought her tea and food, ran her baths, and most of all kept her company. They played cards and Del learned how to play gin rummy. Although she didn't feel physically well, a shadow within her soul had lifted. The sickness and spending time with Hazel, who treated Del like her own child, was cathartic. By the fourth day Del began to feel like herself again. After a week, with the strike still on, she was able to take long walks through the woods behind the apartments. After that she split her time between being outside walking, reading, and playing cards with Hazel. On one particularly beautiful and warm afternoon she convinced Hazel to go for a walk with her. Although it wore Hazel out, she was overjoyed to be outside. They marveled in the beauty of their surroundings, content to walk for long stretches in silence.

Ten days into the strike Del got a call from Millie, the secretary in the front office of the plant. Hazel had shuffled over around nine to tell Del she had a phone call. Del threw on a pair of jeans and a faded U of W sweatshirt and stepped next door. Millie, in her deep and raspy voice, informed Del that the paychecks had come in two days ago and she was welcome to come pick hers up. Del thanked Millie with little enthusiasm. She didn't really want to make the trip to work, without a car, just to get her check, but she also wanted to put the check into her dwindling account as soon as possible. Del had a cup of tea, chatted with Hazel, and went back to her place to change.

The day had warmed to a comfortable sixty-five degrees with a slight breeze. The blue sky was dotted with a few clouds, and although there was no rain predicted Del, used to Washington weather, stuffed her jacket into her backpack. She grabbed a small water bottle from the fridge and her purse, put them inside her pack, and zipped it up. She donned her worn, dark-blue NY Yankees cap and headed out the door, locking it behind her. She wasn't familiar with the bus system in Anchorage so she decided to follow a main road to the downtown station where she could pick up a bus to the plant.

She didn't mind walking because it gave her a chance to slow down and really see her surroundings. The road was lined with trees and thin woods and a few houses hidden by tall wood fences. As she got closer to town it was almost exclusively houses and later businesses, parking lots, and parked cars that lined the street. She was surprised that it looked more or less like many other small cities she had visited, except the mountainous surroundings were stunning.

After walking for almost forty minutes, past tire stores, video chain outlets, a grocery store, and assorted retail shops, she had a distinct craving for something cold to drink and a comfortable place to sit down. On the next block she noticed a small natural food café tucked within the shadow of an old strip mall. As she got closer she noticed the intricately carved and painted sign which read The Morning Sun Café. A few patrons sat outside at small plastic tables. They looked distinctly out of place, in the shadow of consumer excess, with their tie-dyed clothing, ripped, faded, and patched jeans, overalls, Birkenstocks, dreadlocks, and thoroughly relaxed attitudes.

As Del walked inside a small string of bells that hung on the handle of the glass door announced her entry. She walked up to the counter across old, worn, uneven wooden floors. A small squat woman with long black cornrow braids, tipped with rainbow-colored beads, and wearing a bright, loose tie-dye dress took Del's order for an herbal iced tea.

As she was waiting at a table for her tea she glanced around the small café. There were all types and colors of people sitting, eating, reading books or newspapers, and soaking up the atmosphere. Del could make out East Indian sitar music playing faintly from speakers that hung in a far corner of the room.

She decided to sit at a small table by the front door. She sipped her tea and watched the unusual collection of people: the elderly man dressed in worn fatigues and an old black beret, a young couple in T-shirts and jeans, their hands clasped tightly on the table with almost no conversation passing between them, a middle-aged man in a blue blazer and slacks reading the paper, a group of teenagers with long hair and baggy old clothes who occasionally erupted into long peals of laughter, a pregnant woman with a small child, and another woman dressed in a white tank top and jean shorts, her head shaved bald, sitting on the only couch and reading a worn paperback book.

Del heard the bells on the door ring behind her, but she didn't bother to turn around to see who entered. She recognized Greer's voice, which sounded to her like thick, rich syrup. She turned and noticed that he and

Jesse, a young Korean woman who also worked at the plant, had just walked in and were ordering. She thought she should call out to them, and announce herself, but she hesitated. They hadn't seen her yet and she realized that she could simply walk out, be on her way, and not make conversation.

Then again, she thought, *it might be nice to find out how they're getting along*.

"Hey Greer! Jesse!" Del said, waving them over.

"Hey," Greer said.

Jesse waved, with a surprised expression on her face.

Jesse and Greer got their drinks, pulled up a chair and sat with Del.

"I'm surprised to see you here," Jesse said in a mildly sarcastic tone.

Del was taken aback, not sure how to react to the sudden development of an attitude. Generally, at work, Jesse was nice and even chatty.

"I was walking into town and I decided to take a break," Del said.

"Why are you going into town?" Jesse said sharply.

"I'm going to get my paycheck."

"You're walking to the plant?" Jesse said, in a tone that suggested Del was naïve and possibly stupid.

"I was going to take the bus, from the downtown station," Del said, unable to completely conceal her irritation.

Greer, who had sat quietly, suddenly said, "I kin give you a ride dare. Ise goin' ta pick up ma check."

Jesse fell silent and shot Greer a menacing look, which he didn't even notice.

But Del noticed, and she realized that there might be far more going on between these two than she ever would have guessed.

Del quickly steered the conversation to talk about the strike, and for a few minutes Jesse seemed to be her usual self. Del looked for tell tale signs or body language that would suggest a relationship between Jesse and Greer. Greer sat, stoically, his large, dark hands wrapped tightly around his tall glass of peppermint iced tea. Jesse seemed to lean towards him, into space, but she never touched him or reached out to him for affection.

Eventually they exhausted the topic of conversation and an uncomfortable silence fell over the table.

Looking a bit sullen, Jesse announced that she wanted to get her bike out of Greer's van so she could ride home. When Greer suggested he could drive her she rolled her eyes as if to say, sarcastically, "Oh, please."

He walked out to the van with her and helped her with her bike while Del waited inside. Through the window Del could see Jesse, talking to Greer, suddenly throw up her arms, yell at him, and poke him hard in the chest. She then jumped on her bike and sped off as Greer called after with an exasperated expression on his face and his hands held out in surprise.

When Greer turned back to the café he realized that most of the patrons, including Del, were staring at him. He looked down a bit, with obvious embarrassment, as he walked back inside. He sat down across from Del, and she noticed the pained expression on his face and exhaustion in his eyes.

"You wanna get outta here?" Del asked.

"Sure," Greer answered quietly.

They drove to the plant in silence. Del was taking in the ambiance of Greer's old blue '78 Ford van. The only windows in the van were in front and back. Del surmised that it was probably an old cargo van. The walls and floor had been carpeted with dark brown, plush shag carpeting. A twin mattress sat, neatly made, on a homemade wooden platform. Underneath the bed was an assortment of clothes, boxes of food, an old cooler, and an old boom box. On the dash were scattered beautiful and perfect looking shells which Del picked up and held, feeling the shape and texture of each.

Greer noticed Del looking around curiously.

"I got dis ol' van from my younger brother," Greer said. "Use' to deliver furniture."

"It's quite a van," Del said. "Why'd he part with it?"

"He died," Greer said flatly.

Del swallowed hard and felt her face redden.

There was no more conversation until they got to the plant.

The plant was located near the airport in an industrial area, which was crisscrossed by small roads and railroad tracks. Hopping out of the van, Del could smell the fish.

"I'll meet ya back 'ere in fifteen minutes," Greer said. "'K?"

"Sounds great," Del said, surprised by the implication that he would give her a ride home.

Greer walked up the front steps to the office and Del walked through the large door into the plant. The plant was disturbingly quiet. The only sound was the radio, which was playing classic rock. She felt like she was a kid visiting her school during the summer break. The floor had been recently scrubbed and the smell of the citrus cleaner was pervasive and numbing. She walked through the plant, through the back door, and up the back stairs. The locker room was quiet, as was the break room. She walked by the stacks of cardboard, past the closed up supply/first aid station, and down the hall to the main office. She picked up her check from Millie, who pulled it out of a large stack on the edge of her desk.

She pressed Millie for news about the strike.

Millie shrugged and told her, "They don't tell me nothin'."

Del walked down the front stairs to Greer's van. Greer sat in driver's seat smoking a cigarette and playing a reggae tape on the stereo.

She opened the door and slipped into the passenger seat, closing the door hard behind her. Greer looked up from his hands on the wheel, as though breaking from a trance, and he gave her a wide distant smile.

"You wanna do somethin'?" Del asked, surprising herself.

"Sure, why not, right," Greer answered.

They drove off the lot, under the warmth of the afternoon sun, their minds distant from one another while they enjoyed the comfort of each other's company.

At Greer's suggestion they drove out of town to a fairly remote private lake. As they trespassed over a fence on the edge of a stranger's property, Greer told her this was one of the places where he had lived during the summer, especially since the strike. He had spent his days lying on the small strip of beach in a cove hidden from the rest of the lake. Greer showed her the spot, but then remembered that he had some food in the van. He told her he would run and get it.

Greer came back with the cooler, a bag of food, and an old blanket to sit on. In the cooler were a couple of beers, some chicken from KFC, cheese, bread, and mayo. In the bag there were chips, crackers, and some oranges. Greer apologized for the scarcity of his provisions because he hadn't gone to the store lately. Del assured him that it was fine and there was more than enough food.

With a large serrated knife, and after some struggling they made themselves chicken and cheese sandwiches (Greer called them cutters) with chips and crackers on the side, which they washed down with beer.

The conversation was sparse, since they were both quite hungry. After they had finished Del asked him some non-intrusive questions about how he liked Alaska and work. He said he was happy to be working and that he truly loved Alaska, but he missed the warm sun and beaches of Barbados.

Somehow they got on the subject of drugs and after Del made a long speech about how marijuana should be decriminalized, Greer asked her, "You wan' a smoke?"

"You mean a cigarette?" she queried.

"No, no," he said smiling, "Da green stuff, right."

"Oh," Del said, feeling foolish. She thought about it for a few seconds and said, "Sure, what the hell."

Greer leapt up and said, "Be righ' back," and he headed for the van.

As Greer ambled through the woods Del wondered why she had said yes. It was something about being in the moment, by the lake, a cool breeze rustling her hair, and the sun beaming down upon her. She felt undeniably relaxed, and in her placidity she wanted the feeling of being stoned.

Greer came back with a small hand-carved pipe and a plastic bag of some of the largest buds Del had ever seen. Del had only smoked about six or seven times, and the only stuff that she or her friends could get was generally homegrown crap-weed. Greer packed a large bowl, from one bud, and insisted on Del taking the first hit. She sparked up the pipe and inhaled deeply. She coughed slightly, but it didn't really burn her throat.

"This is some kind bud," Del exclaimed, after she exhaled.

Greer nodded in agreement.

She didn't feel anything until after they had almost finished off the bowl. When she asked Greer if the stuff was any good he assured her that it was some serious creeper weed.

"Jus' wai'," he assured her.

Then she was instantly stoned. Her perceptions changed, time fluctuated, and her head felt like it was floating.

"Where'd you get this stuff?" Del asked.

"Dis Jesse's," Greer said. They both laughed until they could hardly breathe.

They caught their breath and there was a period of awkward silence.

"So what is the deal exactly between you and Jesse?" Del asked suddenly.

For a minute Greer looked puzzled, as though he was chewing on the question.

"No deal," he said. "Trouble don' set up like rain. She wants somethin' but she young, young and I'm married."

"Oh, I see," Del said, a bit embarrassed.

Greer noticed her discomfort and said, "Don' worry, no big deal, hear."

She felt relieved.

Again a long period of silence elapsed.

The warmth of the sun felt good. A slight breeze blew off the lake, which was cool and smelled slightly like marsh and fish. The lake rippled slightly. She lay back on the grass, her hands behind her head. She watched the clouds as they moved slowly across the sky. A black raven flew overhead. She felt at peace, without a care in the world.

When she woke the sky was darker; the color of the clouds suggested rain. She heard Greer snoring, some ten feet away from her. She sat up and looked over at Greer, who was fast asleep. The lake was completely calm except for the occasional fish jumping to feed. Soon after she sat up the mosquitoes began to buzz incessantly around her head. She swatted them away, but they were unfazed. She looked at her arms, saw the large red swollen bites, and she began to itch. "Oh shit!" She quickly put on her jacket and got up, all the while flailing her arms like a lunatic. "Greer!"

Greer barely stirred.

"Greer!" she yelled louder.

"Wha? Wha?" he said, waking with a start, his eyes wide with alarm. He sat up quickly.

"Ah, friggin' 'squitoes!" he exclaimed.

They quickly grabbed their picnic gear and darted for the van, pausing every few seconds to swat themselves and move their arms wildly through the air.

Once they were safely in the van they both sighed with relief.

"Rasshole 'squitoes!" Greer said.

"Alaska's state bird!" Del said, repeating an expression she had heard at the plant.

Greer laughed, an infectious laugh, and Del laughed as well.

Soon after they pulled away from the lake the rain began to fall. The drops were enormous, pelting the top of the van with thousands of tiny thumps.

Greer drove her back to her apartment, and although she considered inviting him in, he gave no indication that he wanted to stay.

"Thanks for a great day," Del said sincerely, smiling.

"Sure t'ing, anytime," he said smiling, his voice sounding distant.

He waited until Del got into her place and then drove off. Del heard him leave and she made her way to the shower. After she toweled off she dabbed her mosquito bites with gobs of pink calamine lotion and tried not to scratch.

After a couple of hours the pot wore off and she considered the day's developments. The day was pleasant and Greer was friendly. Somehow she was surprised that she was so ambivalent about Greer. Del reasoned that he was the type of man that would never open up enough for her to really get to know him. It would be difficult for them to ever be good friends. She definitely didn't want to be in a relationship, especially with a married man, no matter how charming or good looking. And still he was mysterious: begging unanswerable questions.

The strike ended two days later and Del was both happy and sad to go back to work. She wanted to make some more money but she had begun to grow accustomed to the relaxing routine she had developed with Hazel. When Cowboy John and Cynthia picked her up on her first day back they informed her that they would be processing small, slimy pink salmon called chum, and it was no picnic. Del tried to not let her good mood be squashed by John and Cynthia's pessimism.

They got to work a little early. There were donuts and coffee out to welcome people back. People stood around in groups, like students back from break, discussing how they had spent the strike. Del heard that a number of people quit and left to find other work. When she walked down to the processing floor she noticed that Greer wasn't standing in his usual place amid the group of smokers. When she asked Jesse if she had seen Greer, Jesse gave her a dirty look and said that he had quit yesterday and headed back to California. Jesse said it in a vexing way that somehow suggested that Del was playing dumb and she wasn't buying it. As Del got dressed she kept thinking of Greer and how hard it must have been for him to make the trek back to L.A. with only a fraction of what he had planned on making. In the back of her mind she wondered if he had left because of her.

Del put on her yellow PVC overalls, her glove liners, yellow gloves, gaiters, and her yellow PVC jacket which read "Richardson, D." on the back.

She was surprised when she felt something in the right outside pocket of her jacket. She reached into her pocket and pulled out a carefully folded wad of newspaper, which had been taped together with masking tape. She walked outside through the maze of steel racks to find a clear place to sit. She sat down, her back against the corrugated steel of the building, and took off her gloves, gaiters, and glove liners. She carefully unwrapped the tape and newspaper. She peeled away the layers, like an onion, until she saw something pink and white poking out from the inside. She peeled away the last layer and marveled at the treasure. In her hand she held a small shell. It was curved like a conch shell, white and flecked with pink. It was incredibly smooth and glassy in her hand. It was the most perfect shell Del had ever seen, so symmetrical and beautifully colored. She smiled to herself, yet felt a little sad. She re-wrapped the shell in the newspaper, walked upstairs, put it in her locker, and then walked back down into the hum of steel and the smell of salmon.

4

HERE

He sat and absorbed the uneasy dullness of the room around him. The office was quiet save the drone of a bevy of mind-numbing machines. The fluorescent lights cast a pale subterranean glow upon the small room, distorting all of the colors within. Outside, the world was bathed in warm sunshine.

Just a few feet from him, separated by drywall, steel beams, brick, and concrete, the unwavering heat had burned away the early summer mist and it began to develop into a humid and languid day. The birds sang in huge fir trees. If he had a window, rather than a few shelves, walls, and a small office calendar, Brian Fetzler would be able to see clear to the snow-strewn colossus of Mount Baker framed by a clear blue sky.

Brian picked up the pile of papers. The stack was a mixture of colors, sizes, and shapes that flexed and swayed in his hand. He placed them directly in front of him because it was the only clear space. He leafed through the pile. There were policies, memos, changes, renewal notices, cancellation notices, complaints, letters, evidence of insurance sheets, and seemingly random Post–Its filled with almost unintelligible scribbling.

He sighed. His exhaling seemed to be answered by the fax machine behind him, which suddenly sprang to life with a whir. He tried to ignore it. He wanted to hear music or some melodic sound to drown out the incessant, dull, droning hum of the computers, printers, and a copy machine that littered his tiny office. But because he answered the phones he wasn't allowed to bring in a radio or wear headphones.

He looked over at his reflection in a large brass plaque his boss had received for some life insurance sales record. He could make out his reflections amid the etched lettering. He looked terrible, drawn and pale. His round face was marked with blemishes brought on by stress. His eyes were puffy and his receding, thinning light brown hair looked greasy and was combed back in an uneven part. He thought about fixing it until he realized that he wouldn't see anyone important today and he really didn't care. He loosened his green paisley tie and undid the top button on his pants because they felt like they were cutting off the circulation to his legs.

Brian worked at Bellingham Insurance, a small firm. His office had only recently been converted from the file/computer room. The only change had been the addition of a desk, a chair, and a phone that usually rang incessantly. And, as with many insurance offices, there was a legalistic and paranoid amount of paperwork, almost all of which duplicated computer records and files, crammed into brimming client files.

Despite the paperwork, today was not as busy as usual, and he realized that he could probably leave the office for lunch for the first time in two months.

He had taken the job with the expectation that it would be easy and because his boss, Jack Feber, was a close family friend. When his dad had mentioned that Mr. Feber needed an office clerk, Brian had imagined an office with a window, time to surf the Web, call his friends, and put his feet up. Now, a year later, he was beginning to realize that Mr. Feber could hire two more people and he would still be understaffed. And while the work chafed him and the office was a dingy hole with no windows, the worst part was putting up with Mr. Feber's secretary, Elenor Jones.

Elenor was a crass, bitter, middle-aged woman with a thick south Boston accent and a knack for saying the most disgusting things Brian had ever heard. Since the day he started, Brian had become Elenor's recipient of unwanted gossip and commentary. Mr. Feber was almost never in the office because he was out on appointments with clients, selling life insurance, and cultivating other money-making ideas, while she was always there clinging to Brian, shadow like. Elenor was an unbelievably needy person, so extroverted that she would drift toward people and conversations at random simply because she seemed to hate being alone.

After a week of quietly enduring Elenor's foul morning demeanor and erratic afternoon mood swings Brian began to earnestly believe that Mr. Feber stayed away from the office on purpose. The realization seemed to be confirmed when Mr. Feber went so far as to drop by after work or during lunch, leaving quickly and quietly if he found Elenor there.

Once Mr. Feber had slipped into the office after five and Brian was just getting ready to leave. Elenor, it seemed, was just getting started. She was sitting in Mr. Feber's office, in his chair, with her shoeless feet up on his desk. She jabbered away on the phone and chewed her gum so loudly that Brian could hear the saliva-accentuated, cracking sounds in the next room.

As Brian was putting on his coat he saw Mr. Feber walk past Elenor's desk in the reception area. Brian stepped back out of view. He poked his head out just in time to see Mr. Feber walk into his office. Brian couldn't see his face, but Mr. Feber went rigid, and his arms shot out askew as though he had just been shot.

Brian could only imagine what Mr. Feber saw.

Undoubtedly, Elenor sat with her feet up on Mr. Weber's desk, which Brian knew smelled because of the last time she went around the office shoeless. Her stockings were probably marred with the usual runs and holes. She was wearing a cheap, tight-fitting, dark green polyester suit. Her hair was cut short and dyed red, with dark brown roots showing. She rarely smiled, probably because her teeth were yellow and stained from years of smoking. Her fake, white, manicured nails curled around the receiver; brows scrunched, lips pursed, as she passing on information about her latest sexual experience as though it was a state secret.

Brian knew five minutes after he met Elenor that he had stumbled into something he would not be able to ignore. She shocked him, not only in her indecency, but in her ability to put up with the most demeaning customers. There were people who called on his first day who made him want to shrink and hide beneath his own desk. Elenor stood by as Brian stammered to customers, such as Mr. Hansen, seemingly afflicted by Tourette Syndrome. Mr. Hansen's diatribes of expletives were so obscene and elaborately strung together that it almost sounded like the reconstruction of a long-lost language.

She would watch and nod as Brian struggled to speak, and then she would gesture for Brian to hand over the phone to her. She could not be rattled, despite the loud profanity that Brian could still hear emanating from the phone. She disarmed them, somehow. It was all attitude. Every word, pause, and inflection suggested that, at heart, she didn't care what anyone thought, and she told them what they wanted to hear if they would shut up and listen.

☕

The phone rang. He glanced at his watch. It was 7:45. The office didn't open until eight so he let the phone ring and the voice mail pick it up. He didn't want to talk to anyone, and he had a mountain of papers to file, stamp, and sort. He knew that Elenor wouldn't saunter in until about nine or so. And he didn't expect Mr. Feber at all. But he knew that as soon as Elenor got there that he would be lucky if he got a moment to himself.

Sometimes, sitting here in his windowless office, he wondered why he was still doing this. His friends, all of whom he had slowly lost contact with, had drifted off to California or Colorado or just down I-5 to work for Internet startups. They all talked about dot-com stock options, hedonistic company parties, and wintering in Telluride or traveling across Nepal. They had invested in the surging stock market, bought new cars, new houses, enrolled their dogs in day care, and hired nannies with master's degrees to watch their newborn progeny. They seethed with surreal amounts of money and affluence, which quickly became blasé, a cliché status quo.

Brian, on the other hand, lived in a small two-bedroom one-bath apartment on State Street that overlooked the bay. On the outside the building didn't look like much. It was made of painted cinderblocks that were now peeling and faded. It sat adjacent to the large, looming, old brick hospital, which was rumored to have been a mental institution at one time where all kinds of evil deeds were committed. He was fairly certain that the stories were pure fiction, and that the rooms were just an expansion of the hospital or a cheap way to renovate the property and make a quick buck. His rent was outrageous, by local standards, but it was close to everything and he had a sweeping view of the bay, from the waterfront to the Cascades, Canada, and beyond. When he sat in his living room and watched the brilliant hues of orange, red, and yellow sunsets he had some sense of luxury. It felt like a small tease of possibility, a distinctive consolation prize for something greater missed.

It had been almost three years since he graduated from Western and he was still here. He wondered what it was that made him want to stay. Was it fear? And fear of what? The unknown, failure, of feeling something? Anything?

Brian had been living with his girlfriend Jennifer for six months. They had been dating for three years. At least that's how most people described it, including Brian's mother. But in reality they weren't really dating, they were together. They had been hopelessly in love. She was so beautiful and full of life, and despite the fact that she was more sophisticated than Brian could have ever been, he had been almost instantly smitten.

He remembered the night they met, at David Greibing's big party. She was wearing a Mariner's cap, the brim curved and pulled down so it hid her eyes. They had been introduced by a mutual friend, yet Brian was convinced that they had met before. They had talked about how they collected vinyl records when they were in elementary school and coveted a few: Brian, *Abbey Road* and Jennifer, *Saturday Night Fever*. They joked about the ludicrous way they had tried to emulate *The Dukes of Hazard* and *BJ and the Bear*. And they remembered the fear of a nuclear attack from Russia after watching *The Day After* in sixth grade.

Jennifer was a freshman at a local community college. She didn't go to Western because she had failed out of three previous high schools and two private colleges, a fact which she had hidden from Brian for over a year.

Their courtship had been a comfortable state of bliss. They spent all of their free time together, getting stoned and watching videos in Brian's room or bugging Jennifer's female roommates by setting up their tent in the backyard and drinking beers by the campfire, a small charcoal fire pit.

Lately, they talked less and less. And even when they did they said very little. She had stopped smoking pot with him months ago, telling him that she had to start acting more like an adult. He started to smoke more. But little by little he was beginning to realize that the high was different, that something had changed. He no longer felt soothed, calm, and without a care. It had begun to make him feel irritable, paranoid, and even tired. He felt as though he had turned some corner to a place that he hadn't realized existed.

In high school he was basically a nerd and, rather than study, spent hours involved in role-playing games with a couple of his only friends. When he went to college he realized that for the first time he could re-invent himself, he could be anyone he wanted. A couple of the first people he met in his dorm were partiers. It seemed like the life: freedom from circumstance, from conscience, and ignorant happiness. Being high then became second nature and an inoculation against the old life.

Two-and-a-half months ago Brian had walked home from an incredibly bad day at work, soaked because he had left without a coat and had been caught in a very wet mid-April storm. Walking to work had proven tedious, as he suspected, but he had little choice because Jennifer's car had broken down the week before and they didn't have the money to fix it. Despite his initial grumblings he had agreed that she should drive his car because she worked farther away and often worked nights.

As he walked up the steps to his apartment he noticed a figure huddled in a corner of the covered walkway beneath a faded, red flannel sleeping bag. He had thought that it was a bum getting out of the rain. He attempted to walk quietly past, apprehensive and a bit pissed. It wasn't until the figure looked up from beneath his stained Panama hat that Brian realized that it was his brother, Toby.

Toby was a wreck: thin and reeking of alcohol and body odor. Brian invited him inside, fed him, gave him clean clothes, and insisted that he take a shower. He set up a makeshift bedroom in their study, which was separated from their bedroom by a shared bathroom.

Brian's brother, Toby, was the most irresponsible person that Brian had ever met. His years of fighting, crashing cars, and drinking himself unconscious every night in his parents' basement caught up with him one night after getting wasted in downtown Seattle.

It was two days before Christmas Eve and Toby had wandered off from his friends to take a leak. He had become distracted and then lost. It was a cold night and the rain was beginning to turn to sleet. He was wearing only a thin, black jean jacket with a T-shirt beneath. Despite the alcohol he had begun to shiver, his breath misting though clenched teeth. As he walked out of an alley he noticed a young woman getting out of an old two-door Oldsmobile. She had left the engine running and the hazards on as she ran into a small convenience store. Toby saw his chance. He sauntered up to the car and tried the handle on the driver's side.

To his surprise, the door was unlocked. He slid behind the wheel and drove off towards his girlfriend's house in Lynwood. He didn't notice the small baby sleeping in the car seat in the back until he changed the radio station to "The End" and turned it up. The baby wailed and Toby panicked. A thousand confused thoughts flooded his mind as he swerved into oncoming traffic. When he woke he was cuffed to a hospital bed. The baby was alive and in intensive care and the mother, a diagnosed schizophrenic, had made it clear that if she ever laid eyes on Toby again, he was as good as dead.

Later he was sentenced to community service and alcohol treatment, primarily because he was a sixteen-year-old with a clean record and visibly distraught parents with a good lawyer.

Somehow, being the youngest, Toby managed to talk his parents into sending him to a local, private school for "troubled youth." Toby survived the school by undermining and skirting every rule that the school had ever established. His two-year stint became one of the most profitable periods in his life. He had managed to make connections with often dubious minor felons to get every type of contraband his fellow classmates desired. He was never caught, and although he barely graduated he managed to leave school with around eight thousand dollars.

The money had lasted Toby all of six months of gambling in Reno and Las Vegas, then traveling down to Rio de Janeiro for a few months of unencumbered debauchery.

Brian, still in an agitated state of shock, invited Toby into the kitchen and told him to help himself. Brian changed out of his wet work clothes. Toby helped himself to an entire box of frosted flakes, a quart of ice cream, and three beers.

Brian threw Toby's old clothes away, along with his sleeping bag, which he had gotten a whiff of causing the bile to rise to his throat.

Jennifer was a waitress at a swanky downtown restaurant. She came home from an extremely bad day at work and was not pleased to learn that Brian's brother, whom she had heard about but never met, was taking up the space in the room she normally meditated in. Plus, she noted that they would all be forced to share a bathroom—a thought which disgusted her.

Brian made introductions and then stood between them uncomfortably, in the silence, until Jennifer invited Toby to share some wine and tell them about his adventures.

At the mention of alcohol Toby perked up and he dragged himself into the kitchen to sit at the small table. There were only three chairs because the white, oval farm table was pushed against the wall to save space.

Toby wore Brian's clean white tank-top, his thin almost hairless chest pale-white under the kitchen lights. On his left bicep he had a tattoo of a flaming heart with a scroll across it that read "BITE ME." His dark hair was buzzed close to his scalp. His eyes were a light-brown and framed by deep dark rings.

Toby, looking relaxed as he leaned back in his chair, began to tell Brian and Jennifer about his trip.

"Well," he started, "I was runnin' with some friends south. We, ah, got as far as Rio. Man what a fuckin' trip."

"Vegas though man, that was a fuckin' cool place: money, drugs, hookers, and lights everywhere. I started out with this killer ride, a red Chevelle. That car absolutely rocked. I took it out into the desert and got it up to 140 no problem. Later, I never saw the trooper. They chased me half-way 'cross the state. Eventually they got wise with the roadblocks. I took it off-road but ended up rollin' it. The thing was totaled. I spent a couple of days in the hospital, a couple of weeks in jail until I could post bond. I flew that shit-hole as soon as I could. Now I got to steer clear of Nevada, warrant and all. I hitched my way south until I got wise and hooked up with some truckers who gave me a lift, and I helped them by being their courier. I've never seen so much fuckin' coke. I even got free samples; it was awesome. I would have stayed longer but I got into some trouble in Mexico. I mean, shit, I didn't know that the guy was a cop or I never would have slugged him. And Rio, man that place was killer. Hot topless chicks on the beaches. Cheap food, cheap beer, cheap drugs. It was the life."

Brian glanced over to see Jennifer's expression. It was a mixture of disbelief, shock, and enthrallment. Brian always thought of Toby as a train wreck: his life was nothing but a mess, yet he inevitably drew people to him. Strangers started by listening to his stories, then they were buying him drinks, and later they were bailing him out of jail or pushing him out of bed. What no one but Brian seemed to know was that most of what Toby told was lies. The truth to him was relative—relative to what someone else wanted to hear. He read his audience and fed them whatever stories would get him what he wanted.

This disregard for the truth, or relative truth as Brian liked to call it, had grown more pronounced, like a tumor, over the years. What had started as childhood stories of imaginary places, friends, treasures, and worlds had evolved into a place populated by thugs, guns, drugs, hookers, and violence. The delusions had somehow become real to Toby, and for the first time Brian was genuinely alarmed.

It had been a long time, over two years, since they had seen each other. They had both changed, becoming more pronounced in their individual neuroses. Brian caught himself on the verge of questioning the authenticity of Toby's stories, but instead took a deep breath. He knew that second guessing Toby would be worthless because he could see in Toby's face that he believed his own bullshit.

"So why did you leave?" Jennifer asked, in a tone that suggested Toby should have stayed in Rio if it was such a wonderful place.

"I met someone," Toby answered, "and her dad sent some guys to kill me. I left town packed in a truck full of pig shit, made my way north, and here I am."

"Wow, some story," Brian said and yawned. "Sorry, I'm exhausted."

"Me, too," Jennifer said, and yawned.

"Man you two are pathetic," Toby said. "Like a couple of old married geezers. But Brian always was a geek."

Brian shrugged uncomfortably and stared hard at the floor, unable to think of a witty comeback. After collecting himself he looked over at Jennifer. She didn't make eye contact with him, but got up and walked into the other room. Toby seemed to sense the tension but said nothing as he looked down at the floor by Brian's feet.

Brian got up, uncomfortable in the silence and tired. "Good night, Tobe," he said coldly.

"Hey bro hang on a sec'. I, ah, got a little favor to ask," Toby said, sounding genuinely uncomfortable for the first time that evening. "I'm a little short on cash. Can you spare a few bucks?

"I mean, I promise I'll pay you back just as soon as I can scrape some cash together," Toby said, sounding desperate.

Brian was tired, and, in truth, he wanted him out of the apartment. He knew that if he gave him some cash he would leave, at least for a few hours.

"OK, Toby, but this is only a loan," Brian said sternly.

"Hey, no prob' bro'," Toby said, patting Brian on the shoulder.

"Stay here," Brian instructed. "I'll be right back."

Brian walked into the bedroom and closed the door behind him. He could hear Jennifer in the bathroom washing her face. Brian went over to the dresser and opened the underwear drawer. He felt around the back until he found a small wooden box, the size of a small shoebox. He took it out and opened it up. In it, he kept about two hundred dollars for emergencies, some antique pieces of jewelry that Jennifer's grandmother had given her before she died, and a couple of antique coins that Jennifer's father had given her. He used to keep his stash in the box, until Jennifer found out, and he moved it into a smaller box that he hid under the bed. He took out a twenty and a ten. He closed the box back up and shoved it under his boxers at the back of the drawer. As he put the bills into his pocket he found himself reflexively check to make sure that Jennifer was still in the bathroom. He felt like he was sneaking around, afraid of being caught.

He took the cash out and gave it to Toby. As he gave him the money he could see in Toby's face that he was disappointed with only thirty bucks.

Just as Toby was about to make some sarcastic remark he sensed Brian's irritation and said, "Thanks, bro, you're still one cool dude."

Brian knew that there was no way he was going to get his money back.

Around three A.M. there was a loud knock on the front door. Brian shot out of bed, alarmed, and Jennifer woke up as well, disoriented and none too pleased. Brian made his way to the door, squinting as he turned on the lights. He looked through the peephole. Toby stood outside the door, swaying slightly.

Brian opened the door, disgusted and enraged, and was hit instantly with the reek of alcohol and stale cigarettes.

"Shit, man," Toby said loudly, slurring his words. "You lock' me out?"

Suddenly Brian was embarrassed, even though he knew that he shouldn't be. He had locked the front door, out of habit, before he went to bed.

"Yeah, shit, sorry," Brian said quietly. "We'll have to get you a key." As soon as he said it he knew he would regret the offer and he began to think of ways he could get Toby to leave, permanently, as soon as possible.

The next two-and-a-half warm summer months passed slowly. Jennifer and Brian fought incessantly, about Toby and everything else. The heat, especially at night, worsened their discomfort. They usually kept their doors permanently open and windows ajar all summer long as a respite from the heat. Now doors were kept uncomfortably closed with fans feebly pushing the warm air around each room.

Toby spent most of his days sleeping, watching TV, or eating, and he went out almost every night because he had met some fellow partiers in Bellingham. When he got home he was anything but quiet. They could hear him in the kitchen flinging open the fridge, slamming cupboards, and chomping on cereal. When he went into the bathroom it was worse—through the thin, hollow doors they felt as though they were all in the same room. As if being awoken in the middle of the night wasn't enough, Jennifer told Brian that she suspected that he was also dealing drugs out of their apartment.

Jennifer had come home early one Wednesday because it was a slow day at work. When she got to the apartment Toby was in his room with the door closed and the music turned up. She thought she could smell the odor of pot, even though she had asked him not to smoke in the house. At one point she heard another male voice and she could make out the words, "—good shit, and how bought a quarter?"

Afraid to confront the slacker directly, she railed at Brian about it. She complained about Toby's late hours, his lack of a job, his eating their food, and failing to clean up after himself in the bathroom, especially after he had been drinking. Brian shrugged and remarked that there was nothing he could do, really, and Jennifer stormed off and silently fumed.

Brian cared about his brother but he wanted him out, though he didn't know how to broach the subject. Each day Jennifer grew increasingly distraught and took it out on Brian. Brian felt trapped between them; the stress took its toll. He found himself staying later at work despite the fact that Elenor was often there making snide remarks, asking personal questions, and being a pain in the ass.

Jennifer was also often at work. She had picked up extra shifts because, she said, "We need the money."

Brian knew that it was only partially true. They needed extra money because they were supporting Toby, but he also knew that her staying away was retaliatory, as if to say, "I'll be home when he is gone."

The rest of his day at work passed slowly. He answered a few calls from customers confused about their accounts, filed accident claims for a windshield and a fender bender, reorganized some of his manuals, entered new client information, generated a couple of auto quotes, and filed. It was uneventful, yet when he left he was completely spent. Brian never understood how he could spend so many hours completing mindless, mostly sedentary tasks, and still feel so fried. He left the office at exactly five and walked the four blocks to his apartment. Outside it felt like a typical hot summer afternoon, except for the occasional brine-scented breeze, which he hoped was bringing the predicted cooler weather. For Bellingham it was rush hour, which meant a few more cars filled with solitary, haggard drivers making their way back home. By the time he arrived at his door his undershirt and dress shirt were wet with perspiration and his throat dry.

After he peeled off his work clothes and tossed them on the floor of the bedroom, Brian got out a bottle of vodka from the freezer, where he had hidden it behind a loaf of bread, and mixed it with orange juice and 7-Up. He noticed that the bottle, that he bought two days ago, was now only half-full. His first thought was that his brother had found it, but he wasn't sure. And he knew he soon wouldn't care. The first sip was harsh, burning his throat and making him wince. After he finished half of his drink he realized that he was buzzing hard and feeling and thinking less and less. He wanted this anesthetic; he didn't want to think, or feel, but just listen to music on his headphones and drift in and out of consciousness.

Brian went into the bedroom to lie down and listen to his CD player. After he flopped down on the bed he reached over to grab his player and headphones. His hand felt a disk but nothing else. He held the disk close to his face. It was David and David, *Welcome to the Boomtown*, and it was the same CD that used to be in his player.

"Fuck!" he yelled, realizing that his brother had borrowed it without asking him.

His anger quickly became panic when he began to think about the possibility that his brother wasn't planning on returning it and perhaps had sold or traded it for drugs. He tried to think, but exhausted and buzzed, he knew his reasoning was poor, his memory uncertain.

He jumped out of bed to check on his stash. He reached under the bed where it should be and his hand groped air.

"Fuck me!" he yelled. He looked under the bed and saw the small wooden box pushed toward the middle and against the wall.

He scooted under the bed, pulled out the box, and flipped open the lid, regretting that he had considered, but never very seriously, putting a lock on the box. He also knew that wouldn't have slowed his brother down much. And the box was almost as important as its contents.

He had bought the small box years ago, on a family trip to Cozumel. It had been rougher wood then; two carved palm trees leaned toward each other, graced the front. Over the years it had always been a stash box, of sorts. It had held his *Star Wars* cards he had bought in the sort of fever that compelled some boys to buy baseball cards. It had also held a gold chain he sometimes wore, old keys to long-forgotten locks, stray coins, buttons, a red maple leaf pin from a trip to Vancouver, an old silver dollar his grandfather had given him, and other physical pieces of memory.

When he had moved to college it was the first thing he packed. Optimistically, he had kept condoms in it and sometimes his weed and pipe sealed tightly in a plastic bag. He wasn't sure if his brother knew what the small box meant to him, but he was thankful it was still there.

As he looked into the box he was fairly certain that there was some of his pot missing, but he couldn't be sure. Still, the realization that his brother couldn't be trusted and that he hadn't really changed began to dawn on Brian. When Toby had been living at home his parents were constantly losing things. It occurred to Brian now that he had always suspected Toby might be taking things for drugs, or alcohol, or whatever, but the idea was never even hinted at by his parents. Even after Toby's release from court-ordered rehab and reform school, his parents seemed to regard Toby's problem as a minor incidence of poor judgment. It was hard to tell if they feared being labeled bad parents or if ignorance was simply the best way they knew how to cope with things.

Because Brian was seven years older than Toby he was always seen as the more responsible one. Toby was also regarded as a miracle because, after Brian's difficult birth, his parents had tried to have another baby, without success, for years. Toby had been a complete surprise, since they had long stopped using birth control, believing that it no longer mattered. When he and his brother were younger Brian tried to look after Toby, yet Toby always found ways to lose Brian. Toby would sneak off by himself, often getting into things he shouldn't. Brian used to call him little Houdini because even if Brian tied a rope to him, which he tried once, despite Toby's screaming, he always managed to escape.

Brian sat in bed and tried to think.

If it's about principles, he thought, *then he obviously has no right to my things, but knowing Toby he doesn't have a clue. To him, everything is his, like he owns it even if he doesn't. I mean, what's mine is mine and he has no right to it.*

Brian's indignation at his brother violating his personal space, getting into his private things, and generally showing no regard for the hospitality Brian had shown him made him angry. His anger led to a disturbing thought which had floated in the periphery of his consciousness, waiting to be realized.

Is there something going on between Toby and Jennifer?

For weeks he had subconsciously begun to grow paranoid about the possibility. There were hints, perhaps imagined, and he began to wonder if the conversations between Jennifer and Toby, their accidentally bumping into each other, and their being conveniently gone at the same time were coincidence or something else.

But there's no way, he thought. *She would never go for him. Would she?*

Now he was not only angry but confused, hurt, and painfully jealous. What he and Jennifer had wasn't always perfect and lately it was truly strained. But they had a history, shared experiences, stories, sex, drinking, and great times.

He felt himself begin to tear up. He loved her deeply and wanted only her. And he thought that she wanted only him. *What if things have changed? What if everything is different?*

He felt as though the world tilted; the rug of all he had perceived to be permanent was suddenly pulled out from under him. He now knew that everything he had believed could be nothing more than wishful thinking.

"Shit," he said quietly.

He was overwhelmed with a sickening melancholy. His whole body was paralyzed by it, and the despair that came after laid waste to what was left. He wanted, in this moment, to cease to exist. He wanted a drink, yet he couldn't move.

He lay there for a long time until he finally fell asleep with the light on.

He woke to the sound of the front door opening.

He switched off the bedside lamp and lay perfectly still on top of the covers in the darkness. He knew as soon as she stepped into the apartment that it was Jennifer. He recognized the sharp staccato of her thick-heeled shoes against the linoleum in the narrow entryway. He heard her open the small hall closet, hang up her coat, and slip off her shoes and kick them into the back of the closet. She walked into the kitchen and he heard the fridge open. She took out a beer and opened the top with a crack and whoosh of escaping carbonation. He heard the squeak of the chair as she sat down at the kitchen table and he heard her unfold the newspaper. Usually, she sat down in front of the TV—after she said hello and gave him a kiss. But tonight was different. Perhaps she had been different for a long time now;

he no longer felt he knew.

As he lay there he wondered if he should walk out into the kitchen casually, maybe strike up a conversation. Maybe ask her about her day, rub her shoulders, and then offer to rub the rest of her in bed. It used to work, sometimes, when they weren't always so exhausted, and before Toby had shown up. He remembered now that they hadn't had sex, hadn't really been together, or even made out since Toby had so unceremoniously shown up on their doorstep. Brian hadn't really thought about the sex part because he had been so consumed with coping, fighting, and trying to figure out a way and a good reason to get up the nerve to throw Toby out on his ass.

Brian lay there barely moving, controlling his breathing, and listening for each and every sound. As he listened he tried to think of what to say, what to ask her. He wasn't ready to confront her; he wasn't quite sure that he knew anything, really. But he felt that something was different, and for now that was enough, or perhaps too much. He heard her get up and walk into the small living room, where she switched on the TV. To Brian it sounded like noise, squawks, and music punctuated by silence. He sat up in bed. He took deep breaths and his heart pounded. His throat was dry. He was now disturbingly sober and dehydrated. Brian was craving water.

I could just go out and get a drink, casually, he thought, *and say, Hi, maybe.*

He suddenly realized how strange everything had become. Here he was sitting on the edge of his bed, nervous about talking to the woman he had lived with for months and known for years. She knew when he took a dump or was having a bad day. She had seen him so wasted he had fallen down the stairs at a friend's apartment and puked on her new shoes. He felt all of that was something, should count for something, but he wasn't convincing himself.

Brian stood up, walked slowly to the door, and rested his hand upon the knob. Again he hesitated. *What is the point, exactly?* he thought. *I mean, what will this prove exactly?*

Nothing, he thought, answering his own question. *Not a damn thing.*

Just as he began to slowly and silently turn the knob he heard the front door open, banging slightly against the doorstop.

Toby was back. He squeezed the doorknob hard, clenching his jaw as he seethed with anger. He wanted Toby out. Right now more than anything else he wanted him, and all his vile crap, thrown out into the street.

Brian heard Toby swagger in, lazily, kicking off his shoes in the entryway. He wore them around the house until Jennifer left him a couple of nasty notes and she began to put them, covered in dirt and grime, into his bed. Toby didn't retaliate or complain, which surprised Brian, but Toby got the hint. He obeyed and, in retrospect, Brian began to wonder why.

Brain opened the door a sliver, peered through, and listened. He watched Toby walk to the fridge and pull out one of Brian's beers, pop the top, and toss it into the sink. Brian winced, and he had to remind himself to stay focused, observe, and stay cool.

"Hey, Jen, wha's up?" Toby asked as he walked into the living room.

"Not much," Jennifer said quietly.

"Hey, ah, mind if I hang in front of the tube with ya?" Toby asked nonchalantly.

"Fine," she said flatly.

Brian could hear Toby sit down on the couch.

For a long time Brian heard nothing from the living room other than the TV. He wondered what, if anything, was going on. His imagination, however, began to whir. He began to silently convince himself that they were holding hands, caressing each other silently, stealthily, or they were kissing quietly, hurriedly pushing back articles of clothing, and exposing themselves to one another. He knew, rationally, that all of these imagined scenarios were insane, but he wasn't feeling rational. He imagined grabbing a gun, which he didn't own, and forcing them at gunpoint to confess. Then Brian would pistol-whip Toby and shove them both out into the rainy night.

He knew that he had to go out into the living room, to see what was up, or to at least make his presence felt. He wanted to show Toby who was boss, that this was his place and his girlfriend. Yet Brian stood motionless, breathing shallowly, as he tried to listen carefully for any errant sound. He heard the sound of someone getting up off the couch.

"Night, Toby," Jennifer said, as she padded toward the bedroom.

"Nighty, night," Toby replied.

Panicked, Brian jumped into bed with his clothes on.

Brian watched Jennifer slowly and quietly opened the door. She gently closed it behind her and stood for a moment appearing to wait until her eyes adjusted to the darkness. She walked carefully to the bathroom, quietly opened the door, and slowly shut it behind her. She didn't turn on the light until the door was fully closed.

Brian could hear her turn on the faucet to wash her face, and brush her teeth. She put her clothes into a small hamper in the bathroom, turned off the light, slowly opened the door, and stepped into the dark bedroom.

She made her way to the bed, slowly drew the covers back, and got in. She avoided touching Brian as she adjusted her pillow and turned on her side away from him.

"I'm awake," Brian said, breaking the silence.

He felt the bed jostle slightly as he spoke. He realized that he had startled her.

"Oh," she said quietly, without moving. "I thought you were asleep."

"No." He waited for her to pick up the conversation, to ask him why he was still awake, how his day was, or tell him about hers. But she didn't say anything. He could hear the TV in the living room and her breathing, slowly, melodically.

"I've been up for a while," Brian said tentatively. "I couldn't sleep."

She didn't respond and didn't turn toward him.

He touched her shoulder, and still there was no response. He ran his hand down her back and slowly slid it into the back of her panties.

"Brian, I'm tired," she said, sounding exasperated.

He cupped each of her cheeks, gently massaging her soft skin.

"Seriously, Brian," she said sounding more annoyed. "Not now."

He buried his face in her hair; she smelled of conditioner, perfume, beer, fried foods, and cigarettes. For a brief instant the cigarette smell set off some tiny alarm in his brain since he knew that she didn't smoke, but then he remembered that customers and busboys smoked at the restaurant. He was becoming aroused: the pressure evident against the fly of his jeans. It had been a very long time since he last had sex.

He whispered to her, "Come on, babe, just a quickie."

"I'm not in the mood," she said. "I'm exhausted, my feet hurt, my back hurts, my head hurts, and all I want to do is sleep."

"Yeah, well, you're never in the mood."

"What the hell is that supposed to mean?" She turned toward him and sat up.

"What do you think?" He took off his sweatshirt and threw it on the floor.

"What?" she asked. "Were you wearing your clothes to bed?"

He shrugged.

"Brian," she said in an angry whisper, "I have had a hard day, a hard week, and a terribly hard time since your brother moved in."

"He hasn't moved in, he just never left."

"Shit. You know what I mean. It hasn't exactly been easy."

"What? You think I'm enjoying this crap? You think I want him here?" Brian said, his voice growing louder and his tone more caustic with each word.

"Shh," she said. "He'll hear you."

"Shit," he said. "Like I care what he thinks. I wish he could hear me. But I'm sure he's passed out by now, drunk on *my* beer."

She said nothing.

"Why can't we at least try to have a normal life?" he asked.

"What would be normal about it?"

"I don't know. Maybe pretend that he isn't here."

"Yeah, right."

"I mean let's go away for a couple of days, maybe to Orcas or Vancouver or somewhere."

"Brian, now is not a good time. The restaurant is understaffed; we just lost two waiters, who graduated. I'm doing well with tips. And can you really afford to take off from work?"

Brian shrugged.

He didn't answer because he didn't know, or wasn't sure. He sat down at the foot of the bed facing away from her. He put his head in his hands. In the next room they could hear the incessant chatter of the TV.

"I'm tired, too," Brian said. He wanted to say something else. He wanted to tell her that he loved her, that things would get better, and that he would talk to Toby soon. But he knew that the words would somehow ring hollow. They would sound forced, and contrived.

"I'm going to sleep," Jennifer said, and she turned over and was soon breathing deeply.

Brian sat on the edge of the bed for a long time. He listened to the sound of the TV and for sounds from Toby. After what seemed like too long in the dark he got up and went into the living room, opening and shutting the bedroom door carefully so as not to wake Jennifer.

Toby was asleep on the couch, sitting up, the flickering TV creating strange images across his serene face and the wall behind him. His clasped hands held one of Brian's half-empty beers balanced precariously against his stomach. Brian gently pulled the beer bottle from his hands and Toby barely stirred. Brian stood and looked at him. It was often hard for him to imagine that they were related. They were so different. Even Brian's memory of when they were little seemed muddled and unclear. And the large age difference ensured that they had done little together, except when Brian was forced to baby sit.

Brian considered, just for a fleeting second, the prospect of killing Toby as he slept and how unbelievably easy it would be. The thought, which seemed to originate from nowhere, disturbed him and he shuddered. The brief malicious notion convinced him that he needed to get out of the apartment. He left Toby where he sat, undisturbed, the TV on. He set the beer in the sink and considered getting another one for himself, but he felt too agitated. He gently opened the door to the bedroom and reached around the knob and locked it. He didn't trust Toby when he was home, and even less so if he was going out. He grabbed an old shirt that he kept in the front closet and his green hooded rain slicker. The afternoon heat had finally given way to a night of cool rain.

Thinking about the cool summer night made him realize that classes would have just ended at Western. Remembering that and the fact that the door to that part of his life was closed filled him with a dull ache. With that feeling he walked out into the rain.

He walked away from his apartment and up toward campus. Through his hood he could hear the muffled sound of small raindrops. Somewhere he heard the distant lonely sound of a train and an occasional car splashing across the wet streets. He walked up the steep, small, tree-lined streets and noticed a few students walking in groups, with backpacks, and talking loudly as if everyone was wide awake at that hour. They looked so young to Brian that he wasn't sure if they were in high school or college. A man flew past him on a mountain bike and Brian jumped, startled, as it slid and skidded on the wet street. Near the top of the hill, breathing heavily, he turned down an alley. Around the muted streetlights he could see the rain which hung about them like bright yellow beaded veils. The gravel crunched under his boots and he looked ahead of him, and slightly down, to avoid stepping in the puddles that had formed in the mud.

It was strange to be out so late, with no clear purpose. Yet, he felt surprisingly focused. He wasn't sure exactly what it was. He thought that it might be adrenaline or endorphins or being somehow unattached, existing only within his mind. The feeling reminded him of when he used to walk to parties, years ago, when he went to Western. The sensation caused him to think of one night in particular, when he and his roommate Stan got stoned and went to the party at Dave's house. That turned out to be the night that served as a strange dividing line between a solitary life and a life coupled with Jennifer's.

Inevitably, he was reminded of her, of Toby, and of all of the things he had forgotten about for the past twenty minutes by simply planting one foot in front of the other and smelling the wet, earthy smell of rain and wet cedar. He tried to think of something else, to let his feelings of anxiety ebb. But he couldn't. He knew where the discussion with himself would lead. He wondered if he was out of options, out of room to save something that didn't seem to want to be saved. He realized that he and Jennifer had moved beyond drifting apart. They had moved into the unpleasant limbo of a relationship where the next step would be someone moving out, moving away, or giving up. He was afraid to be the one to do it. In fact, he wasn't even sure he could. Somewhere, in their shared experience, he believed there was still some residue of love, that there was some semblance of tenderness and the whispers of something else. They had missed that exit, and Brian knew that it was only a matter of time before they careened off the cliff.

He wondered how it would end, and what would be said. He considered packing up his things when she was at work and leaving. But that seemed unbelievably childish; didn't he owe her more than that? He didn't know. He knew that his jealousy of Toby, because of his imagined involvement with Jennifer, had been the strongest emotional feeling he had had in weeks, perhaps even months. But he also knew that deep down that feeling wasn't about her, at least not enough.

He walked down the alley, trying not to think, which proved to be difficult. Looking up he suddenly noticed a strange figure standing near a garbage dumpster on the next block. The large man stood half in the shadows and had turned in his direction. Brian figured he was probably a homeless guy, but he didn't want to stay and chat. He turned and walked back to the next cross street. He walked down the darkened street, lit only by an occasional porch light. He knew that he was deep in the student slums because in front of each dilapidated house there were five or more cars often festooned with bumper stickers for skateboards, snowboards, or some local band. Scraps of individual expression hung from some of the rearview mirrors: beaded necklaces from Mardi Gras, tassels from high school graduation, and small scented air fresheners undoubtedly covering the lingering smells of stale beer, cigarettes, and pot.

He walked down to another one of the many alleys that crisscrossed the older parts of Bellingham behind houses which had overlooked the bay for the better part of a century. As he came to a place where the alleyway abruptly sloped toward town he realized exactly where he was. He turned toward the house closest to him. The back porch light glowed green, a recent addition since he had seen it last. Somewhere inside, behind the blinds, a lamp glowed, casting slight shadows upon the grass. This was Dave Greibing's house. Brian stood and stared for a long time. He looked into the back yard, over the short fence; the grass was long, and a single dilapidated white chair lay on its side.

"This was the place," he thought. "Here."

It seemed like a long time ago now. But, strangely, other than the green porch light, little if anything had changed. He wondered if Dave still lived here, if life had changed for him. He also wondered what happened to Stan and everyone else. He hadn't kept in contact with anyone. He hadn't really seen any reason to. Even now he wasn't sure what purpose it would serve, other than to remind him of how much older he was and how little he had done since graduation. The house, alone, was enough of a reminder. He turned and looked toward town. The streetlamps below glowed, and the paper plant was ablaze with light.

He sighed and stood for a long time. As he looked out over all of these houses, bars, and the plant he was struck by how much of a microcosm this view was. Below him were many lives, tiny universes lived out separately from his own, yet each with its own problems, triumphs, and moments of pure ecstasy. In a way he felt less significant, his own problems less important. Yet he felt even sadder and more alone. He knew he was insignificant, that his life had become unimportant, that he had nothing to look forward to and that Jennifer, the best thing that ever happened to him, would slip through his hands. This epiphany washed through him, and its emptiness somehow gave him comfort. For the first time in a long time he wasn't clinging to illusions; he knew exactly where he stood, and he realized his place, his role, within it. His despair gave him certainty.

Yes, he thought. Things *have not turned out like I thought, imagined or whatever, but I have done nothing with nothing. I have waited for something, I'm not sure what. No more.*

Brian felt a certain resolve for something, change perhaps, he wasn't sure what exactly. For the first time in years he had a feeling of resolution, of definitiveness. He turned around and walked back home. When he got back the apartment was quiet and dark. He hung up his dripping coat, walked into the living room, and fell asleep on the now empty couch.

He woke to the sound of Jennifer making herself breakfast. He wondered if she had woken up, concerned about where he was, why he was out so late, and if she came into the living room to check on him. He thought about his midnight walk and the resoluteness it had given him, but being back here with Jennifer just a few feet away he felt weak again. He wanted her back, as things had been, and he wanted Toby out. He felt crushed, almost suffocated by his longing, his desire to return to something he suspected no longer existed. He put his head down and lay looking up at the ceiling and wondered where last night's feeling of certainty had gone.

As he lay there he suddenly realized it was Wednesday. He looked at his watch. 10:30.

"Fuck me!" He was very late for work.

He heard a plate drop in the kitchen and Jennifer gasped in surprise. He sat up as she walked into the living room.

"You're still here?" she asked with a mixture of surprise and irritation. "I was sure that you left for work."

"Nope," he said a bit sheepishly.

"You are going to work, right?" she asked, now clearly irritated.

He shrugged, got up from the couch, and walked past her to the fridge, careful to avoid the broken glass, but making no effort to help. He pulled out a Coke, opened it, and took a sip. He could feel Jennifer staring coldly at him, and he ignored her. He walked to the bathroom. As he closed the door he heard her ask him again if he was planning on going to work, but he ignored her. He stayed in the shower for a long time.

After he got out of the shower and got dressed, Jennifer was gone and there was a note on the table which read, in large letters, "WORK CALLED, CALL BACK." He crumpled up the note and threw it away. He poured himself a bowl of Frosted Flakes and scarfed it down as he finished his Coke.

He decided that he wouldn't call work. He knew that he deserved a day off and that there was no way he was going to call Elenor to negotiate it. She was never one to be sympathetic. The last time he had called in sick he had to argue to convince her that he was actually ill. It had been an exhausting conversation; Elenor had insisted that the next time he called in sick, he had better have a doctor's note.

Screw that! he thought.

He wasn't sure what he wanted to do today. He felt free and yet slightly disoriented, almost giddy, with the prospect of doing whatever he wanted for the day. He heard Toby beginning to stir in the next room and decided that he didn't want to stick around and face his brother. He went into his room, dug out his old backpack, and grabbed his bag of weed, his pipe, and his wallet.

Just as he closed the door Toby turned on his stereo and Black Sabbath blasted from his room.

Brian walked into the parking lot and realized that his car wasn't there because Jennifer had driven it. Amid all of the recent chaos, they had neglected to get her car fixed.

Whatever, he thought. *I'll just walk.*

He walked up to Forest Street, a beautiful tree-lined street complete with large Victorian, Craftsman-style, and turn-of-the-century custom homes. Each house had a distinct character all its own, set back from the street with lawns, flower gardens, hedges, shrubs, and quaint walkways out front. Even the two recent remodels exuded an old-fashioned feel, like patina on copper. He had never been inside any of them but imagined that they had beautiful wood floors, leaded glass, elegant winding stairways, marble tile, giant wood fireplaces, and other elegant touches.

For many years Brian had given little thought to the idea of a house, and, more specifically, a home. His parent's house was starkly modern, large, and sterile. As he got older and lived in various places, including the shabby, sorry excuse for a remodel on Garden, he began to appreciate the subtleties that existed on this street. In fact, he had begun to relish walking down it and musing at the lives lived in these old resplendent homes. It gave him a certain feeling of hopefulness, of continuity, of things withstanding and even weathering time. Sometimes, like now, the houses were a reminder of a life that would always be out of reach. Compared to these homes his place was a dump with a view.

How strange, he thought, *To live just a few hundred feet from a completely different world.*

A year ago, this very month, he and Jennifer had walked this street en-route to a late breakfast in Fairhaven. Hands clasped, they enjoyed the unusually cool Saturday morning. They had noticed the kids playing in their yards, squealing, with running dogs underfoot, an elderly woman working in her roses, and a teenager washing the family minivan.

Brian sighed.

Had that only been a year ago? he thought.

He could hardly believe it. Everything seemed so different, even though in so many ways things were the same: same jobs, same apartment, same town.

He craved a drink, and then he remembered that he had brought his weed and pipe. *Ah, yeah,* he thought, feeling himself relax.

He walked down to the end of Forest, where it met 15th street, another street with enormous old homes. Many of the houses sat up on raised yards, a few feet above the sidewalk, and were enshrouded by trees, bushes, and vines. He walked by Lowell Elementary, a rundown brick building. In the small playground screaming children ran, chased each other, and played. Brian smiled at their exuberance, but he still felt melancholy and focused on his destination so he could light up. He walked down the steep hill into Fairhaven—a small, once separate town of neat little brick buildings which now housed restaurants, bookstores, small stores, and coffee shops. He walked past the two blocks of downtown and toward the Alaska Ferry landing and Marine Park. He walked past fields of dry grass, vacant lots, and a few dilapidated commercial properties. By the time he reached the park he was exhausted, uncomfortable, his feet hurt, and he was sweating profusely. He rarely thought about how out of shape he was, but this walk was a brutal reminder. He was dying to smoke a bowl.

He followed the well-used railroad tracks adjacent to the park that ran along the water's edge. He found a small, rocky, sheltered inlet and climbed down onto a rock. The tide was out and the rock-strewn beach smelled of musty seawater. He sat on a large, cool smooth rock and pulled out his pipe. He was still breathing hard and felt lightheaded so he decided to wait and catch his breath. He could hear the popping sounds of mussels, just beneath the pebbles, and could see occasional squirts of water. He looked up and across the calm water. He could see Lummi Island and the tip of Mount Constitution.

He leaned back on his arms and closed his eyes. He could feel the sun on his face and a slight breeze that blew across the water, and could hear the distant squawks of sea birds. Sitting and thinking about getting stoned reminded him of college because he used to be stoned most of the time. He had a theory, developed while he was stoned, that it was easier and even preferable to simply exist in an altered reality. When he was stoned he was always comfortable, he never felt self-conscious or worried. He could sit for hours at the same activity and he could focus on that one thing, which was usually TV. Social situations had proven to be easier as well. It was so different than high school, where he constantly worried about meeting new people. Even the paranoia that plagued some people when they were stoned wasn't something he had experienced until just recently.

He opened his eyes and noticed that he was breathing more easily, and he began to imagine the sensation of pot smoke in his mouth. He took out his small plastic bag and unrolled it. Opening it he realized that something was wrong: all of the buds were picked out. He felt around inside the bag but found only shake and scraps.

"Fuck!" He yelled to no one in particular.

He knew that the last time he had smoked he had at least ten or twelve good-sized buds in there; there was no point in smoking shake. Looking inside the bag, and still in a state of shock, he noticed the pot was a variety of different colors. He put his nose inside the bag and took a whiff. It smelled faintly of pot but it also smelled of something else. It was a familiar smell but he couldn't place it. It reminded him of pizza.

"Oregano," he said.

Toby had stolen his pot and put in oregano, for appearances.

That shit head, he thought. *How stupid does he think I am? I taught him that trick.*

When Brian was a senior in high school Toby had found some of his parents' stash and they smoked it. Uncertain how to replace what was gone, Brian suggested that they use oregano. He realized later that his parents probably knew immediately that their sons had made the switch, but they said nothing. For them to accuse Brian and Toby would mean that they would have to admit that they smoked themselves, but because they had often lectured them on the dangers of drugs that would make them mere hypocrites. His parents simply moved their stash and the theft issue was never discussed.

Now Brian was furious; he threw the bag and yelled. He could feel his face flush and he clenched his teeth.

"The last straw. The last straw," he said to himself, and got up to head home.

He walked quickly back toward Fairhaven. Brian fumed and began to think of how he was going to beat the crap out of his brother and then burn all of his things. He knew he would have to be deceptive about it. Toby was in much better shape, scrappier, but he was also unhealthy from smoking, drinking, and drugging.

Walking quickly up the gradual incline he was already out of breath and he slowed his pace. *If I can't even walk this how am I going to take out Toby?*

The walk back to his apartment, up two hills, one very steep, seemed to take forever. He stayed focused by imagining all of the ways he could finally tell his brother off. He mumbled various speeches, some diplomatic, some caustic, and others matter-of-fact. He went over each word individually, trying to gauge its impact and possible effect.

Just before he walked up the steps near his front door his speech had become:

Toby. I need to talk to you and I don't want you to speak until you hear me out. I have been meaning to tell you for some time that you have outworn your welcome. Jennifer and I have been gracious, patient, and more than hospitable, considering. You, on the other hand, have been disrespectful and dishonest with us. You have drunk our booze, eaten our food, sold drugs out of our apartment, you stole my pot, and my CD player has disappeared. The only reason I have allowed you to stay for as long as I have is because you are my brother. But I realize now that I have been too tolerant, too understanding, and too lenient. For your own good I want you to pack up your things and leave. Not tomorrow, not in ten minutes, but right now.

Brian thought that the speech sounded pretty good. It was short, to the point and didn't belabor any particulars. It covered all of the things that Brian had wanted to say but had not had the guts to confront Toby with.

As he turned the key he took a deep breath and thought, "Relax, this needs to happen."

For a brief few minutes Brian was hopeful that he could get Toby out, that, maybe, he could even patch things up with Jennifer and get things back to normal again.

"Toby, Toby," he said, as he knocked on the door to his room.

There was no answer. Brian tried the knob and it was unlocked. He walked into the room and instantly realized that Toby was gone. His duffle bags that had overflowed with clothes, his dirty socks and underwear strewn across the floor, magazines, and shoes were all gone. All that was left were remnants of his occupation: empty cigarette cartons, a old lighter, a half-empty beer, dirty bowls, mugs, plates, and silverware, a couple of crumpled up candy wrappers, and dirty sheets stripped off the hide-a-bed and wadded up into a misshapen ball.

Brian looked over the room and was in shock. He couldn't believe that he had just up and left like that, no warning, no notice and no hint that he would ever leave. Brian's shock soon became outrage. He couldn't believe that he had simply packed and left without telling him, without apologizing.

Christ, Brian thought, *look at all of this crap.*

Brian realized that he wouldn't be able to tell him off, make him leave, and make him understand that he had been an inconsiderate, rude, and terrible brother. This further angered him. He wanted some retribution, some justice. He picked up a lamp that lay on its side on the floor and threw it. It crashed against the wall with a thud of broken glass as it exploded.

He stood amazed, looking at his hands, at the destroyed lamp. He could hardly believe what he had done. He hadn't destroyed anything in anger since he was a kid, yet he couldn't believe how good it made him feel. He knew the feeling would be fleeting, but in that instant, as he threw the lamp and it exploded, he had wished the wall was Toby's face. Its was a sickening realization but he understood, more clearly, that he hated his bother and that he no longer trusted his own sense of self-control.

Brian walked out of the room and closed the door behind him. He got a beer out of the fridge and tried to think of what he should do and what he should tell Jennifer.

Toby didn't leave a note, so it is possible that he is coming back, he thought, *but I seriously doubt it. And I broke the lamp. How am I going to explain that?*

Then he imagined a remarkably simple scheme that would solve all of his problems and maybe even get him back into Jennifer's good graces.

He would tell Jennifer the way things should have happened. He would tell her that he had come home, fed up and angry, and had given Toby the speech he had planned to give and Toby had lost it and threw the lamp, narrowly missing Brian. Punches were thrown, they had struggled, and Brian hauled Toby out and his stuff with him. What Toby had left he had taken out to the dumpster in a furious rage. He had considered burning his things, he would tell her, but his reasoned cool-headed judgment had prevailed.

Brilliant, he thought, smiling to himself with a sense of self satisfaction. *But it needs to look believable.*

Brian downed his beer and pulled out what was left of his vodka in the fridge, which he had taken pains to hide in a half-empty carton of orange juice. He took large gulps of the stuff, wincing against the burning sensation and swallowing hard as the bile threatened to rise up in his throat. He stood against the counter, waiting for the alcohol to kick in. Soon he realized that he was drunk and that it was time to begin.

He walked into Toby's room and picked up loose objects, trash, books, scratched CDs, papers, a small clock, and magazines, and threw them around the room. The papers fluttered about like loose birds and bits of Toby's trash floated or fell to the floor. As the books and magazines crashed some ripped and others broke their bindings, sending loose pages scattering. The dissonance of harsh thuds and whoosh of papers caused Brian to become lost within the moment. He became a minor cyclone of destructive energy. With each object he flung he imagined doing the same to Toby. He clenched his jaw and felt himself begin to sweat.

He also began to yell, in his own voice and his best imitation of Toby. This made it feel more believable to Brian, and in the slim chance that his neighbors were home they would make unwilling collaborators.

He threw himself against the door, wincing as he heard the pop of his shoulder, leaving a large dent in the door. Brian screamed out in pain, which only fueled his fury. He spun around the room, jumped on the hide-a-bed, jumped off, grabbed the cushions, and threw them onto the floor. He careened against the walls, punched the bookshelves and broke them, and cut his hand. Then he spun into the bathroom door; his fists flew and dented the door. He grabbed pictures off the walls and threw them haphazardly; they hit the floor and a small nightstand, and burst into thousands of tiny shards of glass. Then he flung himself into the hallway and the kitchen, turning over chairs, throwing a beer bottle against the floor which sent glass and beer across the kitchen. He ran down the hall, pulled over another kitchen chair as he went, pulled coats off their hangers, and kicked shoes across the smooth floor.

He opened the door and yelled, "And stay out!" slamming the door so hard that a picture in the living room fell off the wall and shattered.

Brian sighed and felt an enormous sense of relief. He felt as though he had really rid them of Toby, the parasite. In his drunken state, as the creeping pain in his shoulder, his hand, and his knee became more acute, he began to believe that he had actually thrown Toby out. The pain was real, the destruction was real, and Toby was gone. He had thrown him out, he was now sure of it, reliving the memory of their fight in his mind. He peered into the spare bedroom where Toby had been just that morning and was perversely overjoyed at what he saw. The room looked like someone had set off a small bomb. Brian thought it looked believable enough and he smiled again at his brilliance. But his head, and the rest of his body, began to throb painfully.

I need another beer, he thought as he stepped back into the kitchen.

Walking toward the fridge he had forgotten that the floor was covered with beer and broken glass. He didn't remember slipping, but he felt himself fall backward, his feet flying upward almost in slow motion. He knew somehow, before his foot began to slide, that he was going to hit the floor. He closed his eyes. Just before the back of his head hit the hard floor he saw himself fall.

For a fraction of a second he watched impassively. He saw the falling, the sensation of fear and struggle against inevitability as though he was watching himself on a grainy eight-millimeter movie, like those that had captured so much of his early childhood. His legs kicked air and his arms flailed, askew, almost comically, as the expression on his face betrayed wonderment and his wide eyes an intense fear. As his head hit the floor it made a sickening thud like a hammer against a watermelon and he blacked out.

Someone was banging on the door.

He opened his eyes and looked up at the ceiling. An intense pain washed over him and he closed his eyes. The pain reminded him of what had happened.

Someone was still pounding on the door and now they were yelling something. He couldn't tell what exactly. He forced himself up and was instantly sorry that he had done so. Sitting up his head pounded so intensely that he almost vomited. His head was spinning and he had to brace himself to keep from passing out again.

He could now make out the words of the person who was knocking.

"Hey, you okay? Open up or I'm gonna' come in. I have a key."

Brian struggled to his feet, bracing himself with each change in elevation. The person on the other side of the door continued to pound and he wished they would stop because it simply added to his headache.

He leaned against the wall as he walked slowly to the door. He took a deep breath, trying to compose himself despite the now blinding pain in his head. He cracked open the door just wide enough to see who it was. The bright light from outside caused him to squint and initially obscured the figure until his eyes adjusted.

It was the maintenance man, Joe. Brian recognized him because he wore a uniform with the name of the apartments and his first name on the front, and he had once fixed one of the light switches when it was broken. Brian had hardly ever talked to the man.

"Hey, ah," Joe said, obviously uncomfortable. "Your neighbors complained about a bunch of noise and I was just making sure everythin' was ok, and all."

"Oh yeah," Brian said slowly, and carefully. "Everything is fine."

"Well I, ah, you know, just wanted to check up on ya," he said, trying to look past Brian and into the apartment.

Brian noticed. He closed the door slightly and shifted his position so Joe would only be able to see into their closet.

"Sure, sure," Brian said, forcing a smile. "I appreciate it."

For a few seconds Brian considered telling the maintenance man how he had thrown out his brother and there had been a minor scuffle.

"Thought about calling the police," Joe said, "but I wanted to check it out myself first."

At the mention of police Brian felt a slight twinge of panic. He would have to explain many things about Toby, their unreported extra tenant, and how they were violating their lease. He would probably have to file some type of report, and he might even have to go in for questioning. The thought made him shudder.

"You, ah, alone in there?" Joe asked.

"Sure, yeah," Brian answered, becoming more uncomfortable with each question.

"Really, thanks for stopping by and your concern, but everything is fine."

Joe shrugged, obviously irritated, and turned and left without another word.

Brian closed the door slowly, and locked it. He leaned against it, holding his pounding head in his hands. He was proud of himself because of the little ruse he had managed to pull off. Brian was never good at lying, not because of a sense of moral certainty but because he was so unpracticed at it. Toby seemed only to lie, adeptly and effortlessly. It was a skill that Brian now envied. He wondered if he could pull off lying to Jennifer, who seemed to know him so well. But Brian also knew that he was regrettably predictable, that his actions and reactions seemed to fall within a certain realm of possibilities. Deceptions, destruction, aggression—these were things that made Brian uncomfortable and yet here he was. He stood away from the door, briefly glancing back at it. He did a double take. Against the dingy smooth whiteness he noticed a small patch of bright wet redness. He felt the back of his scalp and his hands felt warmth. He felt faint and a flood of worries seized him.

Oh shit, he thought, panicked, *I cracked my head open, my brains are seeping out.*

He walked as quickly as he could into the bathroom. He found an old compact of Jennifer's and struggled to see the back of his head in the small mirror. He noticed a small amount of blood in his hair, which had already begun to dry. He also had a large goose egg which sent shockwaves of pain through his entire body when he barely grazed it with his fingertips.

With some tissue and an old towel he gingerly cleaned the wound, took a couple of ibuprofen, and got some ice for his head. He checked the clock, it was almost four thirty. He wasn't sure when Jennifer would be home so he sat down on the sofa to drink beer and watch TV.

He woke to the sound of Jennifer yelling. He was groggy, half asleep and he could only make out the words: "What the…? Holy shit!"

Brian jumped up, startled, ready to explain himself, but then he remembered the plan and he relaxed.

"Brian, what the hell happened? And where is Toby?"

Brian winced and wished she hadn't asked him where Toby was. She sounded concerned, but about whom?

"Let me explain," Brian said calmly, deliberately.

She stood there saying nothing, her hands on her hips. Her face betrayed only surprise, no hint of concern or worry for Brian's welfare.

Brian was confused and hurt by her reaction. This was not what he had expected; this was not the way it was supposed to play out. He had rehearsed it, mulled it over, and yet she already seemed pissed and defensive.

"Well, ah, Toby and I got in a fight," Brian continued, "after I told him that he needed to leave."

Jennifer's expression changed and she relaxed. She walked over and sat next to Brian.

"Brian, that's terrible," she said, putting her arm around his shoulder.

This was what he had hoped for. "Yeah he went psycho on me. It was like I didn't even know him. He was throwing shit around, screaming, and yelling."

He looked at Jennifer. She was definitely listening. She didn't have that distracted, far off look that she seemed to have so often lately.

"Then he just went at me," Brian said. "He started thrown punches, pushing and shoving me. At first, I was, you know, freaked out but after that adrenaline kicked in I started swinging. I wasn't really trying to hurt him but he just kept coming back at me. He was totally whacked."

"Jesus," Jennifer said slowly seeming to think about what he said. "You okay?"

"Yeah, but he stopped at one point and was acting all sorry and stuff and then he hit me with a bottle," Brian said as he turned his head to show Jennifer the dried blood and the large bump on the back of his head.

"Oh hon," she said, clearly moved and concerned. "We need to get you to the hospital."

"No, really, I'm fine," he said, taking Jennifer's hand, trying hard to sound convincing. "I'm just a little sore is all, slight headache."

"Brian, really," she said, clasping his arm as she stood, trying to pull him up with her. "You need to see a doctor."

He wriggled out of her grasp. "I'm fine," he said. "Maybe tomorrow."

She looked at him for a moment. "You're sure you're okay?"

"Really," he insisted, "I am fine."

She shrugged and started cleaning up.

"Oh, I can help," Brian said, meaning it.

"No way," she said. "Don't you dare get up. You need to rest, just relax. You want a beer? Or something to eat?"

"Yeah, sure. A beer would be great and could you make me some of those nachos you make."

"Sure, I'm not sure if I have all of the ingredients, but I can always make a run to the store."

Brian smiled to himself as he turned on the TV, smugly self-satisfied.

An hour later Jennifer came back into the living room and sat down next to Brian.

"That about does it," she said. "But I think were going to lose our deposit."

Shit, Brian thought. *I hadn't considered that.*

"I mean, what a mess he made," she said. "I'm amazed that you weren't hurt worse."

"Yeah," Brian said, unsure if she had begun to doubt his story or if she was impressed that he had so stoically withstood Toby's abuse.

"Oh hon?" she asked. "You mind just getting yourself something to eat? I'm exhausted."

"Oh sure," he said, trying to sound as pathetic as possible.

But Jennifer didn't notice.

"I'm going to bed," she said, and kissed him lightly on the head.

Brian winced for effect, yet was irritated, his head throbbed.

For a while after she closed the door he sat and felt sorry for himself. He tried to analyze their conversation, determine if she was impressed. Nothing seemed to have changed and things seemed more or less the same as they had been for the last few months. It hadn't turned out as he had planned because they were supposed to be having sex right now, and, actually, it was the last thing he felt he was capable of.

Eventually, he grabbed himself a bag of chips and a beer and settled back onto the couch to stare distractedly at the TV. He didn't remember falling asleep, but he woke up in the middle of the night in severe pain. He got up and went to the medicine cabinet and took four ibuprofens and lay down and slept next to Jennifer.

When he woke up he reached over to her side of the bed, but she was already up. He went into the kitchen, which was tidied up, the counters wiped and plates cleaned, resting neatly in the drying rack. There was a note on the fridge which read:

Brian,

    I didn't want to wake you. I got called into work to cover for Amy. I tried to get out of it but Jackson got all pissy about it. Anyway, call me if you need me to come home and if you really feel lousy call the doctor—I can take you. See you tonight—probably around 10.

Love,

Jen

PS – CALL WORK!

He wadded up the note and threw it in the trash. He was irritated. Brian couldn't believe her priorities and her manager's callousness. She obviously hadn't told him, or she wasn't convincing enough. He thought about calling into work but he didn't feel like it. He walked into Toby's old room. Jennifer had piled up what was salvageable and had carried out all of the things that Brian had destroyed. The room looked abused but not completely wrecked. The light flashed on the answering machine, which he had been careful not to destroy. He knew that the message was from work, Elenor asking him what the hell was going on, and why he wasn't at work. Jennifer had probably already heard it. He wasn't even curious. He didn't really care. His head had begun to throb so he took a couple more ibuprofen and drank another beer. He got dressed and decided to head downtown to grab something to eat and maybe drop by the restaurant to give Jackson a piece of his mind.

Outside it was dreary. The rain came down in steady mist, and dull grayness hung about everything like a faint shroud.

Brian pulled his hood up and winced as he barely brushed the lump on the back of his head. As he walked down the hill toward town he became more and more incensed at Jackson. Jennifer hadn't even been scheduled to work and she worked harder than anyone there, Brian was sure. Didn't she deserve a day off more than anyone? He felt his jaw tighten and he clenched his fists in his pockets. He considered taking Jackson out into the alley behind the place and demonstrating his dislike of him with his fists.

No, he thought, *I need to play it cool.*

By the time he had arrived at the restaurant the wind had picked up, blowing cold rain into Brian's face and puckering up his hood. He went to the glass front doors and pulled on the handle. The door was locked.

What the hell, he thought.

Cupping his hands against the glass he peered inside. In the back, near the kitchen, he could see a figure silhouetted against the kitchen lights. Brian tapped the glass. The figure looked up, hesitated, and then made its way toward the door. Once the figure got close enough Brian could see it was some kid in a white apron, probably sixteen or so, maybe a bus boy.

Brian waved at the kid, who was eying Brian suspiciously.

"We're closed!" the kid yelled at the glass and making no moves to unlock the door. "We're open in an hour!"

"Yeah!" Brian yelled feeling a bit ridiculous. "Hey, you think you could unlock this?"

"Sorry," said the kid shaking his head, "boss's orders."

Brian grew increasingly irritated, especially when he surmised that

Jackson was the boss he was talking about.

"Jackson here?" Brian asked.

The kid shook his head again. "This is Jackson's day off."

"Of course it is," Brian said through clenched teeth. "The prick."

"What?"

"Nothing!" Brian yelled. "Look could you tell Jennifer that Brian is here?"

The kid looked at Brian for a minute puzzled.

"It's her day off."

Brian was confused. "No I don't think you heard me! Jennifer Embry."

"Right," the kid said slowly, enunciating each word. "It, is, her, day, off!"

Brian looked away, trying to collect his thoughts. He was sure he had misunderstood, she had to be there, she was filling in for Amy.

When he looked up the kid was walking back to the kitchen. Brian pounded on the door, but the kid ignored him, disappearing behind the partition.

Brian turned and looked across the street.

A large flatbed truck sat idling. In the back sat a large, square box, covered in flapping sheets of white plastic. It looked alive. It looked as though it were spreading its white wings to fly.

5

SINNERS AND SAINTS

The vastness of the desert loomed before her through the smeared windshield. The headlights of her BMW 325i cut a swath through the darkness, illuminating the narrow two-lane highway just ahead of her. At 110 mph the car rattled and the air roared around the car pushing at the doors and windows. She had the stereo turned up as loud as she could stand, and Kurt Cobain wailed at her with auditory intensity.

Occasionally, a truck would pass her going the opposite direction and its lights would momentarily blind her. The lights blasted through the windshield, refracting off every speck of dirt and smeared bug, and then the dark shape would roar past, leaving a vacuum of air in its wake that shook her car and pulled her toward the edge of the road.

She had been making incredible time since she left Provo sometime after dusk. As she had driven away from the small oasis, surrounded by desert, the sky had slowly turned to red. The steep walls of sandstone bluffs, which looked like they had been cut unevenly by a dull knife, loomed in the distance. Just before the last bluish light of day had given way to complete darkness, she had a view of the immensity of space she was crossing. She came up over a rise, at the top of a pass, and the dry, bluish landscape, punctuated by spires of rock, bluffs, and scrub brush, extended as far as she could see. As far as Bridgette could tell, this seemingly dead and dry place could be the rest of the world.

The darkness settled over the desert and the stars shone, unobstructed by light pollution. The night camouflaged the landscape's size and only occasionally, when a bat would fly near the headlights or a small bush would reach out into the shoulder of the road, did she have any indication that she was still in the same place.

Bridgette had decided to travel at night because it would be about eighty degrees, rather than the one hundred thirteen that had been predicted for the following day. Besides, she knew she could really speed at night. She had driven this road, Highway Six, between Spanish Fork and Green River, almost four years earlier. She remembered the rush she had experienced watching the darkness roar around her like she was traveling through the center of a cyclone.

She reflexively gripped the steering wheel tighter, realizing that one minor twist would mean almost instant death. She wondered for a brief minute what it would be like to suddenly turn the wheel, the car flying off the pavement sideways as it spun through the air, rolling over and over, pieces of metal and glass and dust. She imagined how her body would be thrown against the roof and doors as the car flipped, the glass exploding around her. Before she figured out which way was up the car would most certainly crush her. Explosions and fire would follow, the car burning like a solitary beacon in the middle of nowhere.

She shuddered, despite the warmth of the car. Without looking down she fished through her black Coach bag that sat on the seat next to her and grabbed her pack of Camels. She pushed in the cigarette lighter and held the unlit cigarette between her lips until she heard the pop of the lighter. She lit it and inhaled deeply. She began to feel relaxed, less anxious.

She looked up through the moon-roof at the stars. It seemed to her as though a dozen years had passed since she had last seen stars so unbelievably brilliant and bright. They shone with an intensity that would almost make a city dweller uncomfortable—like a billion, luminous diamonds thrown across a dark velvet cloth. She had missed that in Bellingham. She had missed the feeling of the stars being distinctly present, seeming to reach down from the sky with their sheer determined brightness. In Washington, most nights, she simply had to have faith that they were there, obscured by low-lying clouds. And she missed heat lightning, the flashes of light in the night sky devoid of thunder, illuminating distant clouds from within.

The last time she had really seen the stars and heat lightning was over four years ago on a clear July night. The night was air was still; the smell of earth all around her. She lay with her head against Joe's bare chest on a soft blanket in the middle of her grandparent's cornfield. Joe snored lightly, as he always did after they had sex, and she laid awake, eyes wide, staring at the night sky. Every time she watched the night sky it felt to her as though she was seeing it again for the first time. The sky drew her into its cold, protective cloak.

Bridgette remembered how her grandparents would always chastise her for sleeping through the day, for neglecting her chores. They never suspected that she had been out in the cornfield having sex with Joe Reed. But why would they suspect? They simply didn't think that way; they knew nothing of deception because they never had anyone to deceive.

She had learned the trick at an early age, and it soon became almost second nature. When she was very young, before her dad had run off with a bimbo and her mom had one of many nervous breakdowns and divorces, she had learned it was rarely in her best interest to tell the truth. When large sums of cash disappeared out of her father's wallet Bridgette blamed the help. When a Waterford vase was shattered in the front hall she blamed it on the maid. When the car suddenly developed a dent overnight, she convinced her father she heard prowlers. Her parents were oblivious as she emptied out the liquor cabinet, stole their prescription drugs, and borrowed their cars without asking. They believed her no matter what she said. They were never present enough, physically or mentally, to unwind the truth from the lies.

For a few short years she managed to wiggle out of every predicament she got herself into. But eventually the stakes got higher and the lies more complex. By the time she was fifteen she lived two entirely separate lives: one at home and one on the street. Bridgette hung with older kids, whom her parents would have dubbed the wrong crowd. She went from heavy binge drinking to pot and coke. Eventually it didn't matter what it was as long as it got her high. She started having sex, mostly when she was high. Initially, Bridgette hadn't wanted to sleep around, but her friends all did, and they made fun of the prudes who weren't gettin' some. Being high was comfortable; when she was sober she felt eternally empty.

Just after her sixteenth birthday she snuck out of her posh house in Lake Forest to meet some friends in downtown Chicago. They had borrowed her parents' Mercedes and cruised around looking to score some smack. Bridgette had only recently graduated to heroin, and it was like nothing she had ever tried before. The first time she shot up she had the feeling of being overcome with a wave of soft warm peacefulness. It gave her the feeling of completeness like nothing she had ever tried before. She craved the feeling intensely, driving around Chicago asking every street corner dealer for their man Everly—their street corner pharmacist.

Eventually they caught up with Everly. He was standing outside a shooting gallery. As they pulled up he leaned into the car, instantly recognizing a sale. His sleeves were rolled up, revealing tracks, scars, and tattoos. He smiled, showing off his gold-capped front tooth with a diamond set in the center. Everly sold them more than they needed for an elevated price simply because he could. They drove to an abandoned warehouse where they liked to party. They had sparsely furnished the place with a couple of torn-up couches, a mattress, a plastic cooler, blankets, a stereo, and battery-operated lanterns.

When Bridgette stuck the needle between her toes her heart raced in anticipation of the feeling of soft euphoria. She released the smack into her bloodstream and soon felt overcome with delicious warmth.

Then things changed. She began to feel strange. She felt herself blacking out. She lay down and mumbled almost inaudibly as she felt herself slipping into darkness.

She felt as though she was looking at herself from outside of her own body, trapped beneath the ice. The cold water tingled against her skin, the muscles tightening beneath. The water was dark and she was pounding with her fists against the thick white ice. She couldn't breathe. She screamed. No sound came out. She panicked and wailed against the ice, but it was solid. There was no opening. She fought. But the murky, freezing water was all around her and she felt it seep into her lungs. As though a taut string had snapped somewhere deep within her she felt herself unable to struggle, unable to control her fate. She slid, struggling, into the void. No more strength. No more air. The frigid blackness overtook her.

☕

When she woke she was laying on a gurney and being wheeled down a long bright hallway. People ran on either side of her, dressed in greenish-blue hospital scrubs. The lights were so bright. What were they saying? She couldn't understand. Oh, she felt so sick.

When she woke again she was in a dim room. Tubes stuck into her nose and her arms. She tried to move but couldn't. She felt as though she had been dropped off a twelve-story building onto the freeway and had been run over, and over, and over. She felt her eyes close against her will.

The next time she woke someone was holding her hand. She realized it was her mom. She was leaning back in her chair, eyes closed, asleep. Bridgette tried to speak, but no words came. She managed to barely curl her fingers. She felt sick. So tired. She just wanted to sleep, just a little bit.

She woke suddenly as though she had been startled from a dream. She was uncomfortably conscious and every square inch of her body hurt.

"There she is," said a stout middle-aged nurse through a tight smile. The nurse was adjusting the tube that was taped onto her arm.

Bridgette looked around for her mom.

The nurse seemed to notice the longing in her eyes. "Oh, I'll go get your mom. She'll be glad to see you awake."

The nurse turned and slipped through the curtain.

Bridgette heard quick steps in the hallway, and recognized the sound of her mom's footfalls as surely as she would recognize her voice.

Her mom pushed the curtain aside with a harried swoosh and she embraced Bridgette, practically crushing her.

"Oh my baby, my baby," she cooed melodramatically.

The nurse stood in the background smiling. But the smile was uneasy, reserved.

Then her mom's mood changed abruptly, darkening, and she stood back from the embrace, her hands still resting on Bridgette's arms.

"What the hell were you thinking? Christ, I mean you could have died, and heroin!" Her voice grew louder with every word.

Bridgette watched helplessly as mother's expressions changed: her eyes narrowed, her face grew flush, her jaw set tight, and her gesticulations grew more animated and frantic.

"Jesus Christ, young lady, why, why?" She was almost yelling.

Bridgette turned her head away. She wanted to get away, to disappear, but there was nowhere to go. She wanted to die. *Oh, God,* Bridgette thought, *Please let me die.*

She looked back at her mom who was now yelling expletives, one after the other. She grabbed Bridgette's arms.

Bridgette looked at the nurse, whose smile had changed to a mask of fear.

"Mrs. Jonsen, please," the nurse pleaded, as she stepped forward and grabbed her arms.

She brushed the nurse away like she was swatting a fly.

Bridgette realized, to her horror, that mom was having a full-blown episode—strung out on prescription drugs and no sleep. Bridgette's arms hurt where her mom held them in vice-like grips. She struggled to free herself but she was far too weak. She heard the nurse yell something about security. Just as she thought she would be thrown to the floor two large uniformed men shot through the curtain and grabbed her mom's arms. They pulled on her, one on each arm, and Bridgette was lifted off the bed like a rag doll. They had to pry her fingers from Bridgette's arms and Bridgette fell painfully back onto the bed. Her mother was cursing and screaming, thrashing about violently as the security guards dragged her through the curtain. Bridgette tried to tell them to be careful with her, not to hurt her, but she could only manage a whisper.

Her arms ached and she knew that she would have two, deep, handprint bruises.

☕

Bridgette rubbed her left arm resting upon the edge of the windowsill, her hand curled around the wheel. She had dropped her speed down to seventy-five after she passed a police car that had pulled over a semi. The sound of the engine and the wind outside subsided to a dull hum.

☕

It was a long time before she felt well enough to sit up and watch TV or thumb through magazines. The hospital psychiatrist stopped by her room for an evaluation and nurses and a couple of doctors came by to check on her. Mostly she was alone with her thoughts.

She understood exactly why she was there; she knew she was drying out with methadone treatments. But Bridgette wasn't so sure she that she wanted to stop shooting smack. She craved the warm euphoric feeling like a starving person craved food. The pain only made the craving worse.

She began to plot an escape, as soon as she could walk, and hook up with Eddy, Claris, and the rest of her drug buddies. *Then again maybe not.*

She knew that she was flying solo now. Her so-called friends had laid her on the cold, hard concrete in front of the emergency entrance, unconscious and dying. They had laid her there and ran like cowards, their tails between their legs.

Bridgette had overheard the whole story from the nurse, who had been discussing it with the doctor when they thought she was sleeping. The realization that she had been abandoned, like a foundling, possibly to die, made her feel beneath the physical pain. It made her depressed in a way that hurt deeply. It was the kind of pain she couldn't wish away, she couldn't talk herself out of. She wanted smack. More than anything she wanted smack. She wanted to be carried away in its warm arms beyond unconsciousness and into the embrace of death.

Bridgette had shared a lot with her friends, virtually everything, and in the end they were just like everyone else. When push came to shove, they bailed.

For two days after she regained consciousness she hadn't seen much of her parents. Her mother had come by that one time, and almost beat her up, and her father had called from a business meeting in Miami. He had spoken to her as though nothing had happened, as though she was visiting relatives. He talked around the circumstances, making small talk. He never asked her why. She guessed that he simply didn't want to know. When her mother called she sounded drunk or high on Valium. She would ask Bridgette the same questions over and over as she slurred her words. Bridgette knew it had happened before, just after she was born, and her mom had to go into rehab for nine months after almost overdosing on barbiturates and alcohol.

No one else called, or sent flowers, cards, or notes. She figured that her parents probably hadn't told anyone else or that no one cared. Even if they called, or dropped a line, would they know what to say to her? "Sorry about your OD"?

The whole idea is laughable, Bridgette thought. There would be no way to broach the subject and they would handle her with kid gloves. Just as the nurses, doctors, and shrink had. They would smile and speak sweetly to her, and when they thought she wasn't looking they would shake their heads with disbelief or disdain.

They wouldn't understand. They couldn't understand. They would see a young, beautiful woman, frail, in a hospital gown, in a hospital bed with matted hair, and dark circles under her golden-brown eyes. But they wouldn't see the longing in her eyes and the sheer physical will that it took to quell the intense craving. And her wish to die. Like everyone else they saw exactly what they wanted to see.

Bridgette knew that she somehow disturbed them, and their sense of justice, or right and wrong. She didn't fit in with their assumption that junkies were outcasts without means, born poor or destitute or homeless, that they were without family or breeding. Or that junkies were Vietnam vets who were plagued by the demons of memories that gnawed at them like waking nightmares. Somehow they could feel sorry for those kinds of people and they pitied them. But they couldn't pity Bridgette. In fact, she sickened them. Her beauty and affluence wouldn't allow them to see beyond her physical trappings or social position. For them it was almost like looking into a distorted mirror, one which reflected their own inherent weaknesses and addictions, addictions that were socially acceptable. They would look at her with a puzzled and uncomfortable feeling and this confusion would lead to discomfort and this discomfort disdain. Bridgette saw this contempt in their eyes. And she would plead for more methadone, if only to forget their stares and disapproving looks. When she asked, and begged, and pleaded their eyes would further harden, their hearts would shrink, and they would hold their tongues in bitter silence.

She came up over a small rise and her stomach felt as though it lurched into her throat. The enormous diet cola she had at a small, squalid quick stop, was beginning to eat at her nerves and push on her bladder. Her hands shook slightly from the caffeine and she felt as though she was peaking, her endorphins almost spent. The trip back down from that caffeine high would be a familiar and unpleasant one. That uncomfortable fullness would grow steadily worse. A slight headache would develop and grow progressively more intense. Her stomachache would turn from slight discomfort to nausea. And she would wonder why she had bothered getting so tanked up when it simply made her feel terrible such a short time later.

Bridgette finished up her cigarette and impulsively reached for another one. She needed something to assuage her nerves, something to do with her hands.

When she finally got out of the clinic, in Highland Park, smoking had become as second nature as breathing. The clinic staff looked down on smoking, but it was a far better alternative, in their eyes, to shooting smack. For the most part they refused to believe that cigarettes were unbelievably easy to get a hold of. She got her cigarettes from another patient, Frank, who was a recovering alcoholic, heroin addict, and trying to kick speed. The combination never quite made sense to Bridgette, but they hit it off right away.

Frank had come to the clinic after a major, multi-car accident, just four weeks after he got his license. He had been drunk and high on speed when he ran a red light. He didn't remember hitting the brown compact.

He had shared with Bridgette that when he woke up, bruised, battered, and in an intense drug-induced fog, he was informed of his crime, his rights, and that he was now paralyzed from the chest down. Frank said he could tell, despite the haze of the drugs, that the cop who informed him that he would no longer stand, walk, or even piss without assistance had gotten a certain satisfaction from passing on the news.

Over the next several weeks, as the reality of being forever dependent on a wheelchair and catheters set in, Frank said he could finally appreciate the living hell he had been confined to. It didn't really matter where they sent him after he finished his treatment because his cell was being half a man. At one point he got so depressed that he swallowed a handful of pills he had found in his roommate's pocket. He hadn't known that they were laxatives and he spent the next day and a half sitting on the toilet and being fed intravenously.

Frank and Bridgette had met in the lounge on a cold December day—the light, icy blue and the world outside was brown, lifeless, and dead. They had struck up a conversation about cards. Bridgette had never learned how to play anything except Go Fish. Frank taught her Blackjack, Poker, and Bridge. He laughed at her attempt at a "poker face," his combed-down Mohawk shaking slightly. The day she finally beat him he gave her a cigarette. She hadn't smoked in months, but after she inhaled that first drag and the smoke burned deeply into her lungs, she realized that she had exchanged one habit for another.

Almost two hours had passed since she had come down from her caffeine high and her need to pee was intense. She saw a sign for the exit to Moab and although it was almost an hour out of her way, she decided to take it.

Highway 191 to Moab was a two-lane straight stretch, punctuated by an occasional small rise or dip. There was no shoulder or place to pull over and Bridgette's need to pee had become painful. She pushed the accelerator to the floor and watched, out of the corner of her eye, as the speedometer needle crept up over one hundred and fifteen. The car began to shake and rattle. Each small change in the road magnified itself in the steering wheel. She began to feel as if she was fighting the road itself. She gripped the wheel tighter until her knuckles were white and scanned the landscape ahead for a place to pull over.

As she crested a small rise she saw a pair of lights in the distance, just off the main road. When she got closer she slowed down to seventy-five. Until she was within a few hundred yards she wasn't sure exactly what she was looking at. Finally, she realized that the lights were a couple of yard lights for a trailer that sat a few hundred feet off the narrow road.

Strange place to live, she thought, as she slowed to a crawl, killed the lights and the engine, and drifted onto the dirt shoulder.

She let the car coast just far enough onto the dirt driveway so she was safely away from the road. She opened the door and walked around to the passenger side where she wouldn't be seen by a passing car. Bridgette looked around, up to the trailer, down and up the road behind her. Quickly she pulled down her jeans and squatted just above the dirt, her back to the car. She peed so hard that it splattered loudly in the dirt and she barely missed her shoes. The whole process took only a couple of minutes but to Bridgette it seemed like an eternity, with her butt hanging in the breeze and the possibility that someone would see her. When she was done she yanked up her jeans and without even bothering to button them she ran back around to the driver side door. She jumped inside, started the car, threw it into gear, and sped off, unintentionally spraying dirt behind her.

Back in the car she felt a little lightheaded and she decided that she may as well travel into town and get something to eat.

By the time she rounded the bend, just before Arches National Park, she was unbelievably tired. She noticed that she was now in a wide canyon, its floor sloping out before her.

Even before she reached town there were enormous, tacky billboards advertising camping, bike tours, and whitewater tours. Just after one of the signs was a hodgepodge of a campground made up of RVs, tents, and some type of cabins. After a couple of minutes the highway turned into Main Street. She drove through town and was not especially impressed. Moab was a small place of single or double story buildings (mostly brick) shops and restaurants. Most of the places appeared to cater to tourists. Some of her friends back at school had raved about Moab, about its radical biking trails and rafting. She felt like it was a joke that she just wasn't getting.

Maybe I'm just tired, she thought to herself.

There were no cars on the street, which didn't surprise Bridgette, because it was just after four A.M. She wanted to find a place but she also had a craving for coffee, and maybe even breakfast. She drove to the far edge of town and turned around when she noticed that the shops gave way to scrub brush, trailers, and an occasional gas station. She found a place just off Main Street that appeared to be open. It was a small restaurant called the Canyon Casa.

She pushed open the front door and stepped into the dim light. The counter ran along the opposite wall; three tables with the chairs stacked upside down, on their seats, sat to her right. A stereo somewhere played mariachi music quietly. She walked up to the counter and sat down on a black padded stool. She set her bag on the counter, fished out her cigarettes, and lit one. There was no one else in the place.

She stood up and leaned over the bar. In front of the counter hung a large mirror, a couple of pictures and plaques, and the specials listed on a large chalkboard. She drummed her red fingernails on the countertop and smoked and waited.

She waited for what seemed like a long time, savoring each drag on her cigarette. At some point Bridgette wondered if she should leave—she was almost too exhausted to stay. But she was seated and comfortable and she had no desire to move for a while. It felt strange to her to be in a place so quiet. It seemed like whole world was asleep, beyond dreaming, in the deep spaces before consciousness.

She rested her chin on the palm of her hand, her elbow on the white countertop.

Eventually, she heard a squeak: the familiar sound of a door being opened. Light flooded the darkened dining room briefly. A man stepped out of the brightly-lit kitchen. He was short with close-cropped, dark gray hair. He looked tired, even haggard. His posture was stooped in a way that suggested that he had worked long hours picking up, hoisting, or cooking. He wore a white vee neck T-shirt. Over the shirt he wore an apron stained with grease. His belly pushed taught against the apron, making it appear that he was hiding a bowl or half a ball there. The glowing whiteness of his shirt and the dim lights made his skin seem even darker than it was.

As he looked around the room, his eyes rested on Bridgette. He did a quick double take. He hadn't expected a beautiful woman in a black leather jacket to be chain-smoking at his counter before five A.M., especially since he thought that he had locked the outside door behind him. He sighed—his mind was undeniably elsewhere.

Ramon noticed that she was staring at him, and the look made him pause. She was poised, but disheveled, and sat with a bound-up intensity. He chided himself quietly for hesitating, wiped his hands on his apron, and walked over to her. She continued to look at him in a way that made him feel like she was looking into him. Before he had even opened his mouth he was uncomfortable. It was an unusual feeling for Ramon Valenquez, who made his living, essentially, reading faces and moods. He couldn't read her at all, her expression and eyes blank.

Ramon smiled awkwardly and said, "What can I get you?"

She didn't answer him right away but simply looked at him, letting the words hang in the air for a moment.

His smile grew and he almost burst out in an uncontrollable laugh.

"Coffee and...some huevos rancheros with green sauce," she said pointing with her cigarette at the special listed on the board. It was not a request but more like an order devoid of feeling or inflection.

Ramon noticed no pleasantries in her manner or speech, no please, no thank you, and no smile. He wanted to believe that she was just tired, but something told him otherwise.

"Sure," he said, secretly wanting to tell her that the kitchen was closed for a couple more hours. But in a way he felt as though his pride was a stake and he was tired of feeling small and vulnerable. He had come in early today because, as usual, he couldn't sleep. Here, at least, he felt useful.

Bridgette had noticed the short Hispanic man just after he stepped out of the kitchen. He seemed disoriented or somehow lacking in intelligence. He had taken her order so slowly, as though it pained him to stand there and listen. She was tired and annoyed. She had told him what she wanted and she had already made up her mind that he wasn't getting a tip.

Ramon walked back to the kitchen and pulled down a large cast-iron skillet and two more small steel saucepans. Out of the walk-in he got out some cheese, eggs, butter, frijoles, roasted tomatillo salsa, and corn tortillas. In one saucepan he placed the green chili sauce and in the other the frijoles. As the beans and sauce warmed he pulled down a large plate from the cupboard by the sink.

When he first opened Canyon Casa, Ramon had dreamed of making everything fresh, rather than pre-cut, pre-made, and processed. He quickly realized that the sheer volume of food that had to be cooked made prepping and buying processed food a necessity. It was an unpleasant compromise. Somehow he felt as though he had sold a little bit of his soul.

Standing over the old stove, a wooden spoon in his hand, he felt it had been an eternity since he had last cooked in this kitchen. Really cooked. Not supervised, ordered, harangued, filled in, snacked; or carried trays, plates, and ingredients.

The last time he could remember cooking was a week before Agatha left.

Ramon met Agatha four months after he began working on his Masters in Archeology through the University of New Mexico. He was working on a dig outside of Chaco Canyon and she was a twenty-one-year-old Anthropology undergraduate who was sent to assist him. When Ramon had gotten word that he was finally getting an assistant he assumed that it would be a man. Dr. Vorhis, a professor at U of NM, and a venerable prankster, had sent him a short note to the closest ranger station.

The note said:

You are getting an assistant, A. Dewler, who will be there in about two weeks. Supplies and photographic materials you requested are forthcoming.

The day she arrived Ramon had been busy trying to locate some pottery shards he suspected he would find in a new section. She drove up in a beat-up white Toyota pick-up truck. The truck kicked up so much dust that he had seen it miles away, speeding over the wide open valley of reddish earth, scrub brush, rock, and pinion pine. The sky overhead was brilliantly blue and clear. It was a June afternoon, the sun blazingly hot. Ramon's shirt and pants were soaked with sweat and coated with red dust.

As the truck approached he stood up from the shallow hole he had dug and gingerly set down the small brush and trowel. He wiped his dirt-caked hands on his pants. He took off his wide-brimmed hat, pulled a blue bandanna from his back pocket, and wiped some of the grit and salty sweat off his face. He put his hat back on and stretched his back with his hands on his hips. He crouched down, stretching his knees, and picked up his water bottle.

The sun was almost directly in his eyes, and he squinted against the glare. He unscrewed the water bottle and took a large sip, letting the tepid water slosh around in his mouth.

When Agatha swung out of the cab he wasn't sure what to think.

He squinted, convinced that he wasn't seeing things right. *Boy that's some small guy*, he thought.

Agatha turned and pulled her bag from the bed of the truck, her figure silhouetted by the sun. That's when Ramon almost choked on the water in his mouth. He spit it out and coughed, and hacked and coughed.

"You ok?" she asked.

It is a woman, he thought. *With a beautiful voice.*

"Yeah, fine," he sputtered and coughed.

She walked over to him with her backpack over her shoulder. She was dressed in a light tan T-shirt, jeans, and boots, and was wearing a large straw hat. She was thin, tan, and slightly muscular. She stood a few feet from him, calmly gauging the situation. She took off her sunglasses, stepped forward, and extended her hand. Ramon looked into her face. Her eyes were a deep endless blue set off by high cheekbones.

"Hi, I'm Agatha."

Ramon stood there for a moment, embarrassed by his choking episode, and still a bit stunned.

"Hi, I'm Ramon," he said and shook her hand, instantly impressed by the firmness of her grip.

It wasn't until later that he realized he must look like a mess. He hadn't shaved for a couple of days. He was dirty; his clothes were coated with dust and sweat. He was sure he probably stank. But Agatha had a certain effect on him—she made him feel completely at ease no matter how uncomfortable he would usually feel. He felt as though she was holding him and reassuring him even when she stood at arm's length.

They stayed on that dig for another five months and quickly became close. Ramon's memories of those wonderful months were still as bright and clear as the yellow and orange sunrises that they used to watch each morning together—the glow of the sun illuminating the clouds, spread across the sky as though the world was on fire.

When they were finished with the dig she moved into Ramon's place in Albuquerque. Six months later they got married, much to the disappointment of Ramon's family, who disapproved because she was white and eight years his junior. A year later Agatha found out she was pregnant.

They were both elated at prospect of having a child. They planned their lives to the minutest detail, all around their future baby. The spare bedroom became a nursery filled with colorful toys and books. And then, when Agatha was in her sixth month, she miscarried.

They both wanted someone to blame, someplace to put all of the deep and displaced emotions, the numbness of being overwhelmed. The doctors told them it was an unexpected thing, a random incident, but their assurances and words did nothing to quell the pain.

For a long time afterward Agatha didn't talk much, laugh or smile. Ramon wavered between depression, anger, and numbness. He was angry with his family, whose sympathy seemed either forced or took the tone of I told you so. He was angry with Agatha, which also made him feel guilty, and he was angry with God. He felt God had betrayed him. It felt as though He had given him the promise of grace and immortality and then, in a blink of an eye, He had taken it all away.

Every Dia de las Muertos he placed a tiny calavera carving on a small altar he had erected above his television to remember his nino limbos. He bought marigolds and sprinkled their petals on the baby toys he kept. The toys had become part of his ofrendas, his altar of offerings designed to lure back the dead. For Ramon this ceremony was as much about tradition as about healing and living with the dead. He had come to terms with God, in a way, having faith that it was all part of some special plan, with some larger purpose.

But sometimes, like now, he felt questions and despair looming in the shadows—a cross he had to bear, that he didn't want to let go of lest he forget the child he almost had. The child he almost played with, watched grow, walk, talk, play soccer and baseball with, teach to drive, and grow old with.

Ramon greased the cast iron skillet for flavor and placed it back on the old gas stove. He cracked the eggs into the pan and they sizzled and popped quietly. As the eggs cooked he grated some white cheddar cheese. When the eggs were almost done he put the tortillas on the plate, the frijoles on the tortillas, the eggs on top of the frijoles, poured the roasted tomatillo salsa over the top, and sprinkled on some farmer's cheese. Then he put the plate into the oven to bake for a few minutes.

Agatha had loved huevos with white posole. It was the first real meal they had after they left the dig, and Ramon had cooked it for her. He had taken hours to prepare it for her. Most people he knew made their huevos with a red tomato chipolte or jalapeño salsa, but he like to make it with a green salsa made from roasted tomatillos, the way his grandmother had taught him.

Overnight, in a saucepan, he soaked dried white whole-kernel corn mixed with baking soda. He boiled the corn for three hours, replacing the water as it boiled away. Then he drained the corn and rinsed it with cold water to remove any hulls. He boiled, rinsed, and drained the corn a couple more times. He had soaked dried New Mexico peppers and dried chilaca peppers. He drained and finely chopped the chilies and then pressed it through a food sieve. He then chopped up onions, red bell peppers, and garlic. In a saucepan he had put a large drop of oil and cooked the onions, then the bell peppers and garlic, and threw in some dried oregano. After a few minutes he had thrown in the hominy and a couple of cups of chicken stock. All of the ingredients were brought to a boil, and then he added the pressed peppers he had set aside. He let everything cook together, waiting to salt it and add lemon juice just before he served it.

He mixed and heated the soaked beans with bacon drippings, onion, and garlic. After the beans were cooked to a soupy consistency he mashed them. He husked, rinsed, and oven-roasted the green tomatillos he had been storing in the crisper. He cut the garlic, onion, and cilantro. After the tomatillos were slightly darkened and had cooled, he threw them in the blender with the jalapeños, garlic, and onion. He tossed in water, salt, and sugar without bothering to measure them.

Ramon even made the tortillas from masa harina and hot water. He formed each tortilla into a ball, rolled them flat, and cooked them on a seasoned, cast iron skillet on the stove. When the roasted tomatillo sauce was done he made four eggs sunny side up. He put the tortillas on a plate, spread the frijoles on top, laid the eggs on top of the frijoles, put some hominy on the side, and then smothered it all with the tomatillo sauce.

All of the work had been worth it: she had loved every bite.

He made huevos for her after that but with far less deliberation and preparation, yet she still showered him with praise.

After Agatha's miscarriage she lost her appetite. Ramon used to sit at the foot of the bed and watch her as she dozed or stared at the ceiling. Her skin was pale and sallow, dark circles rung her eyes. Sitting there, he feared that he was watching her waste away. He had a nightmare that he had come into the bedroom and Agatha wasn't there. In his dream he walked over to the bed, pulled back the covers, and there was nothing there but dust. He woke startled and disturbed.

In desperation he made her huevos, the smells wafting through the dark stillness. That night he felt as though his long deceased grandmother was in the kitchen with him. Once, Ramon's uncle had told him of how Grandma Valenquez had brought him back from near death after a bout with pneumonia with food, herbs, and love. Ramon had learned to cook from her, traipsing around the kitchen behind her, standing on chairs so that he could reach the counter.

Ramon's cousin Jose had offered to sell him Canyon Casa partly because he was worried about Ramon and Agatha and partly because he wanted to retire. Ramon and Agatha saw it as a chance for a fresh start. They sold their house in Albuquerque and got a loan to buy the restaurant. They bought a small trailer on the outskirts of Moab on three barren acres. The restaurant was an extremely popular place, always bustling with tourist and locals. For almost a year Agatha and Ramon were consumed with learning the ropes and were barely able to keep up with the long hours and the busy schedule. Every night they fell into bed exhausted.

Then they hit a dry spell. A couple of new chain restaurants had opened in prominent locations on Main Street and business at the restaurant dropped off. They suddenly found that they had a lot of time on their hands. They had to let a couple of their employees go, employees who had also become friends. They started to fight about money and what to do to get their business back. They began to avoid each other and a wall of silent tension settled between them.

An old colleague wrote Agatha about a dig near Mesa Verde that was short-staffed. The job was temporary with the possibility of becoming long-term. When Agatha told Ramon that she wanted to go he didn't know what to say. He thought that maybe they needed a break, but he wasn't sure if she would want to come back.

The day she left they stood in the kitchen embracing. He held his face to her hair, breathing in the fragrance. She smelled of flowers, desert heat, and roasted chilies. He didn't want to let go.

"Don't worry, it's only for a few months," she said.

Ramon nodded, but he knew her well, and she looked at him as though she was trying to both remember and forget this moment forever. He knew that she would be gone for a long time.

As he tried to sleep, surrounded by too much quiet, he often thought he heard her opening the screen door. But it was only the desert wind.

While the huevos stayed warm in the oven he washed out the coffeepot and made a fresh pot. When the coffee was done he poured it into a large white mug and set it on a tray. He pulled the hot plate out of the oven, placed it on another, slightly larger, plate, and set it on the tray next to the coffee. He grabbed some flatware and a couple of paper napkins and carefully set them on the tray next to the plate of huevos. He grabbed a couple of small containers of half-and-half and set them next to the coffee. He hoisted the tray up onto one hand and carried it through the kitchen door and into the dining room.

Bridgette was on her third cigarette, and she realized that despite the nicotine swimming in her veins she was undeniably hungry. She saw the short dark man walk out of the kitchen holding the tray with her food on the flat of his hand. Despite his appearance he had an understated sort of grace. His balancing the tray looked effortless, and his face and posture showed no sign of strain.

He set the tray down and carefully lifted the plate of huevos rancheros off the tray.

"Careful, plate's hot," he said.

Then he carefully arranged the flatware, napkin, and coffee cup around the plate as though he arranged a place setting for a visiting dignitary.

"Water?" he asked.

Bridgette nodded.

Ramon walked back into the kitchen to get her water.

Bridgette surveyed her meal. It smelled unbelievably good. She picked up her fork and cut herself a bite. When she put the first bite into her mouth she could taste the flavors of the beans, spicy lemony tanginess of the sauce, the garlic and onion, and the saltiness of the eggs and cheese. She chewed the first bite slowly, savoring it. At first she thought she was just extremely hungry, but she knew that it was much more that that.

Delicious, she thought.

She took a sip of coffee, and it was also perfect. It had a distinct flavor, a hint of cinnamon, but it was not overbearing or bitter. She wrapped her hands around the cup and felt the warmth.

She barely looked up from her food when Ramon brought her water.

"Everything okay?" he asked.

She nodded absentmindedly, her concentration on eating, aware of the sensuality of taste. It was something she had never experienced before. If someone asked about it later she would be unable to describe it, attributing it to exhaustion, stress, and too many stimulants. But at that moment she was conscious of the distinct sensation. Each bite was imbued with reverence and contentment.

As she ate she thought of why she was here, in a small diner in Moab, in the still darkness of the early morning. Her grandfather was dying of cancer. He had been sick for months, but was recently moved to Denver, where he would be under the care of an oncologist. Bridgette knew that her grandparents were now living on hope. On the grace of the good Lord, they had said.

The cancer was advanced, and the proposed surgery wasn't guaranteed. They were going to remove a tumor from his lung, and there was a high risk of infection or complications.

He was weak now. She had heard it in his voice on the phone. She knew when they called to tell her they were going to Denver and he was going to have surgery that she had to be there. She loved her grandfather despite his distant, quiet nature and stubbornness.

After her mom had dumped her at her parents, fresh out of rehab, Bridgette thought she had been left in hell. Her grandparents were quiet, unassuming Christian people who lived their lives exactly as they wanted. It was clear from the day Bridgette arrived at their farm, near the Kansas-Colorado border, that Bridgette's antics would no longer be tolerated. Despite their vigilance she still snuck out when she could, something she now felt guilty about. After a while, her life there revolved around physical work, and her grandparents counted on her to follow through with every project. She found she was stronger and weaker than she realized. She was often sore, tired, and lonely.

Bridgette felt trapped there. After her chores or the day's work was done she would sit in her small room and stare at the walls and imagine a different life. Her grandfather would call her outside, and she would go grudgingly. He would put his arm over her shoulder without saying a word. They would walk along the fields without speaking, listening to the warm breeze rustle the corn.

He was like the big elm that she had played under back in Chicago. It was comforting to know that it was always there, even when she wasn't, and she didn't want to think of losing that. There was too much she hadn't said, and might never say, but still she wanted to be there for him, for once.

When Bridgette had finished her food and second cup of coffee she knew that she had to get back on the road. She felt completely satiated. She slipped some cash under the bill, grabbed her things, and walked out of the restaurant into the cool morning.

The sun was about twenty minutes from rising and the sky was alive with color. Clouds, streaked orange and pinkish red, traipsed across the sky of yellowish blue. The sandstone canyon walls around Moab reflected the light and looked almost the hue of blood. The air was still and the only sounds were the distant calling of birds and an occasional car. A slight fragrance of pinions and dust wafted through town.

Ramon came out of the kitchen where he was tidying up for the morning shift and noticed the girl was gone. He walked down the counter to where she had sat. A cigarette lay smoldering in the ashtray; it had burned away to ash virtually unsmoked. The plate was clear and the coffee drunk. He picked up the bill and counted the money that was under it. She had left twenty-six dollars for a six dollar and fifty cent meal. Ramon figured that there must be some mistake; she must have accidentally left too much. He decided he would try to catch her.

He ran out the door into the early morning sunlight. Ramon looked up and down the street and there was no sign of her anywhere. She was long gone.

Ramon shrugged and put the wad of bills into his pocket. Then he looked up into the sky. It was so beautiful he held his breath. The sun was just about to rise and tendrils of wispy clouds were infused with hues of orange and yellow. The dim light and colors reflected off of the canyon walls in a million hues of red. It looked as if the world was on fire.

Bridgette drove out of town the same way she had come in, through the canyon that surrounded the town, as the sun spilled over the canyon walls. She began to ascend up the slight grade, and to her right on the valley floor she saw motor homes lined up, their engines idling. Their inhabitants were inside, watching TV, or sleeping or eating, all waiting for Arches to open.

She sighed smugly. She was no longer tired, but invigorated. Her senses tingled as though she had jumped into a pool of cold water on a hot day. She thought about her grandfather and blood-red canyon walls just before sunrise.

6

EVEN THE SNOW SLEEPS

It was so dark that each time he opened his eyes he thought he was blind. The darkness was complete; there were no shadows, no outlines, nothing. In his semi-conscious state he was agitated and uneasy. Then he heard something. Startled, he held his breath.

He heard the shallow raspy breathing of someone a few feet from him. After sitting perfectly still for many long minutes he forced himself to reach toward the strange sound. Through his gloves, he felt a face and a body tucked inside a sleeping bag. The person did not stir.

It was difficult to think; he struggled to concentrate and remember where he was and what he was doing here. Eventually, Dave Greibing's mind woke to the reality of his situation. He was trapped on Denali in a small snow cave, somewhere near 17,000 feet in the middle of a bitter storm. The person who lay near his feet was his climbing partner, Jim, and he was dying.

The rattling in Jim's chest was evidence of his slow suffocation. Dave's fears of Jim's possible high altitude pulmonary edema were now very real.

Earlier he had thawed some water and made soup but he could not force Jim to drink it.

Dave shifted a little and a sharp pain shot up his leg; a compound fracture, the bone broke the skin. The pain was unbelievable, but Dave's howls came out as mere whispers. The pain told him he was still alive.

The small cave was eerily quiet, which seemed to exaggerate the sounds of Jim's labored breathing. Outside the wind roared like a million howling demons, just as it had for the last six or ten hours. At one hundred plus miles an hour it literally raked the snow off the mountain into the abyss.

Dave had stumbled into this cave after they were nearly killed in a fall, some undeterminable time ago, and dragged Jim along behind him. The radio and half his gear were lost. Now he sat in the darkness, beyond desperation. He felt the void tearing through him, as though he was being turned inside out. On the climb the numbing cold had become his only constant. He was considerably warmer now. He remembered shivering, but that had stopped, a minute or maybe an hour ago. His perception of time was no longer linear, no longer persistent.

For a long time he sat there, trying unsuccessfully to think clearly or sleep. But he couldn't sleep and yet he was never fully awake. He felt trapped between the waking world and a land of unsettling dreams. The line between these worlds had irreversibly blurred. And with each exhale he let out more heat and moisture than he could replace in the enclave of snow.

He was still afraid. In a way that was the only reason he figured he was still breathing. He was still afraid to die.

He wanted to feel sorry for himself, but he couldn't. He had chosen to go on this expedition. It was a huge step up in a long line of other climbs.

Denali had teased him from afar for years. As a naïve seventeen-year-old he had attempted the West Buttress only to be turned away by the worst storm in ten years. That trip had reminded him how inexperienced he was and how much he had to learn. Unwilling to concede defeat he vowed to come back. Later, he realized his immense foolishness. The mountain was not something to be conquered. The mountain, and the mountain alone, let you climb. He believed that if it was gracious and he had shown enough respect he would make it up and down with only immense pain and memories. If hubris dictated his climb, the mountain swallowed you like the sea swallows a drop of rain.

Dave hadn't forgotten this kernel of wisdom some two hours from the summit. But, he had ignored the signs: high wispy clouds near the summit, increasing winds, and Jim stumbling and stopping to catch his breath. If he had reached the summit he could have chided himself for taking too many risks and making too many bad decisions. But now there was more than one life in his hands, and his feelings of helplessness compounded his dread.

While Dave thought he had considered everything, he hadn't counted on being the cautious one.

After all, he had ridden out an avalanche in Patagonia that had killed three other climbers from another party. On the Eiger his protection pulled out, and he had fallen thirty feet until he slammed into a small ledge, the only thing separating him from certain death. He had summited despite a broken arm and a slight concussion. He had free-climbed Devil's Tower. And he had taken a dangerous solo trip to Mt. Kilimanjaro in the middle of a storm. He had done stupid things and there was always someone telling him to slow down, to take it easy. He couldn't remember the last time he had been in the opposite situation; he had no idea what to do.

It was strange, amid effects of altitude and sensory deprivation, to think about his long affair with the pursuit of a certain type of death in an inhospitable place.

We all die, he thought, *but I want to have some influence on where and why*.

When Dave was eight he had decided he wanted to be an astronaut when he grew up. While his classmates talked about being firemen or sports stars Dave thumbed through books on space travel. For Christmas his dad had given him a full-color, glossy, hardbound book about the Apollo missions. He carried it everywhere. Late at night in his room, when he was supposed to be asleep, he was reading his book by flashlight under the covers. In those late hours he learned all about the triumphs and tragedies of the space program. While he sometimes imagined himself inside a bulky spacesuit, stepping off the lunar lander, making huge leaps despite his weight. In science class, when they were discussing the reality of sci-fi movies, he learned there was no sound without atmosphere. In space there was only silence.

The concept of complete silence was too difficult for him to contemplate. The next summer Dave and his dad went to a late night showing of *2001: A Space Odyssey*. That night, watching Dave Bowman float around inside and outside the ship, the only sound his own breathing, he began to understand the silence of space. He discovered this silence many years later standing on a ridge on Mt. Shasta. The wind had abated and the air was perfectly still, the loudest sound his labored breathing and the thumping of his heart.

On every climb after that he paid greater attention to sounds and the silence. Despite his fantasies he realized he would probably never travel into space, yet he knew that he walked amid a similarly lifeless place. He traveled across frozen wastes of rock, ice, and snow where every breath was a struggle. He began to crave these places of sacred and unbelievable power where he could shed the trappings and armor of civilization. Each move mattered, each decision was crucial; this world was sharp and clear.

The rest of his life was less so.

Just two weeks before he had lain in bed, in his house, in Bellingham. The house was cool and silent, dim in the minutes before dawn. The rain had ended an hour ago. The puddles on his deck caught the dim morning light. A small bird sung sweetly to welcome the dull warmth of another day.

Dave rolled over on his side to watch Bridgette as she slept, her back towards him. The sheets draped the curve of her hip and the cheeks of her buttocks. Her tanned shoulder was visible just above the white sheets. Her auburn hair lay about the pillow, wildly, like a dull flame.

He didn't want to wake her, she was so peaceful. Her tanned frame moved slowly with each breath. He wanted to remember her like this, completely serene.

The previous night they had planned a quiet evening alone together because it was the last night before Dave's five-week trip to Denali. Things had started casually as they drank wine and flirted in the kitchen while they made dinner. They brushed their hands past each other suggestively, but they talked little, and by the time they sat down to eat there was an uneasy tension between them.

There were so many unspoken anxieties and fears, and they were quiet for a long time. Each chewed their food and thought about the next day and the days after that.

Before Bridgette, there was little doubt in Dave's mind that his climbing was more important than his personal relationships, but he had begun to wonder if things between them were far more substantial and serious than he had thought.

He looked up from his food, his fork poised. He couldn't tell what she was thinking or feeling. She was often a closed mystery to him. Even when their bodies were intertwined with sweat and passion she seemed to hold back a part of her.

But perhaps I do that as well, he thought, gingerly poking at a ziti shell.

It was true he had spent most of his life in shallow and superficial relationships. At one point he even reveled in it. His lifestyle often limited long-term commitments and also offered a reasonable excuse. He would break up with women because, he said, "He couldn't stand the distance." In reality, it was the closeness he couldn't stand. He was unwilling to sacrifice, to compromise, in all things, but especially when it came to love or a lack of it. And thus, with Bridgette who was as stunning, intelligent, and self-confident as any woman he had ever met, they had reached a mutual wall, an impasse. If either one gave in they would somehow see it as a loss of themselves.

Bridgette knew that he was staring at her but she didn't look up. She was too busy rehearsing what she would say just before she left tonight. She saw herself telling him off in a way that would leave him with his mouth agape or stammering with disbelief, and she would grab her bag and leave. And yet, something kept her here despite a voice that told her to walk away. The paradox of apprehension and longing intrigued her. There was a certain danger in staying, and potential exposure of her fears. Dave exuded danger. He was brash, impulsive, and passionate to the point of being obsessive. Physically, he knew exactly what she wanted and would willingly try anything in bed. Otherwise he had no idea what she needed, and she had no intention of telling him. He had never really taken the time to get to know exactly who she was. In a way this was why he was so much like so many of the other guys she had dated, and why she figured she could just pick up and leave. Yet she sat there, looking relaxed, moving her eyes across the plate.

"More wine?" he asked, trying to breach the silence.

She nodded, and he lifted the bottle to her glass. Then he re-filled his own.

Now the bottle was empty, and although he was sitting, he could feel the warm buzz of the alcohol. He felt himself relax, and mopped up the sauce on his plate with a piece of French bread.

"Good Merlot," she said, as she set down her glass.

"Uh-huh."

They finished their dinners in silence, lost in their own thoughts.

"You want any ice cream or coffee?" he asked.

"No thanks."

Dave cleared the table, put the dishes into the sink, and filled it with soapy water.

Bridgette offered to help, but he said, "No way, you relax."

As he washed the dishes, his back turned toward her, she realized for the first time that Dave wasn't just like the other guys she had dated. He actually cared about her, but he didn't worship her like so many of her other boyfriends had. He did not lose himself in her and require constant coaxing or ego mending. Dave's emotional strength, or detachment, made her lean on him more than she ever thought she would. In a way he was the only man, other than her late grandfather, whom she actually believed would be there from one day to the next. While her grandfather had been rigid and unbending in his ways, Dave seemed malleable, able to go with the flow. But even in his mellowness and easy-going nature she could sense a conflict somewhere behind his ice-blue eyes.

He also didn't act like he wanted to possess her or own her as so many other insecure men had. She believed he intrinsically knew that hers was a will that could not be contained, and he showed no desire to try.

When they were completely alone together it was the only time she stopped thinking about the past, the only time she let herself be.

She smiled, sizing him up from behind.

He whistled a tune she didn't recognize.

She got up from the table and she put her arms around him. They stood there for a few minutes, her head upon his back and his hands resting on the edge of the sink. He turned towards her and they kissed. The taste of wine and garlic mingled between them.

They kissed more deeply, their tongues exploring the warmth of each other's mouths.

Dave un-tucked her blouse and ran his hands to the clasp on her bra. Bridgette ran her nails along his back, underneath his T-shirt. He undid the clasp on her bra and ran his hands along her skin until they brushed against her breasts. He lowered his head and kissed her neck and her ear as he gently cupped her breasts, his thumbs rubbing her nipples.

She unbuttoned his pants and slid her hands around to his smooth butt. She made her way to his front, where she grasped and stroked him. They moved slowly together, until they were at the edge of the table. Dave lifted her onto the table and slid her skirt up around her hips. With her hand stroking him more forcefully he slid his hand into her panties. She pushed his jeans down with her feet and he stood in his boxers, jeans around his ankles, his erection protruding from his fly.

She moved her hands back to his butt and pulled him close to her. They moved against each other, the only thing separating them a thin pair of silk panties.

They were both breathing heavily, their faces flushed.

They craved the feeling of bodily transcendence. They were so close.

Despite their desire and the deliriousness of the moment, they paused. It was a second they knew they would always remember, whatever the outcome. The risk they craved, the warmth, and the absolute loss of pain seemed overshadowed by other things, by future things.

Dave knew he might never be back, that this might be the last chance to see Bridgette, to have a child, even if by accident, even if he wasn't around to see it.

Bridgette also knew this could be their last night, and the very thought of it, the crushing burden of the realization, pressed against her heart.

But mostly they were afraid.

Not of pregnancy, or AIDS. They were afraid of uncertainty, of losing the best thing either of them ever had.

They paused and sighed against the world. They held each other for a long time, in the kitchen, in silence.

They made love later that night. They dozed, and woke to share a pint of Haggen Daz.

Just before they fell asleep Bridgette asked him, "Are you scared?"

He lay there, silent, in the half-light, listening to the soft rain against the window. He felt both empty and full, beyond comfortable, feeling the pull of sleep.

He let the answer come, without judgment or contemplation.

"Yes," he whispered.

They fell asleep and did not dream.

When he woke in the icy cave he was startled. He didn't remember sleeping, but he had dreamed. He thought of Bridgette and the moments he had wasted not appreciating her enough, not wanting to get too close. He felt the darkness. He felt as though he was being buried alive. He could barely turn his head, and his limbs lay like heavy afterthoughts. It was strange to wake in a place that seemed unconscious even of itself, a place where even the snow sleeps.

In the blackness his eyes and mind were deprived of input and he began to see things: shadows that were not there, shapes and forms, and small bits of colored light. That was why he barely recognized the greenish glow at the periphery of his vision. He ignored it. The light grew, and when he turned his head, he had to squint against its intensity. As it faded, it illuminated the figure, where the wall of the cave had begun.

Dave's mind was slow to register the figure and the distortion of space. By the time he began to feel panicked, the figure spoke.

"How ya holdin' up?" asked a man's voice.

Dave knew that the voice came from the figure, yet he heard it all around him. The voice was familiar, yet he felt that he had never heard it before.

Dave tried to concentrate but he was so exhausted. His own voice felt lost. For a long time he tried to respond until slowly he thought, "I'm...OK."

"Good, glad to hear it," the voice said. "You don't recognize me do you?"

"No." Dave tried to shake his head, which lay limp, staring at the figure.

"When you were ten we went to the Grand Canyon. It was hotter than hell that day. But we walked to the rim, the sun dogging us every step of the way. We stood against that small chain, separating us from the chasm. We stood there a long time. And then you said something that I'll never forget."

"This is what God must feel like," Dave answered.

"Yes," the voice said.

"Dad?"

"Yes."

And the light behind the figure shifted within, illuminating a man in his mid-forties in a dark business suit and tie. His hair, receding slightly, was perfectly combed and his smile glowed. He sat cross-legged, yet did not seem to be touching the snow.

The sudden vision of his father startled Dave so badly that he bit his tongue. He couldn't feel it, but realized he had broken the skin when he tasted blood.

He wanted to look away for a moment, to try to concentrate and focus. But he was afraid that if he did his father would disappear, like he always seemed to disappear from his life.

"Don't be scared, it's just me."

"But you've been dead for..."

"Ten years, two months, and eleven days."

"But, but you look so alive. Am I dead?"

"No, son, but you are between worlds." He ran his hand through his hair. "Part of you has traveled on and the rest, well."

His father's words were terse and matter-of-fact, as though he was relating the score from the game the night before, or the fluctuations of the DOW.

"I'm not ready." Even as he said the words he felt the whole of their futility and sadness, the ache of being, of existing, that kept him barely alive.

"We never are. You always were a fighter, Dave, but what's left, really?"

"Plenty," Dave said with trepidation, since he wasn't really sure what he had left, what he hadn't screwed up. Everything with Bridgette was great, but here he was thousands of miles from her, or perhaps at the deepest center of hell, and maybe she had already forgotten him. He was always transient, shifting from place to place, from life to life. And now, only now, was he ready to stay.

"Then why are you here, son? Why are you still doing this dance with death? Death always wins," his dad said with a look devoid of emotion but a certain wry smile in his voice.

"But I want to live, there is still too much…"

"Yes, I know," he said, as he rested the palm of his hand against Dave's cheek.

Dave could not feel the touch.

"There is something I need to talk to you about. Your mom never told you much about the accident, did she?"

"Never. She packed your things, took down all the pictures after the funeral. That was the worst part. She erased you, the hope…of you. Mostly, before you died, that was what us kids were all hanging on to, empty promises, almost nothing."

"Yes," his dad rubbed his chin, "because your mother was more than just sad."

Dave looked puzzled.

"She was consumed with a hatred that could almost be confused for love. See, your mother never told you but the accident, well, I was having an affair. The woman was someone else from the firm, Gina Thomson, and we had just left her house after a mid-morning screw. And the worst part is that I wasn't even in love with Gina."

"Gina?" Dave said exasperated. "She used to come over with her husband. Barbecues. My birthday. Christ!" He was overcome with lucid memories of his childhood, remembered things he thought were only dreams, fragmented illusions. Now there was a paleness to the memories, a shadow of context that changed everything. Dave felt the anger towards his father rise up.

"How could you? To mom? She did everything for you."

"Yes, well, I'm not proud of it. It was never easy. Dave, I hadn't loved your mother in years, and she was holding on to nothing but memories."

"So you faked being happy? It was an illusion?"

"More or less. Dave, Gina was driving when I was killed. A truck ran a red light and cut the car in half. I died instantly. Gina, well Gina was paralyzed from the waist down. Your mother never forgave her. Or me."

"What'd you expect?"

"I don't know what I expected. I think I must have believed that with me out of the way she could get on with things, that she could be happy again. Your mother gave up everything for her family, and it cost her her soul. She punished herself through me. Her bitterness ate at her from the inside."

"Mom was so different after you died, fierce, and empty. She couldn't be comforted. She never let go. I can see that. She would stay up late—standing in the living room in the dark. I would sneak out of my room just to watch her, her silhouette framed by the streetlights. She barely moved, barely breathed."

"I know, I watched her, and in a way that was my punishment, my damnation. Dave I know I wasn't the best father, but I raised you the best I could. When I was a kid I never saw my dad, but I was okay with it. I knew he cared about me and loved me. He didn't have to tell me."

Dave was silent. It was too much. He had suspected for years there was something they had hidden from him, that his mother had held back. But this was more than he had expected. In this semi-conscious state, dying more with each breath, Dave wondered why he should bother to fight for his life. His entire life felt like lies and make-believe. The tragedies seemed deliberate, the joyous moments hollow.

"Yes, Dave, the sadness is real. We tried our best to seem happy, a happy family. But the sadness was crippling, and it was always there, even though you could only sense it."

"What am I supposed to do, Dad? God damn it!"

"I simply came to make peace, so there are no more secrets between us."

"I never knew you. I mean, like you said, you were never around, but mom, she was always there. She raised us by herself. And all the while. Jesus!"

"Yes, I know, I'm sorry."

"Why was it so hard to be there for us? For years, after you died, I tried to think of all of the things I could've done. I blamed myself, like I had done something. Everything, always on your terms. If it was inconvenient you walked away. I've realized, although your body died in that crash, you were dead to us already. Life went on without you. We didn't realize, we still pretended we could fill the hole you left."

"I'm, I'm so sorry. I never meant to hurt any of you, especially you, Dave. I never really thought about anyone but myself."

Dave seethed in silence.

"But, Dave, really, I didn't come here to fight."

"So, you want what, exactly? My forgiveness?"

His father looked at him impassively.

"Is that what you want? Or just to torment me?"

"Yes, Dave, I want nothing more than your forgiveness. Your anger, your regrets, that is what is keeping you tied to this physical world. You need to let go so you can stop suffering."

"But I don't want to die!" Dave screamed, his voice hoarse.

"You don't have a choice whether you die or not, son, but sometimes you get to choose where and why."

The cave was suddenly dark again.

Dave sat silent for a long time, slipping in and out of consciousness. He fought to stay awake and think. He couldn't decide if he had been hallucinating or dreaming. He thought about Bridgette, how he wanted nothing more than to be with her and to feel her warmth. He wanted to keep his eyes open. But it was so difficult. Everything was so difficult.

Dave closed his eyes and sighed.

When he opened them again there was a warm bright light that seemed to be coming from outside the cave. With all of his strength he forced himself onto his belly. He began crawling, slowly. As he crawled toward the light he forgot his anger, his resentment, and even his sadness. He focused and moved, unwilling to feel pain, and the sensation of being detached from his physical being washed over him.

The light was now blinding, and warm, and he was no longer afraid.

7

SEPTEMBER

The Fifteenth

The air was imbued with a sharp coolness; the bright sun filtered through the enormous trees. The wind blew infrequent gusts, carrying the fine topsoil from the new construction next door. Hours ago, driving home from the hardware store, he had been reminded of the open, bright skies of Colorado with a new palate of colors infused by the Puget Sound, the abundance of water, trees, and browning vegetation that sometimes appeared as if it had usurped the landscape. Through semi-hidden inlets he could see the breeze on the water and the beginning of white caps.

He stood in his yard, watching and listening. The lot next door had not seen the workmen today in their dusty pick-ups, festooned with ladder racks, toolboxes, and screaming and pounding hand tools. Stan could hear the birds and the occasional small plane that passed overhead. The trees made their own sweet sound as they swayed in the wind that pushed upon their upper canopies, some 100 feet above his head.

The new eight-pound sledge hammer rested on the ground, the flat metal against the toe of his boot as he loosely held the handle. The wedge, already scratched and dented, was ready to be slammed again into a section of seasoned maple and then thwacked hard until it drove home, split the wood, and fell flat against the ground with a metal thud.

He took a deep breath and smelled the intoxicating fragrance of the woods around him—noble firs, cedar, and the rich loamy smell of so much dead matter on the ground, dampened hours ago by light rain. Mixed in was the sharp sent of drying plywood next door, part of the still-naked house his neighbors were building. He also smelt the already split wood, which reminded him of lumber and sawdust, yet richer and somehow more ethereal.

Staring into the upper reaches of the trees and into the tepid blue sky, Stan knew it wouldn't be long until the rains started. The skies would remain overcast most of the day, and looking out the second-story window of his office, at the college, would make him sleepy. He would crave more coffee, even though he knew he shouldn't have another cup. The thick ambivalent clouds would hem him in and make it seem as though the night had merely changed shades and become less dense. Today would be the type of day he would miss, mid-September, the beginning of the term a looming shadow but not yet a conscious, dictative reality that seemed to consume his every waking moment. In two weeks he would be driving to work in the dark, making the hour-long commute to his office in Olympia. He'd drop off his things and have to rush to his classroom. His uneaten bagel would be clamped tightly between his teeth, growing wet in the mist or the rain that escorted him.

He picked up the wedge and tapped it into the narrow crack in the section until it seemed to stand on its own—a strange, hard, dark, alien object protruding like a growth whose only purpose was to be hammered through solid wood. He pulled back the hammer, John Henry style, and swung with all his might. It came down hard upon the wedge with a loud thwack and settled, stubbornly, deeper into the log. He pulled back again and swung. He tried to consciously keep his eyes open to see the hammer hit the mark, since it felt as though he had not hit it squarely on the last blow. The hammer drove the wedge home and it fell easily through the gap, falling on its side, finally ringing on the hammer's edge. Stan picked up the halves and threw them onto the split wood pile with measured satisfaction. He could feel his body for the first time in months. It had become so neglected, a repository, a soft seat of sorts for his mind. Over the summer he hadn't gained but a few pounds, yet he felt different, out of touch with the confines of his physical being.

He split wood for another hour. Each swing was measured, and bending over to pick up the pieces he realized his T-shirt was soaked with sweat. The pile of split wood grew and he imagined their stores for the winter—this wood was their primary source of heat. He was thankful that his and Del's daughter would grow up here amid the trees, aware of where the things that kept them warm and comfortable came from.

Being outside, exposed to elements and the basics of reality, helped Stan to focus on something other than the worries and future plans that often impaired his other thoughts. His mind was inevitably drawn back to teaching, and he deliberately pushed those thoughts aside. He though about the sledge-hammer in his hand and the sensation of using muscle, sweat, and will to accomplish a task. A task which had a beginning, middle, and an end and, when it was done he could drink a beer and admire what he had accomplished. How many other things in life were so abundantly simple and yet so rich. He imagined that the carpenters who had been working next door on and off for the better part of a month had similar sensations. He also imagined that it was still a job, and the grind of rushing to finish each project as quickly and efficiently as possible had to be taxing. It would be hard to have the same level of satisfaction they would glean working on their own houses, admiring their handiwork on a daily basis.

During the school year, with each passing day, he grew more exhausted, and by the time finals rolled around and term papers had to be read he began to question not only his sanity but his choice of profession. There was so much interesting but ultimately empty intellectualizing that consumed most of his working days. He loved the interactions with students and the wit of many of his colleagues, but he hated the posturing, backbiting, and bizarre faculty versus administration intrigue. It was a strange game and, in general, he refused to play. He knew he was lucky to have developed a friendship with the head of his department, Molly Urbana. She was a petite, feisty woman of sixty, with a head of curly, silver hair. She was demure and polite unless provoked, and then she would verbally tear her opponent a new one. Stan had seen her berate graduate students, tenured professors, and textbook vendors in much the same fashion and reduce each to a quivering bowl of apologetic pudding.

He would be teaching much of what he had last year: two sections of Introduction to Eastern European Literature and one of Russian Literature. Both classes were too specific to be entirely survey classes, and each attracted just enough students to allow them to be offered every year. This happened even though there were those in the college that felt a young assistant professor should be teaching 101 classes, re-organizing tenured professors' offices, and polishing their cars. Thankfully, Molly had made it her personal mission to ensure that non-mainstream literature classes were offered and that new blood could tackle something other than remediation of non-Literature majors. He was now in his third year of teaching, he wrote obscure articles, two had been published, he read term papers, and he wondered if this was it. And if it was, why was he still wondering.

Stan rolled another large section of maple out of the pile, found his wedge, and tried to tap it into the wood. Each time he tapped it in a fraction of an inch and swung the wedge fell over without going any deeper. After five tries his hands began to hurt from awkwardly holding the sledge hammer near the top. Once again he tapped the wedge in, but this time he decided to hit the wedge as hard as he could to drive it deeper. He cocked back for his swing and released. The head of the hammer hit the wedge and it flew away from him into the pile. It took him a few minutes to locate it again and tap it back into the section. He cocked his hammer back and swung once again. When he hit it this time, he didn't close his eyes, and in a split second, his glasses were off and he had dropped the hammer. At first he wasn't sure what had happened. Within a minute he felt a sharp pain on the side of his head just behind the temple. The wedge lay next to him; he had taken a line drive from the five pound wedge into the side of his head.

Shit, he thought, *that was way too close.*

He picked up his knocked-off glasses, and inspected them. They didn't even look scratched—another thing to be thankful for, since he couldn't afford a new pair.

The sharp pain had become a dull ache, and he knew it was only a matter of time before he developed an incredible headache. He wondered if he might have a concussion, then laughed off the thought. He was still standing, still conscious. Besides, Del and Lacey would be home in an hour or so, and then he would be blessedly distracted by playing with his daughter. The wood had to be split; soon he would be back at school, the rain would start and these two cords would rot and fester unless they were split and stored. The wood had been a gift from his retiree neighbors who had cleared their land to build their dream home. He had gone over to buck up a few pieces, but they had cut the bulk of it, including this enormous maple, and he had no intention of letting such fine wood go to waste.

"Suck it up, Stan," he said, reminded of some of his football player scholars, who played for a losing team at a small school, played through any number of injuries, came to class with bandaged hands, broken feet, and limps that explained everything.

I can be that tough, he thought. *I am that tough.*

Stan felt invigorated. Adrenaline helped to numb the pain slightly and made him feel he would, indeed, split the rest of that wood that afternoon. But the next half hour passed slowly, laboriously. He began to grow weary, tired, and frustrated with the entire process. He somehow knew he was doing something wrong, because it shouldn't be this difficult just to split a few measly pieces.

Growing up in Denver's suburbs, amid tracks of similar houses with similar lawns and boring written all over them, splitting wood was far removed from his everyday experiences. When he was very young, and they still burned wood in a real fireplace, the split wood appeared as if by magic, in the fall, by the side of the house when Stan was away at school. When they went camping they had to buy prebundled split wood from the nearest supermarket because cutting and collecting wood would ruin the park. His own experiences were limited to limbing a few trees in his parent's yard and tossing his dad's hatchet like a tomahawk.

All that practice turned out to be poor preparation for the actual thing.

In fact, running the chainsaw became a strange act of faith and contortionism: trying to keep his eye on the cut and his body away from the path of the blade should it choose this moment to unwind and shear off his arm or embed itself in his chest. Visceral danger and blood in his mouth when he bit his tongue as a kid, sledding as fast as his snow saucer would carry him, was the closest thing he could think of to compare to the scream of the chainsaw ripping through a piece of timber and flying wedges that attempted to bury themselves in his temple.

He was decent enough with his hands, exacting and patient, even though it seemed as though he had only just discovered them, having hardly ever held a hammer or a drill. He had always regarded this work as something that others did. Like the builders who came and went like shadows in his blossoming and ever rebuilding childhood neighborhood, or the college guys that his parents hired to paint the house, their loud music and laughter that hushed when they realized Stan was eavesdropping on the deck.

Staring at the pile of un-split wood he felt overwhelmed.

There is no way, he thought. *God, I will never finish this.*

Stan walked over to the hose and put his head down for a drink. Standing up his head hurt more intensely, and he contemplated taking something to quiet the pain, but decided against it.

What's a little headache, he thought shaking his head slightly which only made the pain worse.

Stan decided he might as well try to get as much done as he could before Del got home. He rolled a few large pieces out of the stack, set them next to each other, and began the task of trying to get the wedge started. Each time he set it in it fell over, and he grew increasingly frustrated.

"Shit!" he yelled as he hit his thumb trying to hold the wedge. He threw the hammer into the bushes. He took off his glove and sucked his thumb, which had already begun to throb.

"Oh, man," he said, realizing the ridiculousness of his behavior.

In the distance he could hear a car driving up the dirt road to the house. The vehicle was obscured by the trees and the steep driveway that sloped out of sight, but he recognized the sound of their '88 Volvo wagon.

Del crested the top of the hill and Stan waved, animated and smiling joyfully, hoping to catch the attention of his daughter, strapped into her car seat in the back.

"Hey, hot momma," Stan said, after Del had pulled up beside him and rolled down the window.

"Hey, hon," Del said, smiling, which quickly faded to a look of concern. "Uh, Stan did you know that you're bleeding from your head?" She pointed at her own head with her forefinger.

"Oh," Stan said, surprised, and looked at his faint reflection in the car's window. He could see a spot of blood on his head and a line of blood that dripped down his neck to settle on his white shirt.

"Crap!" he said.

"Shhh, you'll wake her up," she admonished, semi-seriously, smiling.

"Sorry," Stan said. "I don't feel so good."

"What the heck did you do?"

"I hit myself in the head with the wedge."

"What? The axe, you mean the axe?"

"No, no. That little five-pound wedge. I was splitting wood and I went down for a hit and pow! A line drive, right in the head."

"You think you have a concussion?"

"Nah, no way. I'm still conscious."

She gave him a "honey please don't bullshit me" look.

"Really, I am fine, go on in and I'll sit out here until the baby doll wakes up."

"You're sure? 'Cause I still have that article I need to finish, and I need to check e-mail."

"No prob'."

Del turned the motor off but left the radio on, slid out of the car, and gently closed the door behind her.

"I'll be right inside," she mouthed.

"Okay," he mouthed back.

"Where's Duke?" she whispered.

"I think he's sleeping in the back yard," Stan answered. "Doesn't move much."

She nodded and kissed him lightly on his head, opposite his cut, and he winced. His whole head hurt.

"Do you want a washcloth?" she whispered.

"Nah, I'm fine I'll use my shirt," he whispered back, and pulled his shirt up and dabbed at the blood. The instant he touched his scalp, shock waves of pain washed through him, and he suddenly felt weak and sick to his stomach.

He smiled weakly, hoping that Del hadn't seen him shudder. She smiled and walked through the garage and into the house. He watched her go, once again admiring her from the back. He felt himself grow aroused thinking about how luscious his wife was. He found it hard to believe that she was a mom, the mother of his child. His growing attraction to her, his still being aroused by kissing her, thinking about her, watching her walk away—the shape of her hips and her backside—still seemed remarkable. He had known that things were bound to change between them, intimately, after Lacey was born, but he didn't realize he would feel closer to her, his passion deeper, his desire greater.

He smiled as he stepped over to the car, the pleasant thoughts of Del helping to alleviate some of his discomfort.

Stan peered into the back seat through the open window, looking through the gaps in the headrest.

In her car seat slept the closest thing to heaven he had ever glimpsed. Even with her eyes closed Lacey was nothing short of his source of constant wonder. How incredibly serene she looked: her head resting against her car seat, small hands clasping a Pooh bear doll dirtied from so much traveling. She sucked on a binkie, which occasionally moved up and down rhythmically. She wore a small white sailor's cap and a little pink jumper. Despite his aching head he smiled and felt his mood lighten. How was it that every time he saw her, no matter what she did, he was so instantly smitten and amazed? It was as though around her he could no longer trust his eyes, because no matter what he saw, the effect was the same. This had been the case since he had watched her birth. Why so little poetry had been written about this state of deliriousness and so much about erotic love mystified him. Passion and moments of ecstasy were so fleeting compared to this. He wanted to reach in the back and wake her up. To watch her brown eyes open sleepily. However, there would be a moment of silence and then crying and screaming, which could only be silenced by her mother's nursing and quiet rocking.

Better to let her sleep, he thought and he stepped back from the car and sat atop a large, un-split section of maple.

The trees were still now, and a few more small white clouds punctuated the sky above the looming green canopy.

He inhaled the smell of cedar, the saltwater, a few hundred yards from where he sat, the warm engine of the Volvo, and his own sweat.

Stan stood and stretched, realizing he would probably be sore tomorrow.

Splitting more wood would wake the baby, but he was getting restless.

He gingerly picked up the paper rolled up on the passenger seat and returned to his stump to read.

The front page was more or less the same things that had been going on for months now. The president that neither Stan nor millions of others had voted for was waging peace in Iraq. Cheney, his V.P., was now part of a campaign to take the offense against critics of the administration and its pre-emptive strike against a country that was a perceived threat beyond the garden variety of North Korea, Iran, or even Saudi Arabia, which now seemed to have far more to do with 9/11 than any government official would publicly acknowledge. The Veep and his spin masters spun like whirling dervishes, without the benefit of a higher purpose, and still American G.I.'s, who trusted their government, were being massacred. Their stories had been pushed off the front page of the local Olympia paper. Stan found it ironic that a story about the latest soldier killed by rocket-propelled grenades near Fallujah began just above the continuation of an article with an excerpt from Cheney: "…September 11 is 'over with now, it's done, it's history and we can put it behind us.'"

"Yeah," Stan muttered, "tell that to the families of all of the U.S. troops killed since fighting was declared over and America the benefactor of the spoils of a long since spoiled place."

He shook his head, wondering when people were going to "get it." Perhaps they had, but like so many things, the conglomeration of media found the gloss of nonsubstance far more palatable to sell advertising than the pure vile truth that there were good people lured by the promise of retribution.

When did Vietnam begin to look like this? he wondered. He made a mental note to ask his parents about it the next time he talked to them. This reminded him of their remarkable visit the week before.

☕

He, Del, and Lacey had picked them up at the Bremerton Ferry terminal. His parents, Sara and Jacob, had flown into Seattle the night before and stayed overnight at a small bed and breakfast near Queen Anne Hill. He could tell that his parents were tired, unaccustomed to traveling. They had visited a few times over the past few years, and he had driven to Colorado to visit them as well, but they were very settled. Despite it just being the two of them, leaving home caused them unusual amounts of distress. They talked a little in the car, while his parents played with the baby, after insisting they sit in the back with her. Since Lacey was born in January most of their conversations and their visits focused on the baby. Stan was ok with it. He was proud to be a dad, proud that his parents had managed to survive their near divorce, and he was now able to understand so much more about them.

He remembered looking in the rear view mirror as they cooed for Lacey's attention, despite her heavily lidded eyes and their looking slightly carsick on the winding road. It was easy to see the same consuming love that he felt for his daughter conveyed in so many nuanced moments, smiles, and chuckles.

That afternoon his parents and the baby had napped, and Del and Stan tiptoed around as they often did when Lacey slept. Del did research for a freelance article she was proposing, and Stan read a gripping novel by Dan Simmons, a long-time resident of Colorado, whose transportive prose provided Stan with a pleasant distraction.

Stan helped Del make dinner, which mostly consisted of washing dishes and setting the table. His parents played with the baby, who was now very interested in her walker and used her strong, plump little legs to propel herself across the vinyl floor. Stan smiled as she tried to pronounce gampa and gama, but mostly pointed, smiled her charming smile, and asked for what she wanted with dat or dis.

Del, Stan, and his parents talked about world events, primarily what an idiot Bush was, especially when it came to Iraq and world affairs. They also talked about the pervasive atmosphere in popular culture, and now politics, of anti-intellectualism. Stan's dad told them about something he read that detailed how the leader of the free world didn't read books or articles but concentrated on newspaper headlines, relying on his people to give him unbiased opinions.

Stan's parents were long-time Democrats, at least since the 1960s. Stan, on the other hand, had a far more cynical view of politics, and saw very little difference between candidates from either party. It seemed that money controlled the means of governance, and if you had it you could shape public policy for personal gain. In fact, the 2000 election had so turned Stan off to politics, with the appointment of a president by the Supreme Court that he no longer felt the need to vote in any election.

For dinner Del served chicken and fresh vegetables, from her garden, over rice with some white wine. The freshness of the meal was intoxicating in a way that only home-grown ingredients could be. The tomatoes were sweet, ripe, and succulent, the zucchini absorbed the flavors of the olive oil, garlic, salt, and basil while adding texture, and the red bell peppers added a slightly tangy crunch.

After dinner they had pie Del had made from the apples in their yard. It was tart, and the crust flaky; with a little half-and-half over the top it was melt-in-your-mouth perfect.

Del put Lacey to bed and they all stayed up and talked. Stan's father asked him if they had heard the recent story about the climbers who had been killed in Nepal.

"Yeah, I remember seeing the headline for that online," Del said, "but I didn't read the article."

"It's probably in last week's paper," he said.

"Hang on," Stan said. "I'll grab it." Stan grabbed the paper from the burn pile and flipped to the blurbs in the International section. He scanned the articles until he found one entitled, "Trio of American climbers killed."

Stan read it aloud.

"Three American climbers and a South African were killed yesterday en-route between Tingri and Kathmandu when the jeep they were traveling in careened 2000 feet after being hit by a rockslide. Witnesses said the driver was attempting to negotiate a section of washed-out road when the rockslide hit. Members of an international climbing team, returning to Kathmandu, had passed the section just minutes before and claimed the American climbers and one South African were ill and suffering from exhaustion. The three men had successfully completed a hazard-filled ascent of Cho Oyo despite frequent bad weather and avalanches. Cho Oyo, at 8201 meters, is the sixth highest mountain in the world and is located on the border of Tibet and Nepal. The mountain is relatively easy to access, especially in the fall, and thus is one of the most popular 8000 meter peaks to climb."

"And, let's see. I don't see any of the climbers' names mentioned."

"Strange, huh?" Jacob asked. "They die in a random freak accident after making a dangerous climb, while another group of climbers is spared."

"That seems to be strangely ironic," Sara said sarcastically. "And you know, Stan, how your father loves strange news."

"News of the weird," Jacob said, correcting her.

"Right, for the weird."

He gave her a mockingly baleful look, which made her scoot next to him and give him a hug and a smooch.

"So sweet," Del said.

"I'm supposed to say, 'yuck' right?" Stan asked, rolling his eyes for effect.

"Only if you want sweets," Sara said, and gave Jacob another kiss, which he obviously enjoyed, since he heartily laughed as soon as she finished.

His laugh was catching, and they all chuckled. Eventually they moved on to family news, talking about Del's interesting family, and trying to schedule their next visit. After yawns all around, they finished their port and went to bed around eleven.

Getting ready for bed he remembered why he always enjoyed his parents' company. They were thoughtful, tolerant, and critically minded. He often felt out of place living amidst backwoods conservatives, dropouts, loggers, former mill workers, and the truly poor.

Fifteen minutes after they settled in Stan heard some commotion in the hall.

There was terse whispering, a door closed, steps running down the stairs, and the front door closed.

"Stan," Del whispered. "Go see what's the matter."

"They went out."

"I heard. Go catch them before they leave."

"Leave? They're probably going out for some air or a walk."

"What? At eleven." She looked at the clock. "At 11:26?"

"Well, okay, I'll go see."

Stan slipped on his jeans and went down the stairs. He knew they would be gone. He hadn't heard the car start, but he noticed Del's keys were missing from their hook by the phone.

He walked outside. It was a warm and clear night. The stars shone brightly despite the glare of the porch light. He walked out to the driveway and sure enough the Volvo was gone. The car seat had been taken out and set on the hood of their Toyota truck.

"What the hell?" Stan walked inside.

Del was waiting on the stairs. "Are they out there?"

"No, and they took the car."

"They took the car? Why?"

"Got me. They left the car seat; it's on top of the truck."

"Something bad happened."

"What do you mean something bad happened?"

"I mean where else would they go in the middle of the night?"

"I don't know? Probably not out for a drink."

"Or a burger."

"No."

"They went to the hospital."

"No," he said, but he knew she was right, there was no other explanation. "They know how to get there, I think. Remember, I pointed it out when we got into town." He had remarked that was where Lacey had been born. His parents had missed the birth, but had flown up a couple of days after Del and the baby were released. He wondered if he had pointed it out the last time they were here as well.

"Should we call?" she asked.

"The hospital?"

She nodded.

"Not yet. Let's wait about fifteen minutes."

"Should we drive there?"

"And wake up the baby? What could we do?"

"Stan, do you want to drive there?"

"Not yet, let's, let's wait and see if they're there."

The next fifteen minutes passed incredibly slowly for Stan, who felt his stomach begin to tighten as he considered the possibilities. Neither of his parents had been sick, or had any conditions he knew about. The uncertainty was overwhelming. The more he considered the possibilities, the more he worried.

They walked to the kitchen and stood. He stared at the clock as though he could move it or stop it from moving for fear of what he might learn.

"I'll get the number," Del said, and went to find the phone book. She turned back to him. "Are you okay?"

"Not exactly."

She walked to him and hugged him hard. "It's going to be okay. I'm sure everything is okay."

He felt better, but he never had Del's faith in the positive possibilities of outcomes. He saw the worst that could be: a stroke, a heart attack, death.

I'm not ready, he thought. *There is too much. I always thought I would have more time than this.* He was reminded of stories he had heard of losing loved ones suddenly; when the realization came there is no more time left, so many things that needed to be discussed, yet no more company to keep. He hadn't considered this, he hadn't even really thought about it, even though his parents weren't young anymore. He chided himself for his foolishness.

Del came back with the phone book.

"I found the number," she said. "You want me to call?"

Stan felt he should but he was worried his voice would fail him or that he would learn more than he was ready to accept. Better to have Del filter it, process it, and he would deal when she was ready to tell him.

"Yes, please."

She asked for admissions, and then asked if the Gillman-Reinharts had been admitted. She made a sour look at the response, said, "Good bye," and hung up.

"No, she said there was 'no one there admitted under that name.'"

"Seriously?"

"Yeah."

He couldn't believe it. "Where else would they go?"

"Who else could we call?"

"Um."

The phone rang as Del held it, which caused her to jump slightly. "Hello?" she said. "Are you okay? Where are you?" A pause. "Yeah, that's what we figured. Okay, good, oh. How soon?"

Stan, anxious, held out his hand for the phone.

"Yeah, uh, Stan wants to talk to you."

Del handed Stan the phone.

"Hey," he said.

"Hon," his mom said. "We are at the hospital."

"What happened?"

"Your father, well, your father is okay."

"Mom, what happened?"

"Your father is having some heart problems. His heart started racing at your house and it wouldn't stop. The doctors call it arrhythmia. Sorry we had to leave in such a hurry, we didn't want to wake you."

"And I guess you had no time for a note."

"I felt your father's pulse and I knew we had to get him there as quickly as possible. Sorry, hon, there was no time."

"You should have woken me. I could have driven you. Did you find the hospital okay?'

"Yeah, we remembered the general direction even thought it's so dark out. And then we followed the signs."

"So when will you know?"

"Well they just admitted him and the doctor is taking a look at him now. They're going to give him some medication to help bring the blood pressure down. Did the baby wake up?"

"No, she's fine."

"Stan I'm on my cell. I'll call just as soon as I know something. It might be an hour. They're talking about keeping him for awhile."

"Awhile? Dad happy about it?"

"Not especially. He doesn't like all of the fuss, and he is already starting to feel better. But they are worried about a heart attack or a clot."

"You mean a stroke?"

"Probably nothing, sweetie. I'll call you when I know more."

"When we called they said you hadn't been admitted."

"Oh, yeah, the receptionist told us someone called looking for us. They can't release patient information, that new law."

"That's ridiculous."

"I think so, too."

"Do you want me to come down there?"

"You don't need to. Why don't you wait 'til we know more, okay?"

"All right. I'll be up."

"Love you, sweetie, and try not to worry."

"I'm okay, Mom. I love you. Tell Dad I love him."

"Okay, bye."

"Bye."

"So, she going to call back?" Del asked.

"Yeah, she said it could be an hour or so."

"You okay?"

"I've been better, and worse. At least I know that he's safe. I feel like I should go."

"If you need to go, go."

"I'm not sure I could do anything. Maybe I should wait until I hear more."

Stan thought about taking their somewhat reliable truck and leaving Del alone. He worried about seeing his dad hooked up to machines, confused and agitated, and his parents bickering. It filled him with a palpable dread.

"Yeah, I'll wait," he said. "Let's watch some TV."

They sat on the couch and watched some talk shows and chuckled, distracted by the inane jokes. Though he tried not to, he kept worrying about his dad. He knew he would probably be fine, and he knew there wasn't much that he could do.

After an hour and a half his mom called again to let them know that his dad was being kept overnight for observation and she would be driving back. While Stan worried she might get lost, she insisted that she had excellent directions and her cell phone. Stan told her he would be waiting up for her on the couch.

Exhausted, Del went up to bed. Stan got some blankets and a pillow, propping himself up to read. He didn't remember falling asleep, but woke to the front door opening.

Disoriented, he leaped up from the couch to see his mom. She looked haggard and worn out. He insisted that she go to bed and Stan dragged himself up the stairs to sleep for a few more hours.

They had all awakened early and, after some coffee, had gone to see his dad at the hospital. It was a surreal experience. His dad was up, the bed adjusted so that he could read the paper with his reading glasses propped on the end of his nose. He looked scholarly except for the hospital gown, the IV, and the wires attached to his chest.

Stan never liked hospitals, their sterility and bland institutionalism, even though he knew they generally served their purpose well. It was such a different place from the college, and he wondered how strange it would be to report here every day.

They joked with Jacob and he held the baby. The doctor was still gone for lunch, but when she got back they would find out when Jacob would be discharged. The approximate answer he had gotten was around lunch time. Del offered Jacob a bagel with butter, but he insisted that he wasn't hungry.

Jacob explained that his racing heart beat was probably a freak occurrence, since all of the tests indicated that he was fine otherwise.

He stood at the end of his dad's hospital bed. Stan felt helpless, childlike, and uncomfortably anxious. His dad looked pale and his hair was unusually grey, even on his chest. He also looked drained, exhausted. Stan watched his dad holding Lacey.

For a moment the room became quiet, Stan's face flushed, the hair on the back of his neck stood on end, and he had an epiphany so profound that he had to turn his head to wipe away the tears. He didn't just feel elated and lucky and blessed that despite everything his dad was still with him. He knew there were things he had been given, things beyond his control, things he may not actually deserve and could never earn.

The Third

John had been channel surfing when he stumbled across the rapid fire images of monks spinning prayer wheels in a monastery in Nepal, the image of climbers in their colorful outfits making their way up a steep snow face, and a street scene in Kathmandu, where rickshaws, yaks, cars, and pedestrians intermingled in a chaotic dance. The image cut to a scene of what used to be a truck at the bottom of a steep cliff face. The shot was grainy, taken with a digital camera, perhaps from a camcorder. He turned up the sound.

"…the climbers had been traveling back to Kathmandu, along this roadway, after a harrowing climb of Cho Oyo."

The image changed again to an unsteady, amateur video shot of the crumpled wreckage at the bottom of the cliff face. Then the camera panned up and caught the faces of two Nepalese men, dressed in dirty, dark ski jackets, looking down the cliff at the carnage. Their expressions were void and passive, their arms folded serenely, but their dark, almost black, eyes betrayed something else entirely. The resolution was imperfect but John could clearly see a look in their eyes that disturbed him. He couldn't tell if it was recognition, a manifestation of suffering, or weariness of bearing witness to yet another daily horror heaped upon them.

The camera held the shot for several seconds and the men remained still, save the wind which slightly ruffled the collars of their coats and made a hollow sound in the microphone. Unconsciously, John moved to within a few inches of the screen. His impulse was to lay his fingers upon their weathered faces, but he sat back and merely watched.

The image cut back to the anchor in a fine pressed suit, coifed hair, manicured nails, capped teeth, and glasses that looked to be an affectation rather than a necessity.

Just as she spoke he turned off the TV.

He shook off the image of the men's eyes even as the residual representation refused to let go.

It was time for him to get out of bed—after all, it was well after one in the afternoon. He distracted himself by thinking of all of the mundane tasks he needed to accomplish before the show started.

The room was a mess, as usual, but housekeeping would be up sometime soon to clean up the empty beers and the half-eaten pizza. He took a long shower, feeling road dirt coated after a long day of traveling complete with delays and unexpected inconveniences.

He put on black slacks and a black silk, short-sleeved, shirt. He didn't bother with an undershirt and left the top two buttons unbuttoned . He grabbed his wrap-around sunglasses and slipped into his black leather shoes. The room key was one of those annoying cards. He left it on the nightstand next to the invoice for the room service. He grabbed his laptop/overnight case, which essentially contained his entire life's work, and picked up his black battered guitar case, which was propped up near the door.

The hallway was eerily quiet, as all large hotels seemed to be, and it smelled vaguely of disinfectant and new paint. He rode the elevator down to the parking garage and wandered around until he found his rental car. Underground garages made him uncomfortable, and he almost always forgot where he parked. The drive down I-5 and 405 to Renton was uneventful, and once in town he stopped off for gas and a pack of gum. It was a cool, sunny day and so traffic was unencumbered by rain. He missed the rain while living outside of Santa Fe where his boyfriend owned a gallery. Still, he was tanner than he had been in years, despite his job, which sometimes kept him up all hours indoors.

When he arrived at the venue he was escorted by one of the corporate organizers and a technician to the stage. Workers were rolling in stacks of chairs and tables; others were moving supplies in large crates and boxes. He walked onto the stage and looked out into the mostly empty space. This moment always made him more nervous than the actual presentation.

Nothing had been done; it was just pregnant possibility.

The empty space of the auditorium that he hoped would be filled and the gravity of responsibility he felt for so many things gnawed upon him. John found himself reminiscing for a time when things were different, when he was free to come and go as he pleased, and no one seemed to mind. He could drink, smoke, and sleep anywhere he wanted. He was always nervous before he went before a crowd, but today there was something else. He felt emotionally concave, on the verge of imploding.

This sucks, he thought. He didn't want to feel like this, especially not today, just hours before a presentation. He had to remind himself to work on convincing himself, that things could have turned out very differently. And he had to concentrate on why he was here.

John was here, mostly, because of a lot of other peoples' misfortunes.

Initially he had been asked to help a friend of a friend market new software that enabled the easy copying of music files. With a lot of convincing he brought his other friends on board—mostly members of his band, Burn. Within a couple of months they had sold what they owned, borrowed from relatives, and charged up their credit cards to come up with the initial investment to help get the company off the ground. With a lot of advice and a venture capital firm owned by a friend's uncle, they had quickly grown into a company of over thirty employees.

He had ridden the bubble almost all the way to the top, and a few months before it burst he sold his shares and got out. Greed had kept others there, including most of the founders, who had been financially ruined by the dot-com crash. Leaving turned out to be the easiest decision he had ever made. His life had become late nights at the office, eating take-out food at his desk, losing touch with his music, and estranging his boyfriend.

Ironically, he left the company with over a million dollars and a passion to do something with it. For months before he quit, John had fantasized about what he would do with his shares. He made promises, the way he would change things, if he could only get out.

He quit with little fanfare. His partners told him that he was crazy and should re-consider.

"The pot of gold," Todd, one of the co-founders said, "is less than a year away." John had stared at him for a long time, noticing that strange and disturbing look in his eyes. It was the same look he remembered seeing in himself when he had become a strung-out drug addict—one part desperation and two parts self-obsessed delusion.

He had shaken his head in reply and said, "I'll see you 'round."

He sold his condo in Belltown, moved to New Mexico, and formed a nonprofit that promoted arts for underprivileged children, primarily in the rural Southwest. With his business connections the charity became wildly successful and branched out across the country with chapters in seven states. At one point a former vendor in San Francisco, impressed by John's enthusiasm for fund raising, asked him to speak at a company community-outreach dinner. The speech was a hit, especially since John's prop was his guitar, and one thing led to another. Now he spent a month out of every year crisscrossing the country to raise awareness of the importance of arts in public schools and solicit donations. Asking for money had never been something he had been very comfortable with, but, based on his enthusiastic presentations, he knew his donors would probably find it hard to believe.

Over the last year, as the recession had deepened and companies and individuals folded, he had become uncomfortably dependent on a couple of major donors and corporations. He was speaking at Volunteer Week for one of these companies tonight.

It was the kind of corporation that would never have given him the time of day a few years ago as a college dropout and entrepreneur. It gave him a certain satisfaction to be allowed within their hallowed halls to bend their ears for awhile about something many employees and executives assumed was an American birthright—equal opportunity. The idea that even poor kids deserve the enrichment the arts bring, not just a regurgitation of skills that would help them to pass the latest round of standardized tests, was entirely alien to many members of his mostly white upper-middle class audiences.

The technicians had him stand in for a quick sound check. The presentation didn't start until 5:30, just after the employees clocked out, and walked to the corporate auditorium. After his presentation they would be fed a buffet dinner at company expense, and he would shake hands while offering encouraging words.

He told one of the organizers he needed to run a few errands before the show started.

Distracted, the small blond man waved him off and shouted over his shoulder, "We'll see you at 4:30."

"Right," John said, trying not to sound annoyed.

He walked out into the bright sunlight, his guitar case in one hand and his bag in the other. He walked around the parking lot for a while until he found the rental. It was always interesting to see what kinds of cars his audience drove. Most of these cars were no more than five years old, lots of Japanese mid-size to compact. There were quite a few gleaming SUVs, sports cars, and even a few old beaters. He saw only a dozen or so cars with bumper stickers or other evidence of personality.

Basically vanilla, he thought.

Although this would dissuade some from believing he could make an impact tonight, this evidence of ordinariness only strengthened his resolve. He knew his enthusiasm and outgoing personality did not suit everyone, but when he was up on the stage he felt as though the energy of the universe flowed through him, as if he could use his voice, his body, and music to reach inside people whose lives had been so much like his own—bereft of passion, without a purpose.

He put his things in the trunk and sat behind the wheel. The inside of the car was warm from the sun. He turned the car on and put the window down, resting his arm on the sill. The radio played quietly. He really had no place to go, no place to be. He sat in the car and watched the other cars in the parking lot. In twenty minutes he saw only one other person, three rows over. Feeling conspicuous John slid down in his seat, which made him feel even more obvious. A man in a dark suit went to his car to fish something out of the trunk, a gym bag or something. It was hard to be sure from where John was sitting. John changed the stations until he heard the melodic sounds of a guitar. He turned it up. He recognized the piece, "Recuredos de la Alhambra," by Francisco Tarrega.

The sounds of each individual note, beautiful and melodic, reminded him of many years ago in the metro in London.

The experience had been slightly surreal—rounding the bend in one of the many curving, white-tiled, reflective passageways to see a boy, sitting on a wooden box playing a stunning but worn, old flamenco guitar. The sound from the guitar itself was light and distinct, echoing down snaking passageway. The boy tapped the face of the guitar percussively, fleetingly, and precisely. Even the way he held the instrument, as one would hold a beloved deep in the throws of ecstasy, belied hidden truths about the music, channeled through its player.

By his playing alone John realized that this was not a boy but a young man of perhaps sixteen or seventeen. He played for several minutes as John stood there transfixed, enraptured, and amazed by a level of playing he had never heard outside of a conservatory or a professional studio.

The young man looked up and John felt his eyes look through him or past him as though his presence was entirely unnecessary for the performance. His dark eyes were set deep into his face and framed by long strands of limp hair that had fallen out of his battered fedora.

John was carrying his own guitar and his backpack. He could feel the fatigue of the past few months pulling him downward, collapsing his lanky frame. His feet ached and his knees wobbled, but he continued to stand, unwilling to move and break the spell that the young man held on him. He closed his eyes, and for a few brief seconds he heard only the notes, the purity of intent, the melancholy and exquisite nature of absolute sadness.

He thought about his guitar safe within its case, an expensive Robert Ruck that his parents had taken out a home equity loan to purchase, and he felt embarrassed, ashamed. He could play, sure, but what value would his Brazilian rosewood instrument have in the hands of the musician who sat before him. A young man, not yet twenty, with his guitar case open and strewn with a few coins and bills upon the worn velvet. A young man who played as though he had lived the music he played or perhaps the music lived through him.

He heard steps behind him. A heavyset older woman, dressed as though she worked in an office, walked up to the boy and stood. He could smell her perfume, something like rosewater. She stood and waited patiently until the young man finished. John was drawn back into reality soon after the reverberations echoed and died.

Leaning down, the older woman quietly said something to the young man, in Spanish, and he picked the money out of the case and handed it to her. She put it into her worn black purse, smoothing each bill, and placing each coin carefully into a coin pocket. Then she stood with her arms crossed and stared toward the exit. John reached into his pocket and pulled out his last ten-pound note, knowing he would have to skip eating until he got on the plane in a few hours. He handed the money to the young man who looked up and smiled slightly, the lines around his dark eyes creasing. The young man looked down again, their short, silent conversation over. John adjusted his pack and turned, walking around the passageway to where it met the stairway and blinding sunlight.

John smiled and looked across the expanse of the parking lot. He could smell the delicate smell of rosewater and hear the movement of slender fingers, like evanescent summer rain.

The Fifth

Lacey sat on the couch and raptly watched her video. Del watched her from the doorway, feeling a little guilty sitting Lacey in front of the TV, even though it would only be for a half hour or so. The hypnotic effect and everything she had read about children's development more or less indicated that, at the very least, it was not beneficial to her daughter's growth. But she had resorted to the distraction out of desperation. Lacey was at a stage where she didn't want to be put down, ever. She still woke Del in the night to breastfeed and insisted on being carried around for much of the day. When Del put her down, other than in front of the TV, she screamed, cried, and carried on. She knew there were many people, including some of her loose collection of new mom friends, who would say that Lacey should be left to cry.

This instinctively seemed wrong to Del. Fortunately, she had stumbled upon new studies and anecdotal evidence that showed that carrying Lacey around was fine and would actually encourage her to be more secure and independent in the long run. Whenever she doubted herself and her parenting choices she reminded herself of all of the screwed up kids she had seen having the kind of nightmarish interactions with their parents in public that she could never imagine having in private. She also knew that those insecure, disturbed, or at least emotionally detached children would only become more so as adults—the kind of people she knew too well and tried hard to forget.

Normally, Stan would be helping to carry Lacey around, because he was still on summer break, but he was at a seminar in Seattle. Del thought it was wonderful to have him home, even though she knew he often felt he was in the way, disturbing the delicate domestic balance that Del and Lacey had carved out for themselves. She was so used to doing things without help that she rarely delegated duties to Stan. On more than one occasion they had argued about whether Stan was helping enough, and Del had more or less stated that he should spend more time jumping in rather than waiting for instruction.

Stan had learned helplessness when it came to many things around the house. His mother and his sister had taken care of him growing up. In college he more or less stumbled by, eating poorly, doing his laundry when there was literally nothing left to wear, and sometimes cleaning up after himself and his roommates. Del never considered herself to be a paragon of housewifery or motherhood, yet she surprised herself by how good she was at it. Her discipline, patience, reserves of energy, and positive attitude had, generally, made things easier.

Stan being home had other benefits, as well. They had been having considerably more sex. Despite the fact that she was often sleep-deprived, at least slightly stressed, and taxed from the demands of Lacey and her freelance work, they often found time to be alone together. With so many things going on, and so much on her mind, it often took her awhile to get into the whole experience. But when she did, and afterward, it was usually wonderful, in a trembling, goose-bump kind of way.

Sometimes she wasn't in the mood, even though Stan was rarely not in the mood; this had created friction between them, sometimes even a sterile distance. She knew it also had something to do with all of the things he had on his mind, primarily work and beginning the long school year. She noticed his demeanor changed, every year, and as the year progressed he became more withdrawn. Summer was his release, she supposed. He was back to himself and back to wanting her most of the time.

Del sat at the kitchen table, staring at her laptop, her notes strewn out before her. She didn't need to reference them. She had been working on this project for five months and had virtually memorized them. She had talked to an editor about the idea last fall and it had taken her months of stolen hours to do the research and get halfway though the article. She knew she should feel proud of having come this far, but instead she felt anxious and tired of writing and editing the same piece of work.

She got up and walked over to the den to check on Lacey. Del peeked through the crack in the door, worried that she might scream and cry at the sight of her. Lacey was still staring blankly at the video of toys set to classical music. The educational aspect of the video, Del knew, was only to assuage some of the guilt that parents felt as they planted their children in front of the idiot box so that they could steal a few minutes for themselves, or put the house back in order for the umpteenth time that day.

Duke, their elderly black lab, lay behind Lacey on the couch, snoring.

Del walked over to the sink and nearly tripped on a small stuffed bear. She placed it on the counter, even though her initial instinct was to kick it across the kitchen. She stood at the window and looked out at the garden and the forest beyond. The grass, the ferns, and the small bushes were unusually dry, and some had even turned brown in the long summer heat. The garden looked surreally verdant against the landscape.

It had been overcast and misting earlier, but it appeared as though it would burn off—the sun was stealthily peeking through the clouds. She opened the window and inhaled the cool morning air. Soon she could make her way out to the garden. If she closed the gate and put Lacey in a spot in the sun with her beach tools she would sit and dig contentedly for at least an hour or until she discovered why people don't eat dirt.

Del looked back over at her notes and computer. She had begun to hate the sight of it, the stress that the mere thought of it brought to mind. The unfinished project had taken on a life of its own, as though the project itself was no longer the focus but the void that the as-yet-to-be-determined part took up. It had occupied too many of her thoughts, yet she rarely found inspiration from it. She walked back over to the table and sat down. She ran her finger across the mouse pad and the computer whirred to life. She scrolled up to the beginning of the article.

The title read: "How to eat it too—the musings of a (freelance) organic gardener." And below it her first by-line: "by Delany Gillman-Reinhart." She thought the title was catchy, but perhaps too cute, too pert. A friend of her dad's cousin, who was an editor at *Sunset,* indicated there was definitely a market for the piece, but perhaps not at his magazine. Del had envisioned it as a step-by-step, detailed account of her neophyte organic gardening and the notion, held by many, that one could live literally off the fruits of one's labors without it seeming too laborious. She had written in a sort of musing journal style with notes up to this month. Each time she read it through she sensed that it was missing something, something compelling but invisible, which, if included, would make it instantly complete. Del dwelt on it even as she wrote, and it seemed to cheapen the rest no matter how smart her phrasing, wonderful her description, or poignant her observations. She felt that if she figured out what it was she could finally finish.

She looked up again, out the window and into the yard to watch the birds. Gray jays, black-capped chickadees, red-breasted nuthatch, sparrows, and a larger stellar jay fed off the bird feeder that hung from a sun porch over the deck. The jay flew with an exaggerated swagger, his tall black plume rising above his head and long tail. He flew at the feeder, ate, and flew to a nearby stump to loudly proclaim himself with a shaq-shaq-shaq.

As soon as the jay was far enough away from the feeder the smaller birds swooped in, sometimes two at a time, scattering bird seed looking for the choice bits, and flew off, making the long clear feeder sway slightly. Occasionally, a bird would land on the deck and clean up fallen seeds.

In the winter, Del would see fewer of them and later notice their absence. She would wonder where they had traveled to or if they survived. Many people had talked about it being an especially cold and wet winter and she worried a bit that the mule deer, coyote, and red fox would have a very hard time surviving in the rare snow and cold that marked an unusually bitter winter in this part of the world.

Perhaps she would keep the feeders full through the winter. But the idea somehow interfered with her notions of what was natural.

She thought, *Is helping them, by feeding them thorough out the winter, such a crime, a selfish thing to help more survive?*

Watching the birds made her ache to be outside. The tomatoes were now so ripe that some were literally bursting. This had been the driest summer in almost a hundred years, and while many things were drying up, or were already dead, watering the garden had produced a bumper crop. The tomatoes were succulent, sweet and virtually perfect, far better than last year. She had heard that tomatoes usually got blight in Western Washington, but not this year. The zucchini were huge, the peppers large and crisp, the carrots continued to grow, and only the lettuce had really bolted. Her biggest adversary had been the slugs, and she had used organic slug bait, ash, and beer to ward them off. She was intrigued by the idea of using copper around the beds next year, which the slugs disliked crossing.

What could I write today? she thought. She sighed, got up to make herself a cup of tea, and the phone cord to check her e-mail.

She spent a few minutes sorting her e-mail, deleting spam, trying to avoid viruses, and writing back to a few of her friends and her mom. There was an e-mail from Stan's parents containing their itinerary. Del had completely forgotten they would be arriving in two days. She had a moment of panic until she realized Stan would be home tomorrow, and they had no major plans for the weekend.

As usual she decided to go to her ISP home page and check the news. She skimmed the headlines and noticed: "Climbers Killed in Nepal Identified." Absentmindedly, Del checked the time, and realized that the video had been over for awhile, and yet there was no noise from the den. Panicked, she raced to the door and swung it open. Lacey sat on the floor playing with her set of blocks. She looked up, startled. Sensing she was about to cry, Del rushed over to her.

Lacey, predictably, held up her chubby hands and said, "Up, ma."

Del set her on her lap and steadied her as she continued to play with the blocks.

She could feel Lacey's warmth through her sundress and shirt, felt her soft sides, round tummy, and tiny ribs. The sensation of holding her filled her with an indescribable joy.

This is my girl, Del thought. She smelled the top of Lacey's head, inhaling the distinct baby smell—the scent of baby shampoo, cooked carrots, and something else sweet.

Del suddenly had the sensation of waking up, as though she had been asleep for too long, groggy. The stir of being present, within herself, and living, breathing, and holding onto what she wanted flooded through her. Evidence of the everyday, this moment, so transitory as to be gone in a matter of seconds or minutes, but indelible nevertheless.

Del stood, effortlessly, and carried Lacey out to play in the garden now dappled with the sun.

The 10th

Brian watched the water, the way it crested in the middle and formed a v-shaped wake pushing outward. It was cool on the aft deck, and the wind whipped his light rain-jacket around him. He pulled his baseball hat down lower on his head, fearing he would lose it. He stretched and took in the scenery around him. It was breathtakingly beautiful. Rounded islands of evergreens rose from rocky bases out of the cold dark water. The twilight sky was bedecked with clouds and the threat of rain. The air smelled of brine and teeming sea life. The ferry passed small pleasure boats, white sailboats, and an occasional fishing boat as though they were anchored. Large white gulls flew along with the ferry.

He watched the seagulls, their eloquent grace and perfect synchronization belying their hope of a handout.

The ferry began to slow and turn towards Lopez Island. He considered going to the bow of the boat, but decided to stay put and watch the water. The boat slowed and docked, letting off passengers, cars, trucks, and bicyclists. Brian watched the water swirl and splash against the large dark pilings tied with cable like smooth, round cord wood. The water here was green and gulls and black crows were settled upon the huge pilings, further streaking the tall columns with their white excrement. He could smell the pitch and wood, the stronger smell of saltwater, diesel smoke, and exhaust. Over the past few months these smells had become a comfort, a signal of permanence to Brian.

Eventually, the new passengers and vehicles were settled and the ferry's powerful propellers thrust it back into the Sound and on toward Shaw Island. The boat quickly picked up speed, and Brian's yellow coat flapped again in the breeze as his hat tried to try to fly off. He looked down into the water and wondered, as he did on every trip, what it would be like to simply jump. He knew he probably wouldn't die, although he might. The water would be unbelievably cold and would take his breath away. Then someone would yell, the ferry boat would go into man overboard mode, whatever that looked like, and he would be scooped out of the water like so much fish. If they didn't get to him soon enough, his limbs would be paralyzed by hypothermia and he would quickly slip from sight. The weight of his clothes would pull him downward until he breathed one last breath of saltwater and drowned. Again he decided it probably wouldn't be a good idea.

The boat reached Shaw, the disembodied voice again announcing their arrival and that passengers should disembark if this was indeed their destination. He continued to marvel at the water, its shapeless, protean shape, the color, and so much else that he knew he was experiencing but could barely recognize.

Brian felt a bit anxious and excited as the ferry made its way out from the dock and across the short stretch to Orcas Island. He had spent his day off visiting with his brother, who was in a residential treatment facility in Seattle. Brian had managed to avoid seeing his parents despite their insistence that he come see them when he was in town. He had little to say to them since he had seen them at his brother's hearing.

Toby had been accused of helping his roommate hide the cocaine he was dealing. His roommate had managed to work a plea agreement with the DA's office, but he would still do hard time.

After Toby was arrested, their parents told him that it was unfortunate, but they weren't going to be able to pull any strings for him. The best they could do was to help him pay for treatment. This hadn't really bothered Brian much, since it seemed overdue for a kid in his twenties. But he didn't know much about the law and he figured a few months in jail and some treatment might straighten him out. Later his dad had called him at work. His dad had talked to the DA's office and Toby would get a 21- to 27-month mandatory prison sentence.

Brian remembered his disbelief. He had made his dad repeat it, and as it sank in Brian broke out into a cold sweat. He was afraid for Toby.

He thought about the day of the hearing. He remembered waiting in the foyer, outside the courtroom, for the hearing to start. It smelled of mildew, coffee, and old cigarettes. He and his parents sat on chairs across from one another, the voices and footfalls echoing around them in the cavernous space lit primarily by natural light. They sat for over an hour. His mom clutched her purse tightly and looked uncomfortable, while his father did something on his PDA.

"So what exactly do you do at The Resort?" his father asked, breaking the silence.

"I already told you three times. I wash dishes," Brian said, sounding more irritated than he had meant to.

"Who are you in charge of there? I mean who reports to you?" his mother asked, her knowledge of a kitchen limited to what she saw on the Food Network.

"No one, just me. I answer to the restaurant manager and the chef, or basically everyone else," he said.

"So, what are your advancement opportunities? Say toward being the manager?" his father asked.

"None, really," Brian lied. "I don't want her job. She has no time, no life, and she's always at the restaurant." This was true and had filled Brian with respect and pity for her.

His parents looked at him vacantly, uncomfortable forced smiles on their faces. They didn't speak much the rest of the day.

They had sat through the hearings of many other more nefarious criminals before Toby Fetzler's name was called. He looked ridiculous with his shaved head and orange jail jumper, his hands cuffed in front of him, a fact his mother talked about repeatedly with a tone of astonishment and indignation. Brian held his tongue.

His brother had a public defender, but the entire affair was cursory since he pled guilty. The judge explained to Toby that due to minimum sentencing laws he would have to give him at least 21 months in prison.

Toby nodded, trying to look cool and collected, even though Brian could see a sheen of sweat forming on Toby' forehead. His face was pale, and his eyes set with rings. He was sentenced to 21 months in prison and would then be released for drug and alcohol treatment in private residential facility.

Brian's visit to the treatment center had been his idea. Toby was okay with it since he complained that the family had abandoned him. No one had ever visited him in prison, a fact that Brian often felt guilty about.

It had taken Brian half the day to get to Seattle. He had to get up before dawn and take the ferry to Anacortes, take the Skagit County Transport bus to Burlington, the Greyhound into downtown, and another bus to see Toby. By the time Brian got there he was spent, even though he had snoozed a bit on the bus.

Toby was waiting for him in front of the TV, in the rec room as the staff called it. It was a sterile room on the first floor with white vinyl floors, a dark grey couch, a couple of easy chairs, and an old ping pong table. For the first hour after Brian got there Toby wanted to watch TV, specifically his soap, which he said he had become addicted to.

While Toby watched TV Brian thumbed through the most recent newspaper in the room, a *Seattle Times* that was over a week old. It was mostly the same news about Iraq. But there was one article, a small one, about a group of unidentified American climbers that had died in a truck wreck in Nepal. The article struck Brian as somehow unreal. It was hard for him to imagine climbing a mountain, let alone in Nepal, just to die in an ordinary car crash.

"Soap's over," Toby said and switched off the TV.

Brian folded the paper and laid it on the table next to the couch.

"How's work?" Toby asked.

Brian discerned that he was probably just making conversation, but there was always a strange tone in Toby's voice, like white noise. It meant that he was working you over for information, disrespecting or belittling you, or had some other angle. Regardless, it was all about him.

"Fine, the same. How's the food?" Brian asked.

"Fine. The same."

So you got your own place there on the Island?" Toby asked.

"No," Brian said tersely, lying. "I stay in the old shit-hole maid's quarters."

"Fuck me!" Toby said. "You stand for that shit? I got my own suite here."

"Yes, courtesy of Mom and Dad."

"Yeah, well fuck them. I did almost two years, two fucking years."

"Yeah, I've heard it, two years. What exactly were you expecting?"

Toby gave him a menacing look that quickly changed to a Cheshire cat grin. "I just got caught, won't happen again," he said, folding his arms.

"You mean you won't do it again, or you won't get caught again?"

Toby shrugged, tight-lipped, eyebrows raised.

"Ok," Brian said willing to change the subject. "You seen Mom and Dad?"

"Yeah, they've been by once," Toby said, holding up his middle finger. "They said they were coming by today, heard you were in town or some shit like that."

Brian's eyes widened. "You told them I was coming. You shit!"

"Hey don't look at me. They don't even call here."

"Strange. I wonder how they knew."

Toby shrugged again.

Both were silent for a few minutes.

Brian pretended to play with the zipper on his jacket. "So how's treatment?"

"Pretty much bullshit," Toby answered. "They got me on this twelve-step program and all."

Brian nodded.

"I mean, I really haven't made it past the first step. Something about being powerless or whatever. See, in group, we're all supposed to share and all that bullshit. I went through all kinds of withdrawal shit in prison. I was really sick for a while. And, well, I don't really give a fuck what all these other dickheads think."

"Yeah," Brian said quietly.

"They beat the shit out of me you know, broke two ribs and my arm," Toby said quietly, almost whispering, looking down. "They said I was lucky I wasn't their type or I would be in worse shape."

Brian didn't know, and he knew it showed on his face, in his eyes. He had suspected. His parents had alluded to it, writing about Toby being changed by prison.

"I had nightmares for a long time," Toby said, looking away, past Brian. His face was slack, his eyes vacant.

Unconsciously Brian turned to look over his shoulder.

"Hey, ah, you stayin' for lunch? I gotta take a smoke break," Toby said, suddenly buoyant.

"No," Brian said, turning back. "I have to get back for work."

"What, they can't get some other sorry ass to wash the dishes."

Brian winced. He thought of defending himself but really, what was the point. He washed dishes, he had a small cabin on the resort's property, he ate well, and he had plenty of time to walk the beach, collect shells, sketch, read, and think.

"Well I guess I'll see you later," Brian said.

Toby was already up out of his chair and tapping his pack of cigarettes. "Yeah."

No handshake, no hug, no contact, no nothing.

Walking to the bus stop, that would take him back to the Greyhound, he began to feel relieved. It surprised him, since he hadn't noticed how tense he had been. His jaw was now sore from clenching it. And when he got on the ferry he felt even more relaxed, almost sleepy.

He made his way to the front of the boat to watch it come into the dock. He walked though the partially enclosed smoking area and through the double doors. Inside it was much warmer than out on deck, as filtered sun filled the cabin. People were gathering their things, children ambling along behind their parents, some making their way to their vehicles below. As usual he didn't recognize anyone. He could smell food from the grill and his stomach grumbled. Hunger wasn't really that important, since he would eat when he got to work in a couple of hours. He stopped at the water fountain and took a long drink. He stepped away, smoothing his jacket over his flat stomach.

At the front of the boat he stepped into the semi-enclosed area where an old man and a young woman were finishing their cigarettes.

He walked out to see the Orcas Hotel: white with a red roof like a sentinel on the hillside, the tall fuel tank, bluish white. The dock seemed to grow larger as they approached. The boat slowed and they docked. He could see people waiting to get on and family members waiting in anticipation for loved ones to return.

Brian walked down to the car deck and out onto dry land.

He would hitch a ride past Eastsound to the resort, walk down the road, and down the beach to his cabin. Then he would finally be home.

The Fourth

Not much had happened since Bridgette had arrived at the makeup counter early that morning. It was about a half an hour until her lunch break and she was tired. She was tired of standing, of smiling that fake smile, of asking dismissive passers-by if they were interested in a makeover or the special of the week, or more ridiculously sized samples for every purchase over $19.50. She was happy for the discount the store gave her, the commission she made, even though it was minimal, and the social interactions she had with most of her co-workers. Today, however, Jane was working. And Jane and Bridgette didn't get along.

Ever since Bridgette found out that Jane had been badmouthing her to customers and employees she had basically wanted to strangle her. When Bridgette had mentioned it to management they promised they would look into it, but it went nowhere. Jane was the number three associate for total sales at the counter, and had been a model employee for two years.

So when they were scheduled to work together, which lately seemed far too often, Bridgette kept her distance. Occasionally, standing at the opposite end of the counter, she'd throw Jane an icy cold stare and Jane would flash her eat shit and die grin right back.

A young man walked by in a business suit, and Bridgette wondered what Mike was doing at that very moment. She wanted to call him, but personal phone calls were discouraged and she knew Jane was likely to narc on her. Besides, Mike was probably in another boring budget meeting. Finance. How she had fallen for a guy in finance was something she just couldn't figure out sometimes.

She looked at her gold watch. Twenty minutes until her next break.

Shoppers, mostly middle-aged women, other employees of the mall, and some younger mothers with small children browsed through the racks of expensive clothing and passed the display cases. She wondered what she looked like to them. Her makeup was flawless and long white jacket spotless and pressed. She turned the mirror on the counter and looked into it. Her eyes sparkled, her brows were perfectly sculpted, her lips a deep burnt red, her eyes lined lightly, and her cheekbones barely shadowed. She noticed the beginnings of the lines around her mouth and eyes, the thin crow's feet that even concealer couldn't hide, the slight laugh lines around her mouth—an irony since she had laughed little in the last few years.

Am I that old? she thought.

The question was largely rhetorical since the answer was staring at her cruelly magnified, framed in chrome. As she stood up and smoothed her coat, the notion of plastic surgery occurred to her for the tenth time in so many weeks. For years she had seen it as inevitable. Hadn't her mom started having work done when Bridgette was 16? Even then it hadn't seemed all that strange. But Mike was pretty much ambivalent about it.

When they were out at dinner last week, she had asked him, if he thought she should get her eyes done or maybe a lift. He had stared at her for a long time, not saying anything.

"Is that what you want?" he asked.

"I don't know," she answered. "I think so."

"How much does it cost?"

That question. He always asked that question. At the dinner table she could feel her face grow slightly flushed. She had to take a few deep breaths before answering.

"I don't know," she said.

"Oh," he said, now uninterested.

They ate in silence for most of the rest of the meal, but Bridgette knew that Mike probably hadn't even noticed. She knew, rationally, that most of his day was about money, but she wanted it to be different with her, with them.

Bridgette and Mike had been dating for almost a year, and she had begun to wonder when he would finally pop the question. They each still kept their separate places—hers, an apartment near Eastlake, and his, a house near Bothell. They spent overnights together, when she didn't have to work. They were certainly exclusive, and yet whenever the conversation drifted toward marriage he would make some remark like, "After I become a manager I'll have great job security."

It would be quaint if he was being old-fashioned, but she knew he squirreled away much of what he made while she spent all if not more than what she made. He had been working with the same firm for almost six years, he owned his own house, and he had paid cash for his two-year-old BMW. She had run up debts, borrowed money from her dad, been sent to collections, and owned an almost-new BMW that ate up much of her salary.

In fact, their cars were how they met. Mike was having his car serviced and Bridgette was going to get an oil change at the dealership. She was on her lunch break and was trying to complete a few errands before she had to get back to work. She didn't have an appointment, which usually didn't matter since she simply flirted with the guy at the service desk and he would say something like, "I think I can squeeze you in," with a wink and a knowing nod. Sometimes he wouldn't even charge her. "On the house," he'd say.

He never asked for her number, which she was grateful for—he wasn't her type, and the wedding ring was definitely a turnoff.

But that day it was a new guy. He was humorless, wore thick glasses, and had his hair slicked back.

Bridgette walked up and smiled her luminescent smile. She was looking especially fetching in a low-cut black sweater and tight black Capri's.

The guy didn't even smile back. "You have an appointment?"

She didn't, of course. "So what happened to the guy that used to work here?"

"Oh, Stephen?" he said. "They fired him."

"Oh," Bridgette said. "So you couldn't just squeeze me in?" And she gave him a little wink.

He stood there expressionless. "Sorry, miss, but you'll need to make an appointment." He flipped the pages on the large book in front of him. "Looks like the next available appointment is the day after tomorrow, say two o'clock?"

Bridgette knew her schedule by heart since she didn't rotate until the Holiday season. "No, I have to work. Are you sure there's nothing sooner?"

"Sorry, miss." The greasy guy looked down at her cleavage for a split second and then looked up.

"Hey," a man standing behind her said. "She can have my appointment. I can come back in a couple of days."

Well, well, Bridgette thought, as she turned around and sized up the stranger. He was wearing a tailored suit and dark tie. He was around 35-40, tall with dark hair, and well groomed.

"Thank you," Bridgette said smiling broadly.

"No problem," he said, smiling.

"Keys, miss," the greasy attendant said.

"Oh yes, of course."

She waited outside for the stranger in the suit, fighting the urge to light up, to introduce herself. He came out after a few minutes and she thanked him again. They exchanged cards, agreed to meet for coffee that weekend. And to

Bridgette the most remarkable part was he didn't look at her cleavage once.

She looked at her watch again and realized it was time for her lunch break. Jane was busy talking to a customer at the other end of the counter, and so Bridgette left without telling her.

She'll figure it out, she thought.

She walked out into the shadows of the parking garage. She was working the swing shift today, which meant her whole day was basically wasted. By the time she got off around eight Mike would probably be dozing in front of ESPN or CNN. Sometimes she called, hoping to have a conversation, and woke him. He was understandably tired, and their exchange consisted of mostly one-and two-syllable words.

She waited until she was almost to her car before she got her cigarettes out. She put one between her lips and got in her car. She wouldn't light it until she got to the restaurant, where she could smoke it slowly. She had been able to cut back to around 10 cigarettes a day. Mike had convinced her to quit, especially after he reminded her about premature aging. He was basically a health nut, always trying to get her to drink protein shakes, and eat her vegetables.

On their second date he had gone on for almost twenty minutes about how much he hated smoking. He didn't know that she smoked and even though she had planned on lighting up outside after dinner, she had fought her craving for nicotine. She was anxious, sweating, and began to shake a little. Her desire was so intense that it obscured her thoughts. All of her intellectual energies became focused on when she could get that smoke.

He had invited her to a movie, but she left right after dinner because she felt sick. It was only a partial lie, and he said something about how she looked kind of pale and maybe she should lie down. He wanted to follow her home but she insisted on him only walking her to her car. She apologized, and he gave her a peck on the cheek and told her he wanted to see her again, illness or not. She had smiled weakly and slipped into her car. At that moment Bridgette just wanted to be home, to be left alone.

As soon as she got out of the parking lot she lit up. She stopped shaking. She took deep pulls on her cigarette, enjoying each drag. She felt calm, comfortable, and satiated.

Bridgette arrived at her usual lunch break spot a few blocks from the mall, her cigarette hanging loosely from her lip. It was a boring restaurant, but they had an okay bar menu and there were always a few other smokers, so she didn't feel like the pariah she felt around Mike.

She figured that he knew that she still smoked sometimes, but they never talked about it.

It was utterly unexpected that Dave had called the day after her second date with Mike. She was getting out of the shower, getting ready for work. She was screening her calls, listening to the answering machine. Suddenly his voice came on. It was exactly like she remembered it: deep, rich, soft. She hesitated, wondering if she should pick up.

"Hello?" she said lifting the receiver. "Sorry, I didn't hear the phone."

"Oh, hey," he said. "This is Dave, Dave Greibing."

"I know," she said teasing. "It hasn't been that long."

"No, I, ah, suppose not," he said. "Anyway, I was packing up the house and I came across some things of yours."

"You're packing the house?"

"Oh, yeah," he said. "I'm moving to New York to be closer to my business partner and my clientele."

"So your guiding business has taken off."

"Well, in a manner of speaking. I partnered up with a guy I met a few years ago. Maybe you remember him, Josh Fern?"

"Oh, yeah, the guy with the funny accent?"

"Right, he's from South Africa. Anyway, he was looking for a new partner running expeditions to South America and eventually the Himalayas, and well, we got along well together."

"So, when are you moving?"

"I already closed on the house, and I'm renting it back from the new owners for about a month or so, at least until I can get all of my crap packed up."

"Oh."

There was an uneasy silence.

"I could mail your stuff to you."

"Sure."

"Or, well, I'm going to be in Seattle this weekend. Maybe we could have coffee, and you know, catch up?"

"Well I…" she said.

"Oh yeah, I understand," he said.

"No, wait," she said. "Let's meet this weekend."

"Really?"

"Sure, it will be great to catch up."

"So your husband won't mind?"

"I'm not married."

"Your boyfriend?"

"No, and don't you be getting any ideas."

"Yes, ma'am."

She laughed.

"So you want to meet at the Market?" he asked.

"You mean that funky Indian restaurant we went to years ago?"

"Yeah," he said. "You think it's still there?"

"I'm sure," she said. "If not we can wander around until we find someplace else."

"Okay, so how about one on Saturday?" he asked.

"How about later, say six or seven? I have to work."

"Ok, um, let's say seven then."

"I'll see you then."

After she hung up she was excited and nervous.

What the hell? she wondered, surprised at herself.

It had been a very long time since she had last seen him, at least four years. She was certain he had changed little, something that she wasn't sure if she was pleased or disappointed about. She hadn't thought about him for months. He had become a subconscious anecdote, and then he called. Instinctively, she started thinking about what she would wear. *Nothing too slutty, but definitely something he will remember. Something sexy.*

Then she thought about Mike. Of course, she wasn't going to tell him. She wasn't crazy or stupid. They weren't exclusive, plus it was only old friends getting together to talk about old times. She laughed at the thought. They were never old friends. Many things, but never friends.

The week dragged by. Work seemed more boring than usual, and she only saw Mike once for lunch. He was unusually chatty, but also seemed a bit distracted. Even when she was sitting with Mike, taking in his dark features, she found herself thinking about Dave. It took all of her concentration to stay focused. The rest of that week she went through almost a pack of cigarettes a day. She chain-smoked on her breaks, at home, in the car, in the bathroom.

Dave had never seemed to mind her smoking, although he rarely smoked himself. He told her that it added to her allure, her sexiness, and said it reminded him of after they had done it. She found herself thinking about sex a lot that week, especially how it had been with Dave. She and Mike hadn't really done anything yet, even though she was sometimes tempted to just show up at his house in nothing but a negligee. There had been a few guys since Dave, mostly short timers, or one-night stands, but no one memorable or even that interesting.

On Saturday she found herself pacing behind the counter, nervously rearranging the display cases and smoking every chance she got. After work she raced home. Bridgette took her time getting ready: painting her nails, shaving her legs, picking out the perfect outfit. She wore something she knew Dave would like: tight jeans, a tailored, white silk blouse, and her new high-heeled black boots.

She was late for their date, of course, intentionally. He was waiting outside the restaurant when she arrived.

"Hey," he said smiling, his perfect smile.

He looked good. He was tan, wore a thin, dark red sweater and tan chinos, and had cut his hair short.

"You cut your hair," she said, amazed.

"Yeah, I figured it was time. Josh said that some of our clients have more faith in the clean shaven."

"Business people?"

He nodded. He said nothing about her being late, he never did.

They looked inside the restaurant.

"Was this place this much of a dump the last time we were here?"

She laughed. It was definitely dumpy and looked as though nothing had changed but much had aged.

"It's been a long time," she said.

"Yes, yes it has."

They walked in and she noticed that he still limped, slightly. She said nothing, but remembered the months of physical therapy and the exhaustion, and she knew he didn't want to be reminded. They sat down and began to talk. They caught each other up and started to talk about old times, slipping easily from one topic to the next. She found herself reliving some wonderful memories which until today had seemed wholly out of reach.

She found herself irritated when the waiter came by to take their order—she had become so engrossed in their conversation.

She was surprised how comfortable it was talking to him again, as though mere weeks had passed and things had ended amicably. They had an easy effortless rapport. Dave listened, his light blue eyes sparkling. His every move was grace and bound sinewy energy. Watching him, even here in this restaurant, she was reminded of a video she had seen of him climbing. She had found it on her own at his place years ago, he would deny it existed. It was shot with a telephoto lens by a buddy of his. He was climbing somewhere in central Oregon, maybe Smith Rock. The way he moved, smoothly, with sublime concentration and finesse that belied his strength was amazing to see. For a short time afterward she thought she understood, or at least sympathized with his obsession with climbing. But after his trip to Denali and Jim's death things between them had changed.

They ate chicken curry and lentil soup and drank tea. The food was delicious, spicy, tangy, and rich. By the time she was halfway through her meal she was stuffed. As usual Dave ate with gusto. Like everything he did, he consumed life. She thought about offering him her leftovers but somehow that seemed too familiar. Watching him eat made her think of sex. There was something instinctively carnal in the way he held his fork, stuck it into the chicken, and slid it into his mouth.

"What?" he said, noticing her looking at him, half-smiling.

"Oh, nothing," she said, and smiled.

A split second of self-consciousness flashed across his face until he read her mind, just as he always had when he wanted the same thing.

"Are you done?" he asked. "Do you want to get out of here?"

"Oh, I'm fine you finish, there's no rush."

He smiled at her mischievously. "Waiter, check."

They walked around the Market, consciously avoiding touching each other. She reached toward him once, grabbing on to his arm as they walked through a gauntlet of tourists, and the first brushing of her fingertips on him, even through his clothes, seemed to send cold electric shocks through her body. She wondered if he felt it, too.

Eventually they wound up back at her place with the pretense of having coffee, maybe a couple of drinks, and she would get her stuff.

They drank their coffee standing on her deck. Music played near by, a diesel engine purred in the distance. After a while he put his arm around her shoulder. She looked over at him.

"You looked cold," he said.

"Yes, I am. Let's go in."

They sat down on the couch and soon afterward he leaned into her. They kissed at first slowly, then almost ferociously. Later they ended up on the floor, then made their way, naked, back to her bed. The made love deliciously, feverishly, knowing each other so well and yet being so much like strangers. It gave Bridgette a sense of erotic vertigo. She still knew his body, which seemed not to have changed at all. She wondered, at first, if she would still be attractive to him. She quickly learned, though the intensity of his touch and the caress of his tongue, exactly what he thought. They didn't speak when they made love, which was how they had always been. Language seemed to distract from the pure visceral pleasure.

At some point she had looked into his eyes and saw the grief there. It was what he had brought back with him from Alaska, a deep sorrowful darkness. Not even the façade he had put up for the evening could keep her from seeing what had kept him drunk every night for months, had made him weep uncontrollably, had caused him to roll his truck after a night at the bar.

She had tried to talk to Dave then, to tell him that when her grandfather died, she wasn't sure she wanted to live. The heroin had called to her through the strange warp of her subconscious. She considered it for a very long time and even went so far as to start formulating a plan to get it. But she found herself coming back to the image of her grandfather in the hospital, the cancer consuming him. He had refused the pain medication. For days he sat there stoically, all of his energy consumed by lifting his conscious mind beyond the physical world through prayer.

She told Dave about when her grandpa had awakened in the middle of the night, sweating, and she told him to take something for the pain. And he had said, "I'm still alive. He still wants me here."

Dave had listened to her story half-heartedly, and said, "You weren't there. You couldn't possibly understand."

She had reached out to comfort him and he had pushed her away then, literally, and she had had enough.

Sometime late that morning they had fallen asleep. She woke a few hours later and reached over. He was gone. She wasn't exactly surprised. She let out a sigh of relief and sadness. Somewhere, in the back of her mind, she knew this was the only way this could work out. She wrapped a blanket around herself and walked into the kitchen. On the counter sat the box he had brought. On it was a note.

> *Dear Bridge,*
>
> *I'm sorry to sneak away but I didn't want to wake you and I have an early appointment. Here are some things of yours. It was great to see you and now I remember why I didn't want you to leave. Take care of yourself. Tell the boyfriend I know you're hiding from me that he better be good to you, or I'll make it a point to kick his ass.*
>
> *I don't know my new address yet but just send stuff to B'ham if you want.*
>
> *Keep in touch,*
> *Dave*

He didn't sign it "Love, Dave." She knew him well enough to know that he tried not to say things to her he didn't really mean, especially love. It was something he didn't take lightly, in fact, perhaps too seriously.

She walked into the restaurant and sat down at a table in the bar area. She lit up, grateful for the smoking section. Eventually the waitress came by and she ordered a diet Coke, fries, and a dinner salad. She looked up at the TV that was on in the bar. A commercial showed a guy climbing up a sandstone wall in some pseudo-American Southwest. The sound was turned down and she wouldn't have been able to hear it anyway with the music on. The commercial reminded her, inevitably, of Dave. She suddenly had a strange sensation, a sense of unease. It was the same thing she had felt just before the park ranger had called her from Denali to tell her they were going to organize a search party. The ranger had to explain to her three times that Dave had listed her as an emergency contact and next of kin, and that he had gone missing in the storm.

She set down her cigarette and reached inside her purse. Tucked inside her appointment book was a postcard from New York City.

"Call me if you're in the area," his name, and his phone number was all that was written on it.

She flipped the card over. It was a picture of the skyline of New York Harbor with a little I heart NY in the corner. She flipped the card against her fingertips.

What the hell, she thought. *I'm sure he's fine.*

She pulled out her cell phone and dialed the number.

It rang five times.

Probably not home, or online, she thought.

Just as she was about to hang up a woman's voice, breathless and crackling with anxiety, said, "Hello, sorry, I was on the other line."

Bridgette recognized her voice. It was Dave's mom. The last time she had talked to her was when she had called to tell her that Dave was missing on Denali. She had lost it on the phone and Bridgette had spent an hour trying to console her and answer her barrage of repetitive questions.

"Hello?" Mrs. Greibing said again, sounding even more anxious, fearful, and upset than the last time she had talked to her.

Bridgette hung up. She took a deep breath and tried not to cry. How she knew she wasn't entirely sure, but she knew she would never see Dave again.

The Second

Dave looked over at his companions, each one more drawn, dirty, and desperate for rest. They were a pathetic lot.

Except for perhaps himself, Josh looked the worst. Each of them had lost at least ten pounds, their clothes were dirty and soiled, dark shadows ringed their bloodshot eyes. They stared off into nothingness. No one spoke, either too tired or unwilling to yell above the sound of the truck to make conversation.

Dave never liked riding in the back of these trucks that climbers in Nepal hired. This one was an older Japanese beast, a lashed-down tarp and some panels covered the area where they sat, protecting them somewhat from the wind and cold that buffeted the mountain road they wound down. The truck bounced uncomfortably along, jarring the passengers and virtually negating a successful nap. His leg ached and he tried to shift his weight to his other side. He was somewhat comforted that at least the driver was experienced—he was the cousin of a Sherpa he had trusted on two previous trips.

The driver had told them when they were arranging to leave Tingri that the roads were bad and they should wait a couple of days until the danger of rockslides abated. Dave knew this meant at least a week or two by the time everything was arranged, which in turn meant rescheduling hotels and flights out of Kathmandu. He had consulted his clients, two American businessmen from Texas. Both were in reasonably good shape, but they were exhausted, they missed their families, and both had pressing business matters to get back to in Houston.

He had told the driver they would leave as scheduled, promising him a little extra if he could get them down quickly, and without incident.

He leaned over and looked out the flapping back of the Toyota. There was no one traveling behind them today. In front, where he couldn't see, a group of Internationals traveled in a truck hired by a competing guide company. It was a cutthroat business, guiding, especially when trying to get it off the ground. This was the first important trip that he and Josh had planned outside of the Americas. They had led a couple of climbs in the Andes, and the trip itself proved to be far more difficult than the climb. There were travel arrangements to make, bribes that inevitably had to be paid, permits to pull, and always the increased level of security to contend with. But it had ultimately been a success, and two businessmen from Houston, Frank and Joe, had booked them while they were skirting between airports and checking their voice mail.

Dave sat back down. He settled onto his pack and sleeping bag, which proved to be fairly uncomfortable. It was difficult for them to stretch out in the confined space, although Josh and Dave had positioned themselves so their clients would have the most room.

On the trip back from a climb his mind always drifted. He had long since played out all of the elements of this climb. The storm was not entirely unexpected and they had been relatively safe waiting it out. They hadn't taken too many chances, but the waiting had cost them precious time and money, and irritated their clients who were impatient to climb Cho Oyo. His leg had bothered him some, but mostly on the descent. He had learned to hide it well. He never talked about it and managed to avoid the pills he had brought, just in case.

He closed his eyes, resting them, certain there was no chance he would be able to sleep.

What woke him was a split second of complete silence. He opened his eyes, and time stopped. Everything in the truck went still.

Then a sound, like an enormous ocean wave splitting itself onto the rocks slammed against the truck, the world shifted, and turned upside down. He felt himself fall. There wasn't time to think, but merely react. Gear and his fellow climbers flew at him from every direction. He slammed against the side of the truck and the semi-hard surface threatened to give way. Someone's arm, a pack, and a large water bottle hit him. He knew everyone was screaming, and yet all he could hear was a low guttural roar, so intense it swallowed up every other sound.

He floated there, weightless, and in an instant of clarity he looked out toward the light that pushed its way through the canvas flapping against the rush of air. He saw sky, clouds, and brilliant snow in the distance.

Dear God, he thought, and the explosion of sound was followed by darkness.

Acknowledgements

This novel is as much my labor of love as it is the substantial contributions of so many people I admire. There are many people I would like to thank for their help in completing this novel. Natasha, my wife, my most ardent supporter, and first reader helped me to find my voice and my purpose in life. My dad, John Ashenhurst, read drafts, edited, and encouraged me. My mom, Jill Welt, believed in this novel and me, and helped finance this creative risk. Yvonne Ashenhurst and Lou Welt have been a sounding board and offered invaluable opinions. My brothers, Eric and James, and sister, Jenny, were always willing to hear my ideas and read my writing. Kristin, Eric's better half, was always a source of positive support. Heather Shoemaker offered interesting and objective perspectives. Kristin Costello spent an entire wedding reception listening to me ramble on as I clarified my novel. The fine teachers I work with, including: Jason Urlacher, Lisa Hornyak, Jan Stegemeyer, Marta Lauritsen, Kara Beloate, and Mack Johnson, listened with genuine interest as I told and retold my tales of woe and the writing process. Robyn M. Fritz edited the finished manuscript and offered sage advice. My students listened as I read aloud from early drafts and applauded when I was done; and taught me about patience, knowledge, compassion, and writing. Also my teachers have helped shape and inspire the writer and teacher I have become. I am forever in your debt.

For additional copies visit

www.oldmeadowpublishers.com

www.NoahAshenhurst.com

or

Order from your local bookstore